DOUBLE ACTION

The STEELE series by George G. Gilman, published by New English Library:

ADAM STEELE 1: THE VIOLENT PEACE
ADAM STEELE 2: BOUNTY HUNTER
ADAM STEELE 3: HELL'S JUNCTION
ADAM STEELE 4: VALLEY OF BLOOD
ADAM STEELE 5: GUN RUN
ADAM STEELE 6: THE KILLING ART
ADAM STEELE 7: CROSS-FIRE
ADAM STEELE 8: COMANCHE CARNAGE
ADAM STEELE 9: BADGE IN THE DUST
ADAM STEELE 10: THE LOSERS
ADAM STEELE 11: LYNCH TOWN
ADAM STEELE 12: DEATH TRAIL
ADAM STEELE 13: BLOODY BORDER
ADAM STEELE 14: DELTA DUEL
ADAM STEELE 15: RIVER OF DEATH
ADAM STEELE 16: NIGHTMARE AT NOON
ADAM STEELE 17: SATAN'S DAUGHTERS
ADAM STEELE 18: THE HARD WAY
ADAM STEELE 19: THE TARNISHED STAR
ADAM STEELE 20: WANTED FOR MURDER
ADAM STEELE 21: WAGONS EAST
ADAM STEELE 22: THE BIG GAME
ADAM STEELE 23: FORT DESPAIR
ADAM STEELE 24: MANHUNT
ADAM STEELE 25: STEELE'S WAR: THE WOMAN
ADAM STEELE 26: STEELE'S WAR: THE PREACHER
ADAM STEELE 27: STEELE'S WAR: THE STOREKEEPER
ADAM STEELE 28: STEELE'S WAR: THE STRANGER
ADAM STEELE 29: THE BIG PRIZE
ADAM STEELE 30: THE KILLER MOUNTAINS
ADAM STEELE 31: THE CHEATERS
ADAM STEELE 32: THE WRONG MAN
ADAM STEELE 33: THE VALLEY OF THE SHADOW
ADAM STEELE 34: THE RUNAWAY
ADAM STEELE 35: STRANGER IN A STRANGE TOWN
ADAM STEELE 36: THE HELLRAISERS

The EDGE series by George G. Gilman, published by New English Library:

EDGE 1: THE LONER
EDGE 2: TEN THOUSAND DOLLAR AMERICAN
EDGE 3: APACHE DEATH
EDGE 4: KILLER'S BREED
EDGE 5: BLOOD ON SILVER
EDGE 6: THE BLUE, THE GREY AND THE RED
EDGE 7: CALIFORNIA KILLING
EDGE 8: SEVEN OUT OF HELL
EDGE 9: BLOODY SUMMER
EDGE 10: VENGEANCE IS BLACK
EDGE 11: SIOUX UPRISING
EDGE 12: THE BIGGEST BOUNTY
EDGE 13: A TOWN CALLED HATE
EDGE 14: THE BIG GOLD
EDGE 15: BLOOD RUN
EDGE 16: THE FINAL SHOT
EDGE 17: VENGEANCE VALLEY
EDGE 18: TEN TOMBSTONES TO TEXAS
EDGE 19: ASHES AND DUST
EDGE 20: SULLIVAN'S LAW
EDGE 21: RHAPSODY IN RED
EDGE 22: SLAUGHTER ROAD
EDGE 23: ECHOES OF WAR
EDGE 24: THE DAY DEMOCRACY DIED
EDGE 25: VIOLENCE TRAIL
EDGE 26: SAVAGE DAWN
EDGE 27: DEATH DRIVE
EDGE 28: EVE OF EVIL
EDGE 29: THE LIVING, THE DYING AND THE DEAD
EDGE 30: WAITING FOR A TRAIN
EDGE 31: THE GUILTY ONES
EDGE 32: THE FRIGHTENED GUN
EDGE 33: THE HATED
EDGE 34: A RIDE IN THE SUN
EDGE 35: DEATH DEAL
EDGE 36: TOWN ON TRIAL
EDGE 37: VENGEANCE AT VENTURA
EDGE 38: MASSACRE MISSION
EDGE 39: THE PRISONERS
EDGE 40: MONTANA MELODRAMA
EDGE 41: THE KILLING CLAIM
EDGE 42: BLOODY SUNRISE
EDGE 43: ARAPAHO REVENGE
EDGE 44: THE BLIND SIDE
EDGE 45: HOUSE ON THE RANGE
EDGE 46: THE GODFORSAKEN

EDGE Meets ADAM STEELE, by George G. Gilman, published by New English Library:

1: TWO OF A KIND
2: MATCHING PAIR
3: DOUBLE ACTION

DOUBLE ACTION
EDGE MEETS STEELE

George G. Gilman

NEW ENGLISH LIBRARY

for
S.A.
in appreciation of
certain sums

A New English Library Original Publication, 1984

First NEL Paperback Edition August 1984

NEL Books are published by
New English Library,
Mill Road, Dunton Green,
Sevenoaks, Kent.
Editorial office: 47 Bedford Square, London WC1B 3DP.

Made and printed in Great Britain by
Hunt Barnard Printing Ltd, Aylesbury, Bucks.

British Library Cataloguing in Publication Data
Gilman, George G.
Double action.—(Edge–Steele; 3)
Rn: Terry Harknett
I. Title II. Series
823'.914[F] PR6058.A686/

ISBN 0 450 05720 8

CHAPTER ONE

THE SIX Ute braves who were hunkered down in the cover of a patch of sagebrush and white fir saplings could see a youngish driver and an older guard riding on the outside seat of the Concord coach of the Central Western Stageline Company that was making unhurried progress through the La Sal Mountains foothills at mid-morning. They could not yet see that inside the travel-stained coach there were two women and one man being carried as passengers.

The fact that Edward Sun looked to be no more than eighteen years of age, which would not have qualified him for the term 'man' in Ute society, was neither here nor there. He was a little over three years older than he looked and whether thinking as a Chinese or an American he had considered himself an adult for much longer than this: more often than not with justification.

Amy Yancy who sat to the young man's right on the forward-facing seat was close to thirty but looked somewhat older. She also looked sick from more than enduring the rigours and deprivations of the journey from Denver.

The other woman's name was Edith Crawford, who admitted to being fifty-six, was sixty-two and in ideal circumstances could sustain the lie. She had also suffered almost two days' riding the stage and two nights that were just as uncomfortable in trailside way stations, so was not looking her best this summer morning. She sat on the same seat, in the corner to Sun's left, and today had given up making the constant effort to keep as much space as the confines of the coach allowed between herself and him. Now only occasionally made her distaste for the young man apparent by pointedly flinching, sometimes with a soft gasp, when a wheel of the Concord hit a rut in the trail and she was jolted against him or he against her.

For his part the young man with the distinctly Oriental facial structure and the pallor of a studious Anglo had ceased to be visibly perturbed by the older woman's bigotry toward him for much longer than this – from shortly after the stage pulled out of the Denver depot and he realised Mrs Crawford was prejudiced against his father's race rather than merely resenting him for being a man.

The mourning-attired Mrs Yancy had remained totally withdrawn inside a private world of grief for almost the entire trip: whether aboard the moving stage or at any of the way-station stopovers for the nightly rest or to switch teams.

Thus had it been a tight-lipped and somewhat morose journey down from the Rockies through Wolf Creek Pass beside the Colorado River and out toward the canyon lands of the Territory of Utah – both within the slow-rolling Concord and also up on the high seat in front of the lashed-down roof luggage. Where the driver, Tod Carmody, and Elroy Washington who rode shotgun were a well-matched team: in that neither ever spoke unless he had something he considered important to say and when this did happen it was invariably terse, pointed and ill-humoured. The men's brooding reserve such that nobody else who drove or rode guard for the Central Western outfit ever wanted to share duty with either Carmody or Washington.

'I don't like it, my friend,' the square-featured, blond-haired, glittering-eyed driver who was thirty announced as he fixed his gaze on the trail ahead after completing a cautious survey of the terrain to either side.

'Me neither, son,' his twenty-years-older, fleshier, darker-skinned and white-haired partner answered without pausing from the way in which he had been watching the surrounding country for several minutes – with fear of the unknown danger stirring just beneath the surface veneer of scowling aggressiveness.

'Anythin' more than an itch?' The more quiet-spoken driver briefly fingered the time-scarred butt of the old Navy Colt in his hip holster before he returned both work-callused hands to the reins and assumed a tensely crouched attitude on the seat – like he was already driving the coach at breakneck speed.

'Not even that, son.' Beads of sweat began to ooze from the pores in Washington's element-burnished skin. He wanted to brush the salt moisture off his forehead, but felt a more pressing need to keep a double-handed grip on the Winchester repeater rifle that he held across his thick thighs, a thumb on the hammer and a forefinger across the trigger. 'Started as just a dryness in the back of my throat. But now I got the hot sweats. If I'm wrong, I'm gonna get outta this business.'

That was a lot for Elroy Washington to say at one time and the younger man at his side began to sweat also, as he recommenced his uneasy watch on the flanking hills and murmured: 'For sure it ain't sweaty heat.'

The man riding shotgun had spoken his piece and felt no need to voice agreement with the obvious. For this early summer day in the northern foothills of the distantly snow-powdered ridges of the La Sal Mountains was filled with arid heat by the sun that glared from out of a near-cloudless sky. The kind of heat that seemed to act to close pores defensively against its searing attack rather than open them – unless a man were to experience dread of an unseen and indefinable presence that he senses means to do him harm.

'You get the smell of road agents or Injuns or what, Elroy?'

'Tod, all I smell is trouble. With a capital B for the bad kind.'

Only when these two partners on duty and friends in free time were under considerable strain did they address each other by their given names. Now, the driver augmented the guard's uneasy surveillance on their innocuous-looking surroundings and as their gazes crossed they were momentarily locked: both men were immediately aware of the extent of their own and each other's terror. Like they suddenly had precognition of a double dying.

It seemed to require a conscious effort to unloose their gazes. And then grimaces of anguish began to spread across their faces as they scoured the terrain for a glimpse of the danger that they knew lurked out there. While Carmody lifted the reins to crack them over the backs of the four horses in the traces and Washington raised the rifle off his knees as he thumbed back the hammer.

Inside the still-leisurely moving Concord, Amy Yancy brought a black-gloved hand up from her lap and swept the fine mesh veil off her pallid face, the better to see through the dusty window as she sensed the threat. A moment later a wheel of the coach dropped into and bumped out of a pothole in the trail, which caused Edward Sun to lurch hard against the matron. But both he and Mrs Crawford were too uneasily intrigued by the actions and expression of the woman in mourning to react as usual to the sudden and unwelcome accidental contact.

'You are feeling unwell, my dear?' Edith Crawford asked and now vented a muted sound of irritation with the man when he leaned across her line of vision – blocking Amy Yancy from her sight as he sought to get a better view through the windows at what had captured the nervous attention of the younger woman.

'No, it's just — '

'Hey, you up there!'

Sun had cut in on Mrs Yancy's attempt to explain: he tilted his head and shouted at the roof of the Concord as he felt the stirring of unexplained dread. Then, as Edith Crawford fixed the scowl more firmly in place and opened her mouth to rebuke the young man, Carmody cracked the reins and roared to the team:

'*Get up, there!*'

A rifle shot rang out, like a muted echo of the sound of the reins, as the four horses responded to the command and lunged into a sudden gallop. And the matron vented a shrill cry of alarm at the abrupt change of pace that pressed her and the other two passengers hard against the back of their seat. The younger woman continued to peer out of the right side of the abruptly hurtling coach, still no more than sensing some brand of threat that had caused Carmody to demand the violent turn of speed. While Sun caught a glimpse on the periphery of his vision of a tell-tale puff of black smoke against the multi-hued greenery that covered the rising ground to the other side of the swaying and bucking and jolting Concord.

He instantly linked the echo-like sound to the briefly seen smoke and snapped: 'On the floor!'

Mrs Crawford gave a gasp of horror and Mrs Yancy shuddered as he clutched each woman by the upper arm and took them forcefully forward with him as he tipped himself off the seat. He had neither the time nor the inclination to wonder if they were responding to his touch or if they had seen what he saw just part of a second after he began the move.

The six Ute braves in breechclouts and feathered headbands had sprung up out of cover after the first shot was fired at the stage, to loose a fusillade of bullets toward the target as it lurched along the foot of the hill directly below the small stand of young timber in which they had been concealed. The range was no more than a hundred yards, and so the bullets made powerful impact – with the timbers of the stage, one of its windows, the luggage on the roofrack and the flesh of Tod Carmody.

Edith Crawford shrilled in terror and pressed her bulky form tight to the jolting floor of the Concord as glittering shards of glass from the shattered window sprayed down on her and Edward Sun and Amy Yancy.

'I will soon be with you, my dearest Cole,' the younger woman murmured.

'Sonofabitch,' the man curled on the floor beside her growled as he saw something close to a gentle smile shape her mouthline while she seemed totally unaware of the blood that oozed from a cut on her pale cheek. Then, as a second volley of gunfire sounded – from behind the pitching and yawing stage now – he felt a compulsion to twist his head and look toward the glassless window in the door. And he saw a spray of blood slipstream across the frame and splash over the pane of the window alongside it. Then, a moment later, as bullets thudded into the boot of the Concord, he recognised the blond hair and the slender form of the driver as Carmody twisted off the high seat and corkscrewed over the side to drop inertly to the trail.

No more than ten seconds had passed since Elroy

Washington's well-honed intuition for danger threatening the stage in his care had proved to be as good as ever. Then he had wrenched his gaze away from the look of death in the eyes of his partner and friend, and found himself staring unerringly at the precise spot on the hillside to the south where the bunch of half-naked Ute braves showed themselves as the first shot was exploded toward the Concord that Carmody caused to spurt.

It was no impulsively triggered accident that one shot rang out in isolation, Washington guessed a part of a second before he saw the man beside him stiffen as the reins slid from his snapped-open hands.

Carmody said: 'Oh,' as if he were just mildly surprised by what was happening, before he began to turn his head to direct a beseeching look at Washington. Which was when the rest of the Indians loosed the fusillade of fire and Carmody died as he stopped a bullet in the side that would otherwise have hit Washington. But it was that first shot, fired by the best marksman among the braves, that had proved fatal as it drilled deep into the driver's head. And left a neat hole between his left ear and eye which now erupted blood as the rigidity was gone from the form that crumpled and twisted and toppled off the seat.

The crud wanted Tod dead and the team runnin' scared, Washington thought bitterly as he saw with grief-misted eyes his only true friend in the world fall lifeless out of sight. And then he heard the second volley of rifle fire and the duller sounds of the bullets impacting with the rear of the Concord: which acted to clear his mind of the emotional turmoil of anger at the cold-bloodedness of the Utes and melancholy for the untimely death of Carmody. His responsibility for the safety of the stage passengers and their property suddenly became his sole concern.

He looked down at where the reins were sagged between the horses, dragging along the trail in the dust raised by the powerfully pumping hooves. And his mouthline formed into a grimace while he briefly considered lunging off the footboard and on to the quivering back of one of the team. Even if he achieved that, though, he felt less confident of being able to stay astride the bare back of the horse as he reached down to grasp for the reins. Hell, he was more than fifty and it was many years since he had been able without vanity to consider himself an expert horseback rider. And even in those days he was strictly a saddle-horse man.

He raised his bleak-eyed gaze from the discouraging view above his toecaps where they rested on the footboard, to peer along the trail stretched out in front of the straining-at-the-gallop horses. And felt a surge of hope. For more than a mile, perhaps nearer two, the trail was a straightaway with undulating rises to the left and a large expanse of rolling pasture to the right. There were plenty of scattered trees in early summer leaf, a few rocky ridges and several hollows and mounds that could provide cover for a great many more Ute braves. But Elroy Washington had a good feeling that there were no other Indians engaged in the ambush.

Probably the bolting team would stay on the trail until they galloped themselves into an exhausted standstill. But even if they did veer a little to one side or the other of the long straightaway, it did not look to the suddenly-less-anxious guard that the stage was likely to come to much harm. The bunch of murdering redskins had made a mess of it. They had picked a wrong spot for the attack and then had killed just Tod Carmody. There was scant chance of the runaway team wrecking the stage on this stretch of trail. And if, after the horses had run themselves into the ground, those stinking half-assed Utes came sniffing around the Concord for booty . . . well, they'd find they had the best damn guard on the Central Western payroll to take on. After what the bastards had done to Tod . . . well, he wouldn't be taking any prisoners, that was for sure.

Elroy Washington's element-burnished and time-lined face came very close to displaying an infrequent smile as he dwelt upon the stupidity of the Utes and contemplated the satisfying prospect of avenging the murder of his friend and partner. But the expression that never spread easily across his features was stillborn as his gaze swept over the seat from which the corpse of Tod Carmody had fallen. And the next moment, after he had submitted to a powerful compulsion to look back across the roof luggage at the scene behind the hurtling stage, the fear of death once more took command of the man's face.

The Utes had ponies.

A seventh brave had been concealed in deeper cover than the others, and had charge of the ambushers' mounts. And now, just a matter of stretched seconds after that first fatal shot was exploded from out of the stand of immature trees, seven braves were flinging themselves eagerly on to the bare backs of the animals. Starting the ponies fast down the hillside, running alongside them and springing up off the ground – like they were giving a carefully rehearsed demonstration of their expert horsemanship.

The mid-morning light of this early summer day was such that a man could see with crystal clarity to the unshimmered horizon on every side. The excited Indians on the hill were only a matter of a few hundred yards away when Washington got his first glimpse of them as they launched into the spectacular display of mounting on the move; and the dread-filled guard was briefly host to an impression that he could see each of their faces as clearly as if they were seated across a table from him. And he saw that each mouth was gaped wide to vent disdainful laughter at him while every pair of dark eyes gleamed with unwavering determination to see him violently dead.

Then the braves, riding in a tight group, were down off the green-clad slope and began to close with their objective on the trail. But they were much less well-defined now, because of the red dust that pumping hooves and spinning wheelrims erupted and billowed out behind. And as the reality of what was happening to him re-asserted a firm grip on the mind of Washington, he realised he had been paralysed both mentally and physically by terror . . . and perhaps a sense of shame impelled him into reckless over-reaction as he sought to match up to his self-assumed position as the best guard riding a Central Western stage.

His Winchester was already cocked behind a loaded breech and his forefinger remained curled round the trigger. And now he turned almost half around on the seat, bringing the stock of the rifle to his shoulder as he aimed the barrel back over the luggage lashed on the roof rack.

A woman was screaming and a man was shouting. Hooves thundered and wheels clattered. Elroy Washington knew there was no point in taking careful aim off the shuddering coach through the swirling dust at the braves astride their galloping ponies. He loosed two fast shots and snarled:

'Take that, you murderin' skunks.'

The fat old woman married to the top-brass officer at Fort Hamilton quit screaming and the uppity youngster who looked like he was a lot more Chink than white cut out the yelling. He wondered if the widow woman riding out to Hamilton to pick up the body of her soldier husband had been hit when the braves started the attack. He had not heard anything from her since that first shot blasted into Tod's skull.

The Utes astride well-rested ponies narrowed the gap on the Concord with a team in the traces that had done many miles of slow hauling before the bolt got started. And there were still seven braves large as life and twice as ugly getting closer by the moment despite the couple of shots he had exploded into their midst. They rode with the same degree of smooth skill as they had mounted, the rope reins held in one hand while the other hand of each naked-above-the-waist Indian was thrust high in the air, fisted around the frame of a rifle. The fact that they chose, to a man, not to answer his fire struck Elroy Washington as an implied insult. And as he pumped the lever action of his repeater a third time to arc the spent shellcase down to the trail and ease a fresh bullet into the breech, acid resentment acted as a potent fuel to the smouldering fires of shame.

'I'll show you, you redskinned sonsofbitches!' he bellowed. And emphasised the extent of his rage with another two fast shots, venting a whoop of triumph when he saw one of the pursuers drop his raised arm, release the rifle and the reins and topple sideways off his pony.

Washington experienced brief regret that there had been no opportunity to see where the brave was hit and blood spurting from the bullet hole. But as he pumped the action again the euphoria at seeing the brave go down became too powerful to allow for any lesser emotion in his mind. And he fired a fifth shot, a sixth and then a seventh in a vain attempt to score a second triumph while he was still relishing the first.

Six braves rode on, still drawing inexorably closer through the swirling dust to the rear of the speeding rig that was raising the turbulent cloud. But suddenly they were no longer charging toward their objective with rifles thrust challengingly but ineffectually in the mote-filled air. For now, as Washington pumped his Winchester, he saw they all had a two-handed grip on their rifles which were aimed from their shoulders toward the Concord – as the braves adeptly steered their ponies into a ragged six-abreast line across the trail, by swaying their bodies to one side or the other while they stayed on the bare backs of their mounts with knees and ankles clenched to the animals' flanks.

To the best damn guard riding the stages of the Central Western line, this was the ultimate insult. And, grimacing his hatred at the Indians who had killed Tod Carmody and now taunted him, Elroy Washington blocked from his awareness the sights and sounds of the headlong chase and concentrated entirely upon triggering a killing shot into the Ute brave who rode second from the left as he viewed the line.

And the white man died doing what in the whole of his life he had never desired more. And he started to vent from his gaping mouth a piercing cry of unbounded pleasure as he saw a neat hole show in the hairless and naked chest of the selected Indian. But he rose too high on his knees on the seat of the runaway stage, in celebration of too small a victory in the fight that was not yet over, so presenting himself as a clear target for the five surviving braves as their second casualty was flipped from his horse.

And of the five bullets blasted toward the man who threw both his arms at the sun-bright sky and arced his upper body in contemptuous defiance of the Utes, three smashed into his flesh.

Perhaps for part of a second as he was held rigid on his knees, facing backward from the speeding Concord, Elroy Washington was able to experience some brand of satisfaction that he had killed two Indians after the band of Utes did for his friend. But then his own life was ended by the three bullets that were lodged in his chest and the expression of ill-humour that formed his death mask was so characteristic it offered no valid clue to his state of mind when he died. Thus, the man might well not have been aware that his life was ended, as Tod Carmody's had been, by the Ute Indians: and so it was a straight two-for-two trade.

The trail that stretched out behind the racing stage from which the bullet-shattered corpse toppled was not so arrow-straight for so long as that ahead of it. Back there out of sight around a curve that arced at the foot of a low rise, a tall and lean man astride a chestnut gelding reined in his mount from an easy walk and in the lengthening silence that followed the final fusillade of distant gunfire took the makings from a pocket of his shirt and rolled, then lit, a cigarette.

On a stream of grey tobacco smoke he growled as he rasped the back of a hand over the bristles on his jaw: 'Sounds like a whole lot of trouble we don't want any part of, uh feller?'

The horse tossed his head and vented a terse whinny. And the rider showed a brief, tight grin as he tugged on the reins and heeled his mount off the trail. Murmured:

'Fine, feller. It sounds like the neighs have it.'

Ahead of where the five triumphant Indians steadily overhauled the slowing Concord, a second lone rider continued to keep his black stallion moving at a leisurely pace toward the scene of the running battle in the wake of the burst of shooting that killed Elroy Washington. This rider did somewhat more thinking aloud than the man who had been coming up on the ill-fated stage from behind.

'Somebody who speaks to his horse and expects to get an intelligent answer from him has to be a little crazy, I reckon,' he said, and sighed when the animal pricked his ears for a word of command, then laid them back down when no such word was spoken. The rider shook his head and went on:

'And a man who talks to himself is maybe even crazier.' He eyed the ears of his horse and this time, drawing no responsive movement, issued the command with a gentle sideways motion of the reins to angle the stallion off the trail as he drawled through pursed lips: 'But a man who rides toward that amount of shooting that's none of his concern . . . he'd have to be crazier than I'm not anymore.' He displayed a grin that was strangely boyish for a man of his age and added: 'If you get what I mean?'

The stallion snorted and shook his head.

The man drawled: 'Let's not get into that again.'

CHAPTER TWO

THE MAN who had been riding the trail in the same westward direction as the stage and who now started to detour to the south to pass by the scene of the trouble was the one called Edge.

He was in his early forties, a tall man of more than two inches above six feet, weighing a lean-built two hundred and some pounds. His face was lean, too, made up of features drawn from a Mexican father and a Scandinavian mother. A dark-hued face, deeply lined, with high cheekbones, an aquiline nose and a wide mouth with thin lines topped and flanked by a sparse moustache that sometimes did not stand out from his heavy stubble. He had eyes that were ice-blue and permanently narrowed under hooded lids. And mostly jet-black hair that he wore long enough to cover the nape of his neck and brush his shoulders. Just a trace of greyness showed against the black. It was a face that could be considered good-looking or ugly, depending upon how the person forming an opinion viewed the capacity for cruelty that seemed to be latent in back of the set of the mouth and the glitter of the eyes.

He did not look like a man who had achieved much out of life from being whatever he was. He was attired in hard-wearing clothing that had seen hard wear – Stetson, kerchief, shirt, pants and riding boots that were all black. And around his waist was a black gunbelt with a tied-down holster in which a standard model Frontier Colt nestled. There was a bullet in every loop of the belt.

His mount was as serviceable as his clothing, but better cared for. And the saddle he rode was not fancy and was hung with the bare minimum of accoutrements for drifting the frontier lands. Including a boot into which was slid a Winchester rifle.

What could appear to be this man's sole item of embellishment was a necklet of dull-coloured wooden beads on a leather thong that was sometimes seen behind his kerchief. But, in fact, he wore this to hold at the nape of his neck a pouch in which was carried a never dull-bladed straight razor. And sometimes he used this razor for purposes other than shaving.

After he had angled off the trail to start up the slope, the smile that never reached his eyes was abruptly gone from his mouth. And his heritage and element-burnished face was in an impassive set as he sat easy in the saddle and seemed to take just an indifferent attitude toward his surroundings.

Adam Steele, who had been riding east while Edge rode west, and who turned off the trail to the south at about the same time as the half-breed, appeared to be similarly only cursorily interested in the La Sal Mountains foothills as he made this attempt to swing around whatever brand of trouble had erupted into gunfire.

The Virginian, whose voice when he spoke his thought process sounded like he had left the state of his birth only recently, was of an age with Edge. But in all other physical aspects he was totally dissimilar. He was a head shorter and, as such, his in-proportion build would perhaps more accurately be described as wiry rather than lean. And his features were of a type that had remained unmatured until he had taken more than his fair share of life's hard knocks – but since his complexion had been darkened by the elements and scored by the passage of time so that his face was a match for the once-prematurely grey hair, he was regarded as handsome by most women who got close enough to him to care one way or the other. It was a face composed of regular features, clean-shaven if he had opportunity to shave, dominated by coal-black eyes that could look harder than the contrasting stark white teeth that could be displayed as easily in a killer's scowl as in a boyish grin of pleasure.

His horse, saddle, overt weapon and his choice of garb were also totally unlike those of the man who had elected to veer of the trail at the same time for the same reason.

The big, black stallion was a finer example of horseflesh and perhaps for no other reason looked to be in better shape, while the saddle on the back of the animal – also black – was ornately decorated with metallic studs in a design that showed Hispanic origin. In the boot was a Colt Hartford revolving rifle with a rosewood stock to which was screwed a gold plate bearing an inscription. The Virginian's style of clothing was patently dudish – a blue-black suit of expensive cloth and cut, under which he wore an elegant cream-coloured vest and a white shirt. A white scarf was fastened around his neck, cravat fashion. His grey Stetson had a black tooled-leather band. His spurless riding boots were black and so were the buckskin gloves that tightly fitted his hands.

Like Edge, he carried an unbulky bedroll with a sheepskin coat lashed to it behind his saddle and his mount was additionally burdened by just two canteens, two saddlebags and a lariat. Adam Steele did not tote a handgun, but the scarf around his neck could be utilised as an offensive weapon when the demand arose and he also carried a well-balanced throwing knife in a boot sheath – which he was able to draw through a seemingly accidental split in the outside seam of his right pants leg.

The Virginian had been unable to see the area where the gun battle started and ended within two minutes or so because he was on a stretch of trail that cut through an expanse of gambel oaks in a hollow: close to where there was a fork in the trail that offered him the choice of continuing eastward or a turn toward the north west. A wooden signpost at the intersection leaned drastically away from the vertical but its two sagging and one elevated arms had promised from a distance to tell him from whence he had come on this spur of the trail and to name the alternative destination should he swing toward the north west.

But since, for a clearly defined reason, he was headed nowhere in particular, the impassive expression that was fixed upon his face as he rode through brush among the trees was a true reflection of his feeling of equanimity toward the trouble he was intent upon riding around. For there was as good a chance of him finding what he was looking for along this new route he was following through the untrampled hills as on any clearly signposted trails. Maybe even a better chance, since the stud farm he planned to run would ideally not have any close neighbours or attract any passing-through strangers.

Because he had failed to achieve what he wanted over such a long time – the plan to raise and run quality horses was just the latest if albeit the most firmly resolute of Adam Steele's ambitions – he remained easy in the saddle and the imperturbable expression stayed on his face as he rode over the rim of the hollow and out of the fringe of the timber. And saw spread before him a vista of rolling hills covered with lush green grass and featured with a slow-running stream, a number of broad and shallow pools and many stands of mixed trees. The kind of good grazing land, well-watered, with adequate supplies of building lumber that at first impression seemed to be just what he had been searching for since a nebulous idea to put down roots had evolved into a clear-cut plan of which he refused to let go.

He could see some duck on one of the pools and a lot more rabbits close to patches of high timber and thickets of low brush. And there was sign left by more than just a few deer in the mud where the Virginian halted his horse so that the animal could dip his head and drink from the clear water of the pebble-bedded, twenty feet wide stream.

After the stallion had drank his fill, Steele heeled him into movement across the sun-sparkling stream. At its centre, it was deep enough for him to be able to lean comfortably down and scoop up a hatful of cool water that he tipped over his head and face simply by replacing his hat. He used a jacket sleeve to partially mop off the refreshing water from his sun-warmed face as he rode out of the stream and continued to eye his surroundings – but less dispassionately than before. For there was something akin to covetousness in the way he scanned this pastoral hill country set against the ruggedness of the distant, snow-topped mountains in the south. But he did not allow himself to become more emotionally involved with this seemingly idyllic piece of country – and it was easy for a man like the Virginian to guard against any kind of feeling that would leave him vulnerable. For he would have been searching for the inevitable flaws in what could never be perfect even had it not been a fusillade of gunshots that caused him to find this place. And so as he headed his mount up a low and gentle grade to where one of the few bare rock-ridged hills in the immediate area promised the best vantage point in every direction, his coal-black eyes searched primarily for the first sign of a threat to his well-being: while he needed to make only a slight conscious effort to combat the temptation to hope that this might turn out to be the place where he was destined to re-establish something close to what once had been so many miles and years from here.

The highest point on the hill was a butte-like crown of granite which he would have been prepared to climb by way of its craggy and pitted side after he dismounted from the black stallion. But what he saw from the base of the smooth and almost sheer western face of the fifty feet high outcrop acted to hold him in the saddle for stretched seconds after he had reined the horse to a halt – his black eyes hard and unblinking and his attitude rigid as he now had to struggle hard against the urge to feel bitter anger. Then, after the impulse to rage had subsided much more slowly than it had risen, he became impassive-faced and easy in the saddle again. No longer resenting the scene he witnessed some quarter mile to the north of his viewpoint – where the trail he had been riding a few minutes earlier ran across the fold between two hills below the rise on which he now sat his unmoving horse.

It was here that the runaway stage had been brought to a halt. Just moments before he moved into a position from which he could see it, he realised. For the brave who had leapt from the bare back of his galloping pony on to the sweat-lathered broader back of the nearside lead horse of the stage team was still astride the bolt-exhausted animal. Gesturing his excited triumph in achievement toward the four other Utes who brought their ponies to skidding, dust-exploding halts, a pair to either side of the stalled Concord.

The sounds of the headlong chase coming to an end, muted by distance, were what had drawn Steele's angry and then dispassionate gaze toward the scene on the trail. And now, as the less obtrusive sounds of far-off voices raised in snarling tones of command reached to him over the same several hundred yards through the same surrounding silence, the Virginian spared the time to glance away from the north and into the east – toward the lone rider whom he had glimpsed for a moment before the more compelling scene on the trail had captured his attention.

But the man who had been too far off across the verdant hills to be seen as anything more than a dark silhouette in the shape of a rider astride a horse was no longer in sight at all on the fringe of an expanse of pinon pines. And, not for the first time recently, Steele was perturbed by the undeniable fact that the wary watch he kept on his surroundings was involuntarily less intensive than once it had been. Not so long ago, before the putting down of roots on country such as this became of such paramount and near all-consuming importance to him, he would have spotted that distant rider earlier. And watched him for long enough to determine at least whether he was a white man or an Indian. Maybe, even, from watching him for long enough he would know if the man in the distance had seen him.

Hell, the sooner he found a piece of country to call his own so that he could quit day-dreaming about such a place, the far better chance he had of staying alive. For with something of solid reality to protect against those who might seek to steal or destroy it, the sharpness that he had once never needed consciously to hone on his five senses and his indefinable ability to be aware of imminent danger would surely return. For it could not have deserted him entirely when it had stood him in good stead for so many years while all that he had cared about was self-preservation.

He spoke aloud an uncharacteristic obscenity and made to back his mount away from the corner of the hilltop rock outcrop, intending to leave the Indians to their robbing business and be on his way. This section of country was too close to a stage route to meet his need for isolation. And if the man who had faded into the timber on the slope of the hill two to the east of this one . . .

Steele clipped the ordinarily terse response to his own circumstances as he halted the back-stepping stallion. Now shot another fleeting glance across the country to the east which continued to appear falsely empty of human presence – the flock of quail that of a sudden beat skywards from out of the pinon wood into which the rider had disappeared might well have been put up by an animal. Then Steele, instinctively moving his right hand closer to where the fire-scorched rosewood stock of his rifle jutted from the boot, urged his horse into the restricted area of near midday shadow at the base of the sheer-faced western end of the outcrop. To watch, his eyes hard and shining and his teeth exposed between lips still curled in the shape of the curtailed obscenity, as the trio of passengers emerged from the travel-stained and bullet-scarred Concord.

First a short and slightly built man who looked to be young. Next a taller and heavier woman with either white or blonde hair who was certainly not young and perhaps was not elderly. Finally, a tall and slender woman with a gait that suggested she was very old – for she readily accepted as essential the helping hand proffered by the young man, both to get out of the stage and to stay on her feet once she was down on the trail. Her hair and face were concealed by a veiled hat.

Because of the clarity of the sunlit air in the mountain foothills, Steele was able to see over the considerable intervening distance that all three whites were deeply afraid of what was happening to them. And yet it was also evident, from the manner in which she had refused his help and now moved to stand apart from him on the other side of the mourning-clad woman, that the other female passenger had emotion to spare for disliking the young man.

The yelling of orders had ended as the passengers stepped down from the stage. And whatever was said now fell far short of the watching Virginian's earshot as the four braves who had remained astride ponies slid smoothly to the ground. When, like the Indian who had brought the runaway team to a halt, they angled their rifles across their backs on leather slings. Three of the near-naked, lithe-bodied Utes drew knives from their weapons belts and brandished the sun-glinting blades to supplement spoken commands that perhaps were not understood by the gowned and city-suited whites. The woman in black was probably weakly silent as she swayed in the single-armed embrace of the man who, along with the second woman, seemed to be pleading with the braves. But then, as the trio of passengers complied with the animated commands to move away from the side of the Concord, it was realised that the Utes were in no mood to be merciful.

Whether this was conveyed by word or expression, Steele was unable to see because all five braves had their backs toward him as three closed in on the prisoners and two clambered up on to the seat and boot of the Concord. Then there was an abrupt flurry of vicious action and a burst of terrified vocal sound that caused the Virginian to fist his right gloved hand around the frame of the Colt Hartford and slide the rifle smoothly from the boot. But he did not thumb back the hammer nor even take a two-handed grip on the gun. And he did not hold back from these actions solely because of the coldly rational realisation that he was out of effective range. Also, he saw that the Indians did not intend to put the whites summarily to death – unless their prisoners invited such a quick end.

For one brave lunged forward, his free hand stretched out in front of him, to fasten a grip on the belt of the dress of the woman in black. Then he jerked her toward him, bringing his knife around in a part arc to tag her veiled hat with its point and flip it off her head. She shrieked her horror and the man from whose token protection she was snatched also roared a response to the sudden assault. Next he brought both his hands up and stretched out his arms as he made to go to her rescue. But the brave who stood immediately in front of him made two sideways slashing motions with his knife – the blade missing the splayed fingers of the white man's hands by a fraction of an inch. And the instinctive and futile attempt to pluck the woman back came to a despairing halt as one knife was held against the throat of the woman in black and another was thrust out, sword-like, toward the face of the man forced to surrender her. This as the second woman gave vent to a forlorn wail that ended with a cry of pain as she dropped heavily to her knees and extended her hands out in front of her, palms upward in a beseeching gesture.

And then all sound within the vicinity of the stalled stage was muted again while, for stretched seconds, the captives and their captors remained in an unmoving tableau and the two braves aboard the Concord began to cut open the roof baggage and boot freight and tip the contents down on to the trail. Crates and boxes too tough to submit to the ravaging knives were tossed down to await fuller attention later. They went about their appointed chore without apparently sparing a glance or thought for what was taking place between their brother braves and the whites. And what happened after the grieving woman was seen to be a quite young and not unattractive redhead was that all three whites were made more secure prisoners.

Evidently in the belief that they would not come to any harm if they did as they were told – or perhaps on the premise that where there is life there continues to be hope – the man and the older woman submitted to having their hands tied while the knife remained hard against the throat of the other woman. Then, always the least troublesome of the prisoners, the woman in black had her hands tied. Lengths of rope that had previously lashed the baggage to the roof of the Concord were used for the bonds. The women's hands were tied in front of them, the man's at his back.

Steele had returned his rifle to the boot as the danger of immediate killing receded. But he felt no temptation to consider that the worst was over for the whites, and he would soon with a clear conscience be able to get on his way again. And it was just a matter of two of three minutes, as the sun inched to the zenith of its arc across the near cloudless sky, before he and the prisoners were given an ominous series of increasingly conspicuous clues to what the Utes had in mind.

Firstly, as the pillage of the stagecoach continued in the same detached manner as always, the white man was made to sit on the ground so that his already bound wrists could be tied to a rear wheel of the Concord. Next, the older and fatter and more voluble woman had a length of rope tied between her lashed-together hands and the centre of the vehicle's rear axle. Then, as a brave ran back down the trail and out of Steele's range of vision behind the mound of high ground to his right, the woman in black was swept easily off her feet and deposited unceremoniously and ungracefully astride an Indian pony. And the brave who had taken charge of her from the very start took a firm grip on the rope reins of the animal.

Knives that were no longer required to pose threats of quick death or agonising injury were now returned to weapons belt sheaths while Steele sensed – he certainly could not hear – anxious queries being voiced by the whites and doubtless ignored by the Indians.

The forceful search for anything of value to the raiding party of Utes continued, with the two braves relieved of guard duty now squatting on their haunches to paw through the debris that had been hurled off the roof.

Steele was not sure if any of the prisoners continued to anguishly question the Utes.

Then the brave who had run from sight came back into view less frantically. He led three ponies by their rope reins and was carrying an extra rifle under an arm and two more on slings across his back. There was also an overload of assorted knives, tomahawks and pistols on his weapons belt and it was apparent he had been scavenging among the corpses of fallen whites and Indians before he gathered the loose horses.

Now, watched in horrified fascination by the two prisoners tied to the Concord and with a brand of temporary serene detachment by the woman on the pony, this brave took a hand in the task of looting the baggage. First wielded one of his tomahawks to smash open the strongest containers, then fashioned packs out of blankets and rope into which the booty was loaded. Two ponies each had a pair of such makeshift packs slung over their backs – the burdens bulky rather than heavy.

Then the work was done, and the five Utes prepared to

indulge themselves in the first rewards of their achievement. As the two women first pleaded and then screamed incoherently at them, four of the braves began to build a fire, collecting fuel from among the debris of the destructive looting. This while the young man held prisoner to the stage wheel appeared to be dumbstruck with dread of the agony that was in store for him – watched with a terrible intensity as the mound of combustible material grew larger at the base of his belly in the vee of his splayed legs.

Hooves began to hit the ground within earshot of the Virginian. Slow moving and not loud, for the horse was as yet some way off, behind him and to his right, heading along at the base of the south-facing side of the outcrop. And even as the distance to the corner of the butte-like mass of rock narrowed, the springy turf under the hooves of the horse acted to absorb much of the sound of impact. Then, when Steele estimated that the animal was some thirty feet short of the corner, the muted thuds of shod hooves on grass came to an abrupt halt. And he fisted a gloved hand around the frame of his rifle again as he shifted his gaze away from the brutal tableau on the distant trail and slowly turned his head to look over his shoulder.

Suddenly, the women became quiet and whatever other sounds were made in the area of the Concord were not loud enough to reach this far across the hill country to where the Virginian heard against the tense silence the scrape of a match and then its flare. Detected the acrid taint of tobacco smoke a moment before he saw a stream of it blown purposefully into view from behind the rock corner.

Then a voice he was almost certain he recognised announced, as the smoke was dispelled in the brightly sunlit air: 'If I meant you any harm, feller, I wouldn't be kicking up this much of a ruckus?'

Steele answered: 'I reckon I'm just naturally the quiet type.'

'Reb?'

'In one, Yank.'

'Sonofabitch, it sure is a small world,' the half-breed growled as he heeled his gelding into sight from around the side of the rock, and showed the merest flicker of a smile at the corners of his lips from which the freshly lit cigarette was angled.

'That is the hell of it,' the Virginian allowed with a similarly brief and not clearly defined expression displacing the impassive set of his features as he unclasped his hand from the rifle and turned his head to peer again at the evil that was taking place on the trail.

'Saw it from the other end of this ridge.'

'After you came up to see if I was fixing to bushwack you?' Steele asked with a grimace that was akin to anguished remorse paying a fleeting visit to his features as the taller man reined his gelding to a halt immediately alongside the stallion.

'Long time ago and a long way from here, Reb. And my memory gets shorter all the while. Unless somebody jogs it.'

Neither looked at the other in the stretched seconds of silence that ensued. And both continued to gaze dispassionately down at the activity beside the stalled stage when the Virginian said:

'Seems to me they're going to roast the kid Apache style, set the team to bolting again to drag the fat lady and save the redhead for cold nights.'

The half-breed took the cigarette away from the side of his mouth for just long enough to arc a globule of saliva at the ground. Then hung it back in place so that it bobbed up and down as he said: 'Looks like that, sure enough. And if we rode on by and allowed it to happen, figure that would be one memory real hard to bury, Reb.'

'Don't they say that there are just some things a man can't ride around, Yank?'

Steele responded with an almost imperceptible sigh. 'No, I never heard that said, feller. But you know what we'll be if you just head on east and I ride on by to the west?'

'Reckon you're going to tell me, Edge.'

'Shits that pass in the day.'

The cigarette had fizzled out part smoked and the half-breed removed it from his lips and eyed it balefully for a moment before he dropped it into the shirt pocket where he kept the makings.

'That's right, feller,' Steele agreed through pursed lips. 'And you know what?'

'Figure you'll tell me.'

'I don't reckon either of us is full of that much crap.'

CHAPTER THREE

DURING THE brief moments while the two violence-forged men who had met just twice before in times of turbulence and killing exchanged quiet-spoken words that in the evenness of their tone seemed oddly divorced from their subject matter, the Utes continued remorselessly to carry out their evil intent.

The Indians spoke infrequently, only in their native tongue, and invariably whatever was said caused short-lived mirth to erupt in all of them. This while their captives remained trapped into speechlessness by the horrifying prospect of what was quite obviously going to be the agonising fate of one of their number – the two women for the time oblivious to what the truncated future might hold for them as they found themselves sapped to emotional exhaustion by the extent of the helpless pity they felt for the tormented young man.

Speechless but not silent.

Every now and then, Amy Yancy was struck by a fit of trembling that attacked her body from head to toe. And when this happened she uttered a low moaning sound as she brought her forearms up to press against her breasts while she cupped her blood-stained face in her wrist-bound hands. This drawn-out cry, which had an eerie timbre to it, lasted for as long as there was breath in her lungs. And the Utes had at first been made uneasy by the strange moaning. But later they laughed whenever the wan-faced redhead astride the pony gave vent to the sound.

Edith Crawford constantly sobbed and sighed and it was as if her throat became parched in direct relation to the drying up of her reserve of tears. For the inarticulate voicing of the woman's abject misery – perhaps more deeply felt by her than the widow because she was conscience-striken over her prejudice – became increasingly croaking in tone as the beads of moisture ceased to squeeze from her eyes. This as she sat on the dusty trail, booted feet protruding from under the hems of her petticoats and the skirt of her dress: as far back from the Concord and Sun as the restraint of the linking rope allowed.

The young Chinese, who had never been loud in his pleas or protestations, was driven into almost total silence when the Utes began to build the fire between his legs and mortal terror of searing pain left him gulping for breath. But then, as the women became quieter while the braves continued calmly and with good humour to go about their brutal business, Sun started to issue sounds that might have been mistaken for speech. In a dull monotone that suggested he was offering up a prayer in a foreign language – so soft the sounds while he kept his head bent it was likely he did not know he was speaking aloud. But then it became apparent, as he slowly raised his sagged head up off his chest, that the sounds he uttered were as incomprehensible to himself as to the women and the Indians. That he was giving vent to an effect one step removed from a silent scream as he struggled toward the limit of his ability to keep himself from pitching into terror-triggered insanity.

Of those in a position to see the anguish scored into his suddenly no-longer-young face as he brought up his head, and from this to detect the nonsensical formlessness of the sound he was making, only Amy Yancy was disposed to take note of it. And for long moments after Sun gaped his mouth to its widest, to give full power to a bellowing scream, she felt sure his reason had snapped.

Her pity for him swelled and this caused the threat of a fresh assault of quaking to withdraw. Then she felt hot anger rising within her as she saw the Utes were crowing with cruel laughter at their prisoner's despair – was not able to hear their triumphant glee because the scream masked all other sounds. She saw, too, that the braves had heaped the fire as high as necessary. The peak was up to his lower chest.

The brave who had obviously, from the first moment the whites were captured, been the leader of the party of raiders now drew a box of matches from a pouch on his weapons belt. But, although the implication of this act made it a powerful image, the woman astride the pony found herself compelled to look away from it. To gaze instead at the sweat-beaded, drained-of-colour face of Edward Sun as his need to draw breath forced the scream to falter. She saw that he seemed to be trying to stretch open his eyes as wide as his mouth. But they were not the glazed and staring eyes of a mad man. In their dark irises and in the manner they switched from peering at Mrs Yancy to gazing into the distant south there was a plea for understanding and a demand for help. Rational and with an underlying threat of fury with her rather than frenzied mania should she fail to understand his tacit message.

On the periphery of her vision, as Sun curtailed the weakened scream and sucked in fresh breath, Amy Yancy glimpsed the bulky form of Edith Crawford and saw that the older woman was shaking her head in pitying acknowledgement of her belief that the young man had finally been plunged into madness. Then, as he gave vent to another piercingly shrill scream, Mrs Yancy realised he was not responding to the scrape of the match on the side of the stage. And she followed the movement of his imploring eyes away from her own face – half-turned from the waist to look in the direction he demanded.

She saw the two men riding at a flat-out gallop through the fold of the two hills to the south. For what seemed to her – and to Edward Sun, no doubt – an inordinately long time, she was filled with a flood of joyful relief that took her breath away and constricted her throat. But it could not have been more than a second before she heard the distant thud of beating hooves and snapped her attention back to Sun. Then was able to emit a shriek that had far more to do with the first flicker of flame of the fire than in helping the threatened young man to mask the sounds of the running horses.

Edith Crawford added her voice to the cacophony, as ignorant as were the now whooping and hollering Utes that she was contributing to her own salvation. Until one of the braves, launching into a body-jerking war-dance that aped the action of the leaping flames, lurched into a turn and saw the would-be rescuers. He halted and did a double-take while his mouth remained open but no sing-song discord came out of it. Then he roared a terse warning and sought to get his rifle from across his back as the other braves peered southward and needed no second look to be certain that imagination played no part in what they saw there.

Both riders had their rifles out of the boot and each had the hammer pulled back behind a bullet in the breech. They rode equally well, even with the reins flying free so they could aim from the shoulder with a two-handed grip on Colt Hartford and Winchester. But Adam Steele was indisputably the better marksman with a rifle and it was he who triggered the first shot. From something over three hundred yards away – the crack of the bullet leaving the muzzle ending a part second of what would have been silence had it not been for the beat of pumping hooves on lush pastureland.

The brave who had raised the alarm uttered an almost apologetic grunt as he gave up the struggle to get the rifle off his back, looked at the hole in his chest and toppled over backward: dead before he hit the ground and the impact caused blood to spurt from the wound in his naked flesh.

The two women shouted in joy now, as Edward Sun's scream took on the tone of true terror.

Edge and Steele fired in near-perfect unison and the first brave to get his rifle and sling over his head took both bullets. One in the head and the other the chest. The impacts sent him into a corkscrewing turn as he fell, and spraying blood from the head wound hissed and steamed in the brightly burning fire.

It took less time for the gloved thumb to cock the hammer and work the revolver action of the Colt Hartford than for the brown-skinned hand of the half-breed to pump the lever of the Winchester. Both men fired as soon as there was a bullet in the breech and one sharp crack was like a rapid echo of the other.

Both shots failed to hit their intended targets – the

Virginian and the half-breed each purposely jerking his rifle to aim high at the first instant after it was too late to stay his finger on the trigger. They needed to do this to avoid the risk of shooting down the woman in black who suddenly hurled herself off the pony.

While the two misdirected bullets were still arcing upward, the revolver action turned again, and a spent shellcase was displaced for a live round to the dictates of the lever action. And the woman in widow's weeds came up off the ground with something clutched in her bound hands.

The Ute who had been holding the pony on which she had sat now swung himself on to the animal's back. And he triggered a shot wildly toward the two white men who had now ridden close enough to the trail for their grinning teeth to be seen in stark contrast to the burnished hues of their skin.

'Mine on the pony, Reb!' Edge yelled..And fired as he rasped: 'Shit!' when the Ute's bullet came close enough to him so that he heard the whisper of displaced air a fraction of an inch from his right ear.

The brave who almost shot off the half-breed's ear with a lucky bullet was himself hit in the neck by a carefully aimed one and was sent pitching off the back of the pony as he sought to wheel the animal which lunged into a bolt along the trail the moment it was relieved of the burden of the rider.

The two surviving braves elected not to waste time and effort with their rifles – directed their full attention to throwing themselves astride mounts and racing clear of the lethally accurate gunfire directed at them.

By which time Amy Yancy was beating frantically at the flames leaping up from the debris piled between the splayed legs of the young man who flinched back against the wheel to which he was tied – both of them sobbing their frustration as the fire seemed to blaze more fiercely under the assault of the slashed-open carpetbag and the immovability of the heavy stage defied the puny physical effort of one slight man to slide it sideways.

Loose ponies, two of them burdened with loot from the stage, galloped off in the wake of the first Ute horse to make a break from the smoke and flame-tainted, noise-filled area of the stage. Two animals with enraged and frightened braves astride them headed into the billowing dust put up by the front runners.

Steele triggered off two rapid shots, the second necessary because he was sure he only snicked a piece of flesh out of the upper arm of the moving target with the first bullet. And the leader of the Ute raiding party swayed and then toppled to the ground, dark crimson spraying in short spurts from the hole in his back as he bounced several times after dropping from the pony.

Edith Crawford was lending a hand with the fire-fighting by then. The limiting factor of the lead line that trapped her to the axle kept her out of reach of anything that could be used to beat at the flames: but she was able to hike her dress skirt and petticoat immodestly high as she raked flaring debris clear of Sun with a booted foot.

A lone Ute raced his pony westward on the trail, his rifle unfired on his back as he pressed himself low and hard against his mount – shrieking and thudding in his heels to demand more effort than the animal was capable of producing.

At the same time, the two white men who had turned the Indians' gleeful triumph into deadly defeat were reining the black stallion and the chestnut gelding to unfrenetic halts at the side of the trail. A few yards short of where the two women sank gratefully to the ground and the young half-Chinese fought against unconsciousness after the fire was out.

'Both of us got one, Yank,' the Virginian recalled evenly as he tilted his rifle and thumbed aside the gate to begin extracting expended cases from the chambers of the cylinder. 'My count gives me two of the others.'

Edge had already pumped the lever of the Winchester. He waited until his mount was still, then took the time to spit. And only then released the reins, threw the stock of the rifle to his shoulder as he swung from the waist, and squeezed the trigger. Because the thud of the unshod hooves of the Ute pony came from some way off now, and there were no other sounds in the wake of the strident din of the recent battle, the single crack of the bullet exploding from the muzzle of the Winchester seemed disproportionately loud to the two women, who both gasped their shock as they stared fixedly out along the trail. It also acted to jerk Edward Sun back from the brink of total exhaustion that had threatened to drive him into unconsciousness. And he leaned his head against the side of the wheelrim to peer with near-empty eyes at the two mounted men.

This as the retreating brave took the bullet in his angled forward back, left of centre. And then tumbled off the pony to the right as the lightened animal raced away with a greater turn of speed. A moment later the one-time rider lay utterly still in the settling dust of the pumping hooves.

'Two and a half each, Reb,' Edge intoned dully as he ejected the final empty shellcase from the rifle and began to reload the depleted magazine with bullets taken from his gunbelt loops. 'Nothing was owed from last time so we stay even?'

'Agreed, Yank. If the horse hadn't been dead way back then, we'd have flogged it to death by now?'

'I guess.'

Steele was first to finish the reloading chore and now he booted the Colt Hartford and slid smoothly from the saddle. Tipped his hat as the women switched their still-shocked attention toward him and glistening tears of deliverance showed in the young man's dark eyes.

'Ladies, son,' he greeted. 'I'm Adam Steele and this is Edge. No other name.'

The half-breed completed reloading the Winchester and slid the rifle into the boot. He looked back along the trail to where the corpses of Carmody and Washington and the first two Utes to be shot were sprawled on the dusty ground at irregular intervals.

Sun had to swallow hard several times before he was able to force out: 'Thanks.'

'Yes, we are deeply indebted to you,' Mrs Yancy said, her voice hardly louder than a croaking whisper.

'If you will be so kind as to free us from our bonds . . .?' Mrs Crawford added breathlessly as she raised her tied hands.

'Certainly,' Steele responded. And left the still-mounted

half-breed to keep watch on the surrounding country as he stooped to draw the knife from his boot sheath. Then freed the older woman and the young man from the Concord and finally cut the ropes which held Amy Yancy's wrists together.

'I am Edith Crawford, wife of Major E. T. Crawford who commands Fort Hamilton, sir,' announced the first captive to be freed, struggling valiantly to regain her composure after an experience which she probably now recalled for its humiliation rather than its danger. 'The other lady is Mrs Amy Yancy who was married to the late Lieutenant Cole Yancy who recently died from sickness at the fort.' She glanced with facile sympathy at the widow and then waved a hand negligently at their travelling companion as she completed the introductions: 'Mr Edward Sun who has no military connection to my knowledge.'

It was apparent to both newcomers that the older woman harboured an active dislike for the part-Oriental who moments before she had helped to save from a searing ordeal. And as her small green eyes briefly surveyed each of them in a head-to-toe appraisal they were left with a strong suspicion that in normal circumstances Edith Crawford would disapprove of them, too.

She was a tall woman – perhaps five feet ten – and because of this her well-padded frame in the elegant and expensive pale-green gown did not appear excessively overweight. But her florid face in a frame of greying black hair stopped a few ounces short of being bloated. She looked every day of her more than sixty years in the wake of terror and mishandling, and the strain of attempting to appear indifferent to the immediate past probably increased the wretchedness of her appearance.

By contrast, the redhead with the dried blood on her cheeks, who was about thirty years of age, had the kind of long and lean face with sharp features that somehow became more attractive when it expressed the darker emotions – from anger perhaps all the way to agony. She was a match for Steele's height and maybe was so scrawnily thin from being sick in her recent state of widowhood. She was not yet ready to make any conscious effort at rising above natural reactions to what was happening to her. And her big, round, pale blue eyes by turn expressed relief and terror while her thin lips were drawn back to display an involuntary fixed grin.

'Thanks again, you guys,' rasped the young man with the good-looking part-Chinese part-Occidental features as he rose to his full five feet three inch height with difficulty: needing to lean his slightly built frame against the wheel to which he had been tied. He had already fought the threat of tears from his dark eyes and now he tried to smile. But the expression became more like a scowl as he gently massaged the inner thigh of his right leg where the flames had burned through the fabric of his pants and scorched the flesh beneath.

'Oh, you're hurt!' Amy Yancy exclaimed. And seemed almost happy to have something outside her own suffering to command her concern.

'It's okay, lady!' the young man was quick to assure her as she swung to look intently at him. He held out his arms to defend himself against her ministrations. 'I can handle it myself!'

The Virginian shot a glance at the half-breed as the pain of the burn forced the young man's hands back to the top of his inner leg.

'Guess he doesn't want anybody else to know how he feels, feller,' Edge said, touching the brim of his hat as he picked up the loose reins of his mount. 'Ladies, kid, Reb.' He nodded to all four of them in turn. 'Been any more Indians around here, my guess is they'd have made a move by now?'

An inflection in his voice added the query as he watched Steele straighten up from replacing the knife back in the boot sheath.

'Reckon so,' the Virginian agreed as he swung back to his horse and remounted.

'Are you just going to leave us here like this?' Edith Crawford demanded quickly. She waved both her arms to encompass the debris-and-corpse-strewn area immediately beside the stalled stage and the bodies, white and Indian, sprawled in the hot sun up and down the trail. 'What about . . .?'

'It's okay, Mrs Crawford,' Sun put in when the dread of being abandoned by their two rescuers acted to constrict the older woman's throat. And Amy Yancy was only able to utter a strangled cry of muted alarm. 'My folks' place ain't so far from here. I can handle driving the rig to the farm. Then my father'll maybe ride the rest of the way into Oro City if—'

'That's fine, Mr Sun,' Steele said, and tugged on his reins to head his stallion eastwards, just a moment after Edge had turned his gelding toward the western stretch of trail.

'But surely you'll help us with the bodies of the unfortunate driver and guard?' Edith Crawford asked.

'They saved our lives, ma'am,' the younger woman pointed out as both riders heeled their horses in opposite directions. And there was suddenly bitterness in her tone, that was as clearly evident as Edith Crawford's anger with the departing men. 'I suppose we must be content they deigned to break their journey to do that!'

'But that one's even going the same way we are!' the older woman cried and pointed a shaking arm after Edge. She wrenched her head around to glare in the wake of the slow-riding Steele. 'And that one I thought was a true southern gentleman who . . .'

Again she either failed to find a way to finish what she intended or did not trust herself to continue for fear of what she might say.

Edward Sun sagged dejectedly against the wheel, obviously not feeling so confident with the situation as he had previously attempted to appear. And he growled, pointedly loud enough for both riders to overhear him: 'Can't deny that it would've been the worse for us if those two guys hadn't happened by when they did . . . but that don't alter the fact they ain't the nicest pair of characters I ever met up with.'

'Amen to that,' Mrs Crawford muttered, her ill-feeling toward the part-Chinese relegated again, as she nurtured disgruntlement with the half-breed and the Virginian.

Amy Yancy added with a shrug of her skinny shoulders that did not dislodge the scowl from her gauntly attractive face: 'Perhaps men who kill so expertly as those cannot be expected to have any of the finer human feelings.'

'You could be right, ma'am,' the Virginian allowed with a casual glance over his shoulder. 'Or it could be I'm always a little rough around one Edge?'

He was facing front again when the half-breed added with a backward glance of his own: 'And maybe I find it hard to warm to cold Steele?'

CHAPTER FOUR

EDGE DID not look back again after voicing the sardonic comment until he had ridden far enough along the western stretch of trail to be almost out of sight of the stage-line passengers: and far beyond the range of vision of Adam Steele. He did not scan his back trail to check upon the whereabouts and activities of these people – rather, he knew he was far enough away from them for the intervening terrain to be host to unknown possible dangers. Thus he raked his narrow-eyed gaze along the trail and over the country, flanking it in precisely the same apparently indifferent manner as he had scanned the grass and timbered hills ahead of his slow-moving horse since leaving the stalled Concord. Not noticeably expecting a fresh outbreak of trouble, but certainly prepared to deal with the unexpected should it occur.

Which was the way it had been for a long time over a great many trails for the man called Edge. Just as it was not his way to dwell upon what had just happened back down the trail. Since, on both counts, too much of a similar nature had involved him after the fates conspired to force him into the life of a drifter. Sometimes embroiling him with people he knew or even cared about, most often not. Whichever, he had surely learned not to reflect upon the recent or distant past during those times he should be watching out to stay alive and have a future.

Adam Steele used to survive by this among other basic rules. But the Virginian had sure been too engrossed in something other than watching out for himself for a long time before he spotted he had company in the hills to the south of this trail.

'Goddamn you to hell, Reb!' the half-breed rasped through teeth clenched in a grimace of self-anger. 'Now you got me at it.'

But then a slight alteration in the line of his curled-back lips and even less of a change in the glittering light of the ice-blue slivers of his eyes made the expression into a grin that stopped just short of being warm. And he shook his head slowly as he dug the part-smoked cigarette from his shirt pocket, hung it from a side of his mouth and struck a match to light it on the jutting stock of the booted Winchester. Allowed smoke to trickle from his nostrils as he scanned this fine looking hill country between mountains and canyon land brightly and warmly lit by the early afternoon sun of early summer. And, without voicing his thoughts now, decided that for old time sake he should not feel mad because he had been tempted to spare a sympathetic thought for a man who was not so sharp as he used to be. For such an uncharacteristic line of thought could not bring him any grief – provided he did not now or later project it along a side track concerned with the premise of *there but for the grace of God or the whim of the Devil . . .*

Suddenly the lean face with its half day's growth of bristles was totally impassive again and the threads of his eyes between the cracked-open lids might well have been made of the ice they resembled, so empty of emotion were they. And for long moments the conscious effort of will he had to make to remain detached from what had happened could be seen in the rigid posture he adopted in the saddle as he maintained his wary surveillance over every point of the compass.

Then it was finished and he was once more the complete loner owed nothing by the world and not beholden to anyone in it. The past was as devoid of substance as the future and there was just the present with himself and his horse and the sum total of all he owned which was carried on his back or on the back of the horse. Travelling between Denver and the next town on the trail which might or might not be, he now saw, the Oro City of which the young part-Chinese had spoken. For, as he rode around the northern rim of a thickly timbered hollow, he spotted the falling-down signpost at the intersection of the trails, short of which the Virginian had angled to the side in a vain attempt to detour around trouble.

Edge had no occasion not to ride directly up to the three-armed sign, where he reined in his mount. And manoeuvred the gelding this way and that as he screwed his head to the side to read the faded lettering on the bleached timber arms. First to confirm that the trail he was riding had come from Denver, then that to swing to the south west would bring him to Yuma, and finally that to the north west lay Virginia City.

No mileages were shown, but the half-breed's geography was sound enough for him to know that Yuma, down close to the border with Mexico, and Virginia City which was near the distant California state line beyond the territories, were both a lot further way from here than was Denver. So, for sure, there would be communities along both trails other than Oro City and Fort Hamilton. But as he gave the gelding his head and the animal took the curve of the north west spur, Edge felt no degree of chagrin with the inanimate sign or those responsible for placing it there. For such signs were expressly for travellers with destinations in mind. And right now this particular traveller was looking no further ahead than for a place in the shade where he might eat and his mount could crop some grass, the both of them resting up for an hour or so, in relative safety from surprise attack.

And he found such a place some two miles from the intersection where the trail, after rising steadily for several hundred yards, was about to drop down an even gentler slope into a broad and shallow valley. There was a small stand of timber to provide shade and fuel for a fire and plenty of lush grazing on the brow of the hill that was featured with little else to north and south, in which directions it stretched more than far enough to suit the half-breed's purpose. Likewise, he had a clear view across a great deal of country in back of where he unsaddled and hobbled his horse and then started a cooking fire and set a pot amid its flames, and out over the land he intended to traverse this afternoon.

It was a green valley where it started out below his campsite, but it gradually deteriorated through a patch of rugged badlands meagrely scattered with vegetation into a vast tract of mesa-dominated scrub desert. The clarity of the air, Edge knew, acted to foreshorten distances and he made no attempt to estimate how long it would take him to reach the badlands and then cross them to get to the rim of the desert. Not least did he refrain from this because he was unable to see if the trail headed in the due-west direction he looked. Virginia City was sure way out at the end of such a crow's-flight line, but a trail for a hundred and one good or bad reasons seldom took the shortest distance between two points.

All of which was of purely academic disinterest to the half-breed as he waited for the salt pork and beans to heat in the cooking pot and then ate the meal, while he paid no more attention to one direction than any other. Then washed down the food with still-fresh water from a canteen refilled only this morning, and smoked a slow cigarette. Maybe he'd follow the route dictated by the trail or maybe he'd swing off the well-trodden way. On a whim or because events would have an influence on his decision.

He chose the time to douse the fire, clean up the cooking and eating utensils and saddle the gelding. And start down into the hilly and timbered bottom land of the valley's eastern end. While a bunch of dead Ute braves motivated him to maintain a more cautious than usual watch over his surroundings – in the same manner that he had been doing since he rode away from the scene of the carnage. For, although it was customary for him to remain alert to the first sign of trouble at all times, he had been aware of a greater degree of tension than usual within himself after he fired the shot that dropped the last Indian. Normally, unless the danger was real and present, he was only vaguely conscious of being on his guard.

The Indians who had hit the Central Western stage and by so doing had temporarily involved Edge in fresh violence were all dead. And as such they should have been forgotten by him, like a whole lot of other men – and not a few women – who had died unpeacefully out along his back trail. But he had a disconcerting feeling about this bunch of braves that, had he been the worrying kind, would have caused him more than a modicum of anxiety. He could not explain it, but he had an increasingly itchy hunch that the seven Utes who died the hard way a few hours earlier were not just a band of outcast renegades running wild and raising havoc in isolation. There was nothing he had seen in the vicinity of the ravaged Concord, and no sign he had spotted on the trail before or after the braves hit the whites, that lent support to his notion that there was big Indian trouble in the offing. He merely felt it: as an occasional prickling sensation between his shoulder blades, in a tightening up every now and then of the tissue at the pit of his belly, the way in which beads of sweat oozed and instantly dried on his flesh at the small of his back and the nape of his neck at infrequent intervals, and how sometimes his lips drew back from gritted teeth and he knew he was involuntarily showing a killer's grin in anticipation of what was to come.

Then, as the warm afternoon lengthened toward cooling evening, the half-breed picked up the first signal that might validate his still staunchly held opinion that the trouble he messed in at midday time was to have far-reaching repercussions for him.

He smelled the dry redolence of recent burning. Not strongly at first, for when he became aware of the arid scent in the air the trail was running through a thick pine wood and the atmosphere was pungent with the smell of the trees. Probably, had he not been so highly attuned today to discern anything that was alien in these natural surroundings, he would have failed to spot it so early. But, as it was, his now actively alerted senses soon began to recognise sign for which he consciously hunted.

Initially just a more powerful smell as he closed with its source and a gentle evening breeze began to stir the air at dusk, blowing for the most part directly into his heavily bristled face. Timber had been burnt, but not just on a stove or a cooking fire. The flames had gone out many hours ago, for although the stink of an old fire must inevitably be stale, there was a particularly timeworn fustiness in this gloomy air: and the atmosphere was so filled with it, this had been no tamely confined blaze.

In the rapidly failing light while the reddening rays of the setting sun got weaker and were further diminished in the wood by the evergreen foliage of the pines, Edge saw where the rider in whose tracks his own gelding had been walking for so long had reined in his mount and discarded a less-than-half-smoked cigar. This rider had steered his horse on to the trail from the north side the best part of a mile back from here. And had ridden without hurry and without pause until this point. Several hours ago, Edge had estimated, without taking the time and trouble to dismount and look closely at the horse apples which were deposited soon after the trail was joined. The horse was well-shod, which did not necessarily indicate the rider was not an Indian brave.

The half-breed could not tell if the discarded cigar had been left to fizzle out before, after or at about the same time as the fire which continued to scent the air. He could see that the rider had dismounted and led his horse on from where the cigar was dropped and left to burn a half inch of tobacco to grey ash before it died. The man who had so abruptly lost his taste for smoking the cigar had died one hundred and fifty yards further on along the trail.

Shadows were deep and numerous in the timber now, and the irregularly outlined patch of blood that had soaked into the dust of the trail might have passed for another one had there not been an ejected shellcase lying close by. The stink of charred timber was exceedingly strong now, but there was still no scent of imminent danger in the softly stirring and fast-cooling air – Edge had never sensed anything more than a portent of what lay in wait at a constant one step removed from the present.

Just as he had done back at the burnt-out cigar, he halted his gelding to peer down dispassionately at the bloodstain, the untarnished shellcase and the disturbed area of dust surrounding them. He read from the sign the way the dismounted cigar smoker who quit so late in his life had got off a single shot from what must surely have been a repeating rifle. Before or after he was himself shot – certainly hit by more than one bullet to spill so much blood. For certainly he was not left here for long to bleed. Before two men, one barefoot and another in moccasins, came to claim his discarded rifle and to drag him along the trail. He was a corpse by then, for no fresh blood was pumped from his wounds to emphasise the way he was hauled. His horse, which had bolted to the south, was led back on to the trail by another moccasin-clad Indian a lot closer to the scene of the fire.

A scene which, in the final heeltaps of twilight before the moonglow became stronger than the wash of the already-set sun, triggered from deep at the back of the half-breed's mind a painful memory of a burnt-out farm on the Iowa prairie seen in the full brightness of a spring day. Then, as he pursed his lips in front of his teeth set in a grimace, he caught the scent of roasted meat permeating the more dominant stink of the burnt-out buildings. And, as he reined in his horse a few feet from where a naked Indian brave was spread-eagled in death beside a dry stone wall, spat noisily after averting his head from the scene. Then, his mind as devoid of ancient memories as his face was empty of expressive responses to what he saw, he glanced down at the stripped brave with two bullet holes in his chest and congealed blood in his mouth and looked at how, in passing, the Ute's death had been avenged.

A freshly lit, much smaller fire, burning in a circle of rocks across the trail from the charred and sooted debris of the old and destructive one, was spiralling smoke appetisingly laced with the aroma of brewing coffee into the sunlit air of early morning when Adam Steele slowed the Concord of the Central Western line to a stop on the trail. Then, a moment later, the door with the bullet-smashed window was flung open, and the slight figure of Edward Sun lunged out.

The city-suited young man who had come so close to burning to death yesterday shrieked: 'Ma, Pa!' as he raced out ahead of the lead horses in the traces. Where he came to an abrupt halt as his frantically searching dark eyes suddenly ended their constant movement in the enlarged sockets. To focus fixedly upon one fragment of the fire-blackened scene as he murmured: 'Holy . . . oh no, please no.'

The Virginian leaned to the side and looked down at the open doorway where Amy Yancy was emerging from the stage ahead of the older and more heavily built Edith Crawford: 'I should warn you ladies . . .' he started. But saw that both women had already seen the particular aspect of the old fire that caused the young man such anguish.

'Savages,' the good-looking redhead gasped, and was able to keep a hold on her composure by glancing at the bullet-shattered brave sprawled under the wall – her abhorrence for the kind that he represented finely balanced with the revulsion she felt for what they had done here. 'Heathen savages.'

The other woman's puffy face expressed a strangely low-keyed brand of sad indignation – as if she were wary of showing a more natural and powerful emotion. And her tone of voice was even more forcedly false as she said: 'If we are all God's creatures, my dear, it is a sore temptation at such times as this to doubt His goodness.'

The two of them moved forward to flank the paralysed-with-shock Sun, and the Virginian wound the reins around the brake lever. Then slid his Cold Hartford from the boot of his saddle which was one of only three pieces of luggage now carried on the roof rack of the stage. The other two were quite obviously blanket-wrapped corpses. When he had climbed down from the high seat, Steele glanced at where his black stallion was hitched to the rear of the Concord and then ambled across to where Edge sat on an exposed tree root close to the camp fire. The half-breed was shaving without using a mirror – a chore he had not interrupted since the familiar Concord had been driven into sight by a man he did not expect to see holding the reins.

Both the young half-Chinese and Adam Steele were freshly shaved, and the two women looked their best given the circumstances – they had washed up, given some attention to their hair and had rescued enough from their plundered and mistreated belongings to make a change of clothing. The widow was no longer attired solely in black and her sombre-hued dress and grey hat were not designed on such severe lines as her previous garb. Edith Crawford now wore a less stylish dress that flattered her stout frame not at all but was better suited to travel in its fabric and cut and to the tragic circumstances of the journey in its drab brown colour.

'Hell of a thing, Edge,' Steele said evenly. 'Two of them are the kid's mother and father.'

'Other one came riding by on the trail.'

'I saw the sign back there.'

The half-breed scraped a final patch of lathered bristles off his throat, then wiped the razor and returned it to the pouch at the nape of his neck. Only now, as he towelled his face dry with a corner of a bed blanket did he look again at the gruesome sight that held the expressionless attention of the Virginian. And said:

'Way I had it figured, you were heading in the opposite direction, feller.'

'I was, but . . .'

Both men beside the campfire under the tree switched their gaze away from another tree across the trail to look at where Edward Sun wrenched himself out of the supportive grasps of the two women with a moaning cry of great distress. And just made it to the dry stone wall before the nausea hit him – so that he was able to fold himself over the wall and achieve some degree of privacy as he vomited in delayed reaction to the brutal manner of his parent's death.

'. . . something came up,' Steele finished. And added: 'That's not meant as some kind of sick joke, Yank.'

The half-breed nodded and growled: 'Yeah, Reb. That would be reaching new depths.'

CHAPTER FIVE

BEFORE THE Indians hit there had been a house and a barn in a yard enclosed by the dry stone wall on the trail frontage and a run of three-stranded wire fencing along the other three sides. The Chinese farmer and his Occidental wife had been in process of extending the wall along one side but had got only so far as placing a single level of flat rocks a matter of fifteen feet from the corner. The couple had needed to haul the rocks from out of a ravine about three hundred yards away across the unfenced fields in which grew a whole array of vegetables, some fruit and even cotton and a little tobacco. But they had not needed to split and break the rocks: this had been done by whatever enormous natural force had cleaved the ravine into the bluff side in primeval times before man was put upon earth to commit inhumanity to his fellow man.

Perhaps in building the three and a half feet high wall around the yard the farmer and his wife had been testing their abilities before starting to construct a more substantial house to replace that which, like the barn, had been timber-built – except for the chimney that was all that remained standing, albeit charred black, amid the burnt-out wreckage of the Sun home and single out-building.

The place and its carefully tended fields – the healthy-looking early summer crops had not been touched by the Ute raiders – were on the north side of the trail, on the fringe of an expanse of mixed timber: the couple having settled on what was the last piece of arable ground before the red rock country began.

On the opposite side of the trail the timber spread a little further westward, although the trees quickly became more scattered and increasingly stunted in growth before they petered out here, too, where the rock took over from the thinning layer of arid and acid, dead soil.

'You uncaring swine, you could at least have cut the bodies down!' Edith Crawford shrieked suddenly to end the brittle silence that had existed for perhaps three seconds in the wake of the nausea-stricken man's final dry retch.

'I'll do it, lady – if the boy can't take care of the chore himself,' Edge said evenly to the gloweringly reproachful woman as he came erect after pouring a cup of coffee from the pot in the fire.

The oak tree that grew at the front corner of the farmstead yard would have provided pleasant shade during high summer afternoons for two of the three people who now hung motionless from one of its limbs in the still, as yet just warm air of early morning. All the corpses were suspended upside-down by ropes that tied their bound ankles to the tree limb. The man who was dead – or as near dead as made no difference from several bullet wounds in his chest before he was strung up to the tree – had not been stripped of his clothing and his arms dangled freely. Edward Sun's parents were naked – thus could their sex be clearly seen and their nationalities guessed at – and their arms were bound to their sides at elbows and wrists.

The farmer and his wife were hanging to either side of the shot man, far enough away so that the fire lit beneath his head would not have harmed them. While it burned the sleeves off his arms, the hair off his head and the flesh off his hands before the intense heat burst open his skull. Harmed them physically, at least. Although perhaps the sight and sound and smell of the partial cremation of the corpse would have driven the helpless couple insane as they waited for the fires to be ignited beneath their heads: maybe mercifully had plunged them into some wondrous state out of mind to where the agonies of the torture could not reach.

'Yes, sir,' Edward Sun rasped out of his punished throat as he turned from the wall, scrubbing at his mouth and chin with a handkerchief. 'I appreciate that you are thinking of my best interests, Mrs Crawford, ma'am. But I thank

Edge for allowing me the opportunity to take care of my own.'

The young man executed a stiffly formal Oriental-style bow toward the half-breed before he headed for the wagon-wide gateway in the centre of the boundary wall. Edge responded with a slight nod as he lowered himself back down on to the tree root and called across the trail as Sun stepped through the gateway:

'Didn't know if the shot feller was some kind of kin.'

'No, sir, but I will attend to him, too, thank you.'

'Anybody else wants coffee, they'll need something to drink it from,' Edge said as the two women started toward him, and quite obviously had to make a conscious effort to keep their horrified eyes from looking at what the young man was doing beyond the wall.

'The way I feel now, I doubt I will ever be able to keep anything inside of me for a very long time, Mr Edge,' Amy Yancy answered. She looked close to the point of nausea, until she sank gratefully down to sit on the half-breed's saddle when he indicated she should.

'And I could get sick to my stomach from simply watching you pour coffee into yourself in such circumstances as these!' Edith Crawford challenged. She had difficulty in supplanting her dislike of the man with expressive revulsion for what he was doing.

'Be obliged if you'd follow the kid's example if you really are going to throw up, Mrs Crawford,' Edge told her. 'On the other hand, be happy for you to take a seat on my blankets if you'll just shut up.'

'Well, I never . . .' the older woman began to shriek.

'Please, ma'am,' the seated woman put in wearily as the other became lost for words. And shared an imploring look between her and the half-breed. 'If there really is to be a serious hostile uprising in this country, the situation will not be helped by us — '

'Very well, my dear,' the older woman interrupted and gave a toss of her head to dismiss Edge from her thoughts. 'You are perfectly correct.' She lowered herself decorously to sit on the blanket and gazed fixedly into the fire.

Steele, who had remained standing throughout, with his

rifle canted to a shoulder in a loose fist as he made a cold-eyed survey of the fire-wrecked farmstead and its surroundings, now drawled:

'We had breakfast more than two hours ago, Edge. Before we broke camp and made an early start. At the place where you stopped to eat at the head of the valley yesterday?'

The half-breed nodded as he set down his mug and took the makings from his shirt pocket. 'That must have been a real early start, feller.' He gestured toward the stage and its patiently waiting team. 'Seeing as how the horses don't look to have been driven too hard.'

'It is doubtful if any of the three of us got more than five minutes' sleep at a stretch,' Mrs Yancy said.

Despite the proximity of the recent death and destruction in an atmosphere redolent of evil, Edge had slept well throughout the hours of cool darkness, and his freshly washed and shaved face showed relaxed evidence of this. While, at close quarters, he was able to see that the Virginian and the two women were bone-deep weary in back of their spruced-up look.

'That's myself, Mrs Yancy and the young man,' Edith Crawford hurried to explain, like she was anxious to have a role in the discussion despite her dislike of one of the others taking part.

'Yes. After you and Mr Steele went on your respective ways, Mrs Crawford and the young man and I attended to the bodies of Mr Carmody and Mr Washington in as dignified a manner as possible . . .' Amy Yancy stole a brief glance at the Concord with the blanket-wrapped corpses up on the roof. 'And then Mr Sun took charge of the driving. But he did not trust himself to remain fully alert during the night, and when it got dark we paused at the place where it appears you did some time earlier, Mr Edge. As I have already said, we slept little. But the horses were in sore need of rest, of course.'

The half-breed lit his cigarette with a glowing stick from the fire as, across the trail and beyond the wall, the youngster was unable to trap just one sob in his chest as he cut the naked, head-burst body of his mother free of the tree branch. Amy Yancy gulped and clutched at her throat with both hands. Edith Crawford made to rise, but froze when Steele laid a restraining hand on her shoulder.

'Reckon he might thank you right now, ma'am,' the Virginian drawled softly. 'But not later.'

The women had not looked at the gruesome scene under the torture tree since they had been able to tear their gazes away from it. Now Edge and Steele glanced briefly toward the shaking but silent young man as he rose from setting down the corpse of his mother – and stepped back up on the iron framework of a burned chair to use the fire-tarnished blade of a handleless knife on the bonds that held his father's body prisoner to the limb.

'I can understand, Mr Steele,' the young widow murmured as she gazed levelly into the middle distance. 'The reason I am here now is because I insisted upon bringing my poor dead husband home for a burial and . . .'

'Came back to warn these people, Edge,' the Virginian put into the pause after Amy Yancy lost the thread of what she was saying or decided that her thoughts on this subject should remain private. 'And to keep from perhaps ending up something like those.' He gestured with a slight movement of the Colt Hartford toward where Edward Sun was gently letting down his father's fire ravaged body to the ground. 'Found the ladies and the kid at their night camp and helped them to move out.'

'You didn't see any trouble of this kind, feller.'

'You know it. You were riding the trail out of the east yesterday morning. All the way from Denver, maybe?'

'All the way from Denver.'

'So you know there's nobody living on the trail for a lot of miles up toward the Wolf Pass.'

'Right, Reb.'

'Saw Indians, plain and simple. Three parties of them. A bunch of less than a dozen, another of twenty or more, and then just four. All of them braves, far as I could tell. Saw them over quite a distance in failing light. Two of the parties heading to where the other was in camp. Those on the move coming in from the north east and the south east.'

Edge nodded. 'So that if the whole bunch was going to

start out after their council or whatever, this would be a likely direction for them to come?'

'Right, Yank.'

'Especially since you knew that another bunch of braves had already stirred some . . .' He glanced through the drifting smoke of his cigarette at the censorious Mrs Crawford and the sadly reflective Mrs Yancy, and ended with a different choice of phrase: '. . . made some trouble over this way?'

Now Steele nodded, and continued with his apparently disinterested survey of his surroundings as he asked: 'If you had seen any Indian activity on your way through from Denver, I reckon you'd have made mention of it?'

'Sure I would.' He rose from the tree root and refilled his cup with coffee as Edward Sun, with the wooden face and impersonal actions of an automaton, silently cut down the stranger. 'You didn't pass by here before? You were heading up the trail from Yuma when the stage got hit?'

'Started on it a long way north of Yuma, Yank. No sign of Indian trouble in the country I came through.'

The redheaded widow suddenly vented a soft cry of alarm and shuddered as a twig in the fire cracked with the heat. For long moments as the two men peered down at her and Edith Crawford eyed her at the same level, Amy Yancy seemed to be still lost in a private world of deep thought from which she had to struggle to find the way out. Then she became disconcertingly aware of the faintly inquiring look in the hard eyes of the men and the concern the woman was expressing.

'Oh, I'm sorry . . . I was miles away . . . day-dreaming.' Abruptly, fear displaced embarrassment as she hugged herself at the shoulders, forearms crossed at her unprominent breasts while her pale-blue eyes darted one way and then another: like she was searching for something tangible to be afraid of.

'It's perfectly all right, my dear,' the older woman assured, with a crooked smile that was quite obviously a tenuous mask to hide her actual feelings. 'For the time being we are in no danger and — '

'Did I say anything stupid?'

'No, of course not.'

'I was thinking of Cole . . . wishing I could be with him again. But that will pass, won't it?'

'Of course, my dear.'

Amy Yancy unfolded gracefully to her feet and chose to look at the impassive faces of the Virginian and the half-breed in preference to the strained smile displayed on the fleshy features of the other woman. And so Edith Crawford found herself at liberty to scowl as a true reflection of how she felt as she came lumberingly up from the blankets.

'My husband caught a bad fever from which he died, you see,' the widow said, still hugging her shoulders, no longer looking quite so fearful. 'I'm on my way to Fort Hamilton to bring home his body. But oh, I told you that already.'

'Yes, ma'am.'

'You did, lady.'

'I really think we should — '

'Well, when the stagecoach was first shot at, yesterday you know?' the younger woman cut in, seemingly oblivious to Mrs Crawford, 'it seemed like the good Lord was answering my prayer. For ever since I was informed of Cole's death, I have yearned to be taken myself. But . . . but . . .'

She looked away from the two men at last, and her pale face with the scabbed cut on the cheek abruptly showed terror in the wake of earnestness. And she seemed to be on the brink of losing total control of herself, until she saw Edith Crawford and allowed the older woman to embrace her.

'I don't want to die at the hands of these savages,' she completed softly, the tone of her voice childlike.

'Nor shall you, my dear,' Mrs Crawford assured her as she gently stroked the red hair, glowering over her shoulder at where Steele was watching Sun, while Edge dropped to his haunches to begin dousing the fire. 'Our young travelling companion told us, did he not, that Oro City is but a few miles beyond his people's farm. The hostiles would not dare to attack such a large community of whites as that is. And anyway, my husband the major will certainly be aware of hostile Indians within the jurisdiction of Fort Hamilton and is doubtless already putting into effect plans to deal with the problem.'

'Yes, yes, of course.' Mrs Yancy eased herself out of the embrace and was again embarrassed at having become emotional. 'Thank you. I'm sorry.'

She flicked her round-eyed gaze at each of them, and even tried to smile at what she considered her foolishness.

'No sweat, lady,' Edge told her as he straightened up from putting out the fire.

Steele said with a tip of his hat: 'No apology necessary, ma'am.'

'I should say not!' Mrs Crawford exclaimed. 'But what is necessary, as I was about to state earlier, is that we should make for town with all possible speed. The army will be alive to the danger, but the major has only limited resources with which to cover a vast area. Obviously it will be better for all concerned if all we whites gather together in one place as quickly as possible so that we may benefit from the best protection the military can provide.'

'That's a matter of opinion, lady,' Edge said as he began to furl his bedroll, with his cooking and eating utensils inside the blankets.

'With which I happen to agree,' the Virginian put in as Sun appeared in the gateway across the trail, hands and face and clothing dirtied by the grim task of attending to the charred corpses. 'Based on what I know of the situation right now.'

'Pardon me?' the young man called tentatively as he came across the trail – his gait rigid like he was afraid he might collapse and he was working too hard to maintain functions that were usually carried out involuntarily.

'I say I didn't?' the half-breed asked of Adam Steele. 'Yeah, kid?'

The Virginian shrugged in response to Edge and arched his eyebrows enquiringly toward the youngster.

'I'd like to bring my folks to town for burial. Since I won't be living out here and so their grave will — '

'We are doing as much for the stage driver and guard, so we must agree to do as you wish, young man,' Mrs Crawford allowed.

'Everything in the house was burned with it. I'd like to cover my parents decently for the trip to town.' He licked his lips nervously as he stopped and became a part of the group at the trailside: eyed the bedroll that Edge lifted off the ground with one hand at the same time as he hefted the heavier saddle with the other. Then, when he did not get an immediate answer, he added hurriedly: 'I'll pay you what the blankets are worth, mister.'

Edge swung the bedroll back a few inches and then tossed it forward, so that it landed at the youngster's feet. 'There you go, kid. Bring me back the hardware from inside.'

'Gee, thanks!' Sun blurted, excitedly surprised to have got what he wanted so easily.

He stooped to pick up the bedroll and the bullet aimed at the centre of his back cracked over its sudden curve to thud into the trunk of the tree beside which the group was gathered.

'Not again! Please! Not again!' As Amy Yancy shrieked the entreaty, she brought her hands up to her head and pressed them to her ears, squeezed her eyes tightly closed and dropped her chin down on to her chest. Strove desperately to withdraw from the reality of this fresh onslaught of violence.

Whatever Edith Crawford intended to voice – perhaps just a scream – in reaction to the gunshot was trapped inside her by the fear that constricted her throat. And she was forced to remain in strangled silence as she wrenched her green-eyed stare from the bullet scar in the tree bark, to the youngster who had been the target and then to the timber beyond the Concord and team from where the shot had been fired. Her mouth stayed gaping wide, but just saliva came out of it.

Then the younger woman was suddenly as silent as the other one. And neither of them offered any physical response, either, as they were brought violently to the ground. Then were dragged savagely off the side of the trail, into the meagre cover of brush and long grass and exposed roots. Amy Yancy hooked around the waist by Edge as he hurled aside the saddle but caught hold of the Winchester to wrench it from the boot. Edith Crawford jerked sideways and then down by Steele's gloved right hand fisted around one of her wrists.

For a stretched second, Edward Sun remained frozen in the act of claiming the donated bedroll. Just his dark eyes moving across their Oriental sockets to register the flurry of frenzied activity at either side of him. Then, as the final echo of the shockingly unexpected gunshot diminished into the distance, the youngster uttered an oath and powered full-length to the ground, then lunged into a roll – across the recently doused campfire, up and over the tree root on which Edge had taken his ease and to a colliding stop against the fleshy form of Mrs Crawford. And now the woman was able to force a passage in her throat through which she snarled an obscenity as a second report closely followed by another thud of a bullet into a tree trunk sounded against the raucous shouting of angry men.

'Pardon me!' the youngster rasped, the Oriental part of his character able to remember his manners even in such a taut situation as he drew back from the cursing woman: but was careful to stay low in the scant cover.

'May God forgive me,' she groaned, and threw a hand up to her mouth as if she feared another obscenity might involuntarily slip out of her.

Amy Yancy sobbed softly as she lay sprawled full-length on the ground, her hands still pressed hard against her ears.

'They don't sound like Indians to me, Reb,' Edge growled as he rolled away from the weeping woman, dragging his arm clear of her so he could take a two-handed grip on the Winchester – his head cocked to listen and try to make sense out of what was being yelled back and forth in English in the timber on the other side of the trail.

'You know me, Yank,' Steele answered evenly as he wriggled around so he could aim the Colt Hartford toward the source of new danger. 'From the South, but I'm not prejudiced. If I have to kill a man to keep him from killing me, I don't give a damn about the colour of his skin.'

The younger woman raised her head and screamed: 'We're all going to be killed, I know we are!'

Edge moved a hand away from his rifle to reach to the

side and force her head back down into the grass. 'Some of us are indestructible, lady,' he growled as he directed a mirthless grin at Steele. 'Maybe on account of heaven not wanting us.'

The shouting across the trail was abruptly curtailed and into the brittle silence the sardonically smiling Virginian murmured: 'And in hell they're scared we'll take over.'

CHAPTER SIX

THE SILENCE stretched time as the newly risen sun seemed to beat down unmercifully through the trees. Then a stray breeze, cool at this early hour of the morning, rustled the foliage and dried the sweat of fear and tension on the flesh of the five people sprawled in the brush and grass across the trail from the fire-razed farmstead. Further back in the timber, where the half-breed had hobbled the gelding to sound a warning should anyone try to get close to his camp from that direction during the night, the horse whinnied. It was just an animal cry, meaningless to Edge who had owned this particular horse for a long time. But its very normality, allied with the effect of the brief breeze, acted to cut through the unnatural quietness. People began to breathe again and to move slightly to ease aching muscles.

'Shit, Dal, there's dead folks under that there tree!' one of the intruders yelled, shocked. He was immediately behind the heap of black and grey rubble that had once been the barn of the Sun place.

'All I friggin' hit was a tree, boy!' came the sour-toned reply from Dal, who was still off the trail beyond where the Concord stood. He would have sounded a lot older than the other one even had he not called him boy. 'Saw the friggin' slugs hit the friggin' bark!'

'Luke means the tree in the yard of the burned-out place, Dal!' a third man interceded

'Yeah, Murray!' Luke came back anxiously. 'You see them, too?'

'I see them,' Murray confirmed from where he was in hiding in the patch of tobacco that was the crop which grew closest to the farmstead buildings. He sounded to be nearer

Dal's age than Luke's. 'See them clear enough to know one of them's Andy Patterson, Dal. Even though his head's all burned to a cinder. I'd recognise that fancy gunbelt of his anywhere.'

Murray had given up shouting. And his tone was close to being reflective as he concluded, like he was merely talking aloud his thoughts. But in the surrounding stillness of this piece of country where the pleasant woodland petered out and the rugged red-rock terrain got started, his soft-spoken words reached to every listening ear. Dal, too, had no forcefulness in his voice when he growled musingly:

'Sonofabitch, Andy Patterson?'

'Dal, there could be some bad Injun trouble brewin' in this neck of the — ' Luke started, and there was deep fear in his strained and quiet voice. It was easy to visualise him looking nervously about himself in the suddenly to him menace-filled woods.

'You sayin' we should start runnin' scared on account of a little old Injun raid that Andy Patterson got hisself mixed up in and leave what we come all the way out here to — '

'You people across there in the trees!' Murray called abruptly. 'Eddy Sun and the other folks! I guess you can hear me real well?'

The widow remained silently unmoving with her face into the grass – perhaps really could not hear what had been said because of the way she had blocked her ears. The other woman and Edge and Steele all eyed the young half-Chinese quizzically when he vented a gulping sound at mention of his name. Sun began to chew on the nails of his left hand as he responded to each questioning look in turn with an expression of entreaty. Then the half-breed and the Virginian exchanged tacit messages, the result of which was that Edge would be their spokesman. While Steele crawled stealthily away into the trees.

'Us and every fired up Ute around here maybe, feller!'

'I see just one dead, bare-assed Injun, loudmouth!' Dal challenged. 'And I ain't havin' no fit of — '

'Shut up, Dalton!' Murray warned grimly. 'You're the one has more mouth than the Mississippi River's got delta!'

'Go to hell, Murray! I'm runnin' this outfit and — '

'Seems you ain't runnin' Murray no more, Dalton!' Luke cut in, still sounding nervous. 'And I reckon I've just thrown in with him!'

'So the friggin' both of you can go to hell!' the outnumbered member of the trio countered sullenly. 'I'm on my own now, and I won't stop at killin' either of you two bastards if you get between me and the bounty money!'

'Just shut up for a minute, will you, Dal?' Murray asked, obviously not taking seriously what the man near the Concord had said. And for a response drew an emphatically noisy sound of a spit. 'You over there?'

'You ain't bored us to death yet, feller,' Edge drawled as Sun stared fixedly across the trail and Amy Yancy felt compelled to face reality again – joined the older woman in gazing apprehensively at the half-breed, one from either side of him.

'Any of you here because of what Sun did to the Randell girl?' Murray asked.

The young half-Chinese gulped again and chewed more ferociously at his nails. And broke out in a sweat as he sensed Edge and the two women looking at him – needed to make a tremendous effort of will to avoid meeting their gazes. In seeing this situation, the half-breed knew that Amy Yancy and Edith Crawford were as much in the dark as he about the frightened youngster's involvement with a girl named Randell.

'Was here minding my own business,' Edge answered. 'Until you fellers showed up and started trying to kill me.'

'No! It was Sun who Dalton was aiming for!' Murray assured. 'He got a little too excited and started in to shoot before — '

'Excited, hell!' Dalton snarled. 'I'd have got him right between the friggin' shoulder blades if he hadn't ducked down!'

Adam Steele, closing in on Dalton's position, expressed a taut grin that showed his teeth but failed to touch his eyes as he murmured to himself: 'Know how you feel, feller. It's a lousy system. Seems it's the moon I keep shooting for and all the time miss.'

'Shut up, Dal!' Murray snapped impatiently. Then

moderated his tone as he continued: 'Listen . . . we just want the Chink and don't mean no harm to anybody else. So if you just send him over here to us, we'll be on our way and you folks can go about your business, which seems to me should include getting out of this piece of country real fast. Because Dal and Luke and me have seen more Indian sign than is healthy . . .'

Luke broke in to confirm this and urge that the deal should be hurried along. And Dalton made a blustering contribution to the talk, accusing the two others of acting like jittery old maids. All of which allowed the Virginian to get within a few yards of Dalton more quickly than if there had just been a level-toned exchange between Murray and the half-breed. He had not needed to swing very wide to guard against being seen as he crossed the trail – elected speed in preference over stealth and darted from one side to the other in partial cover of the Concord while Dalton was angrily voicing his decision to break off with Murray and Luke. Then he became as cautiously furtive as he had been when he had wriggled away from the others. But he was on his feet now, and in a half-crouch with the rifle angled in the general direction where he knew Dalton to be as he watched where he set down each booted foot as much as where he was going. Until the snarling quarrel gave him the chance to lengthen his stride and reach a position where he could see his target – and kill him easily if Dalton reacted recklessless to the snap of a dry twig or the thud of boot on a rock.

Dalton remained squatted down on his haunches at the base of a tree, a rifle aimed from his shoulder alongside the tree – to draw a bead between the lead horses of the stage team and the end of the stone wall, across the body of the naked Ute, at the twice-bullet-scarred tree across the trail. Because of the unevenness of the ground at either side of the trail and the intervening stone wall, the man had no chance of seeing Edge and the others or they him while all of them remained hunkered and sprawled in their respective places of concealment.

Murray and Luke were also out of sight, away to the right of where the Virginian came to a halt beside a tree less than fifteen feet from the unsuspecting Dalton. Murray and Edge were trading words again as Steele stepped forward, rifle aimed at the nape of the neck of the squatting man . . .

'. . . ain't nothing to me, feller. But I'm not about to make him move out so you can gun him down just because you ask it.'

'Damnit, mister, it's your own life and the lives of the women with you,' Murray countered, his anger rising in face of the half-breed's monotoned imperturbability. 'That Chink is worth a lot of mazuma to us and —'

'Shit, Murray!' Luke blurted shrilly.

'What is it, boy!' For the first time, Murrary sounded afraid.

'Why's just one of them over there doin' all the talkin'?'

Steele had halted his forward move and turned just his head when Luke exploded into voice so abruptly – to glance in his direction, fully expecting to see the boy. But there was no sign of him, and Steele faced front again, a brand of self-mocking grin tugging at his mouth now. That at once became an expression of triumph as one query was answered with another. And Dalton froze from head to toe in his rifle aiming crouch – sensing the presence that warned him he could supply the explanation for which Luke had asked. Then the breath that was trapped in his lungs by paralysing terror came out with a hissing rush when the muzzle of the Colt Hartford touched the sweat-beaded flesh at the hairless nape of his neck and he heard the click of the rifle's hammer being drawn back.

'Drop the Winchester or don't bother breathing in, feller,' Steele drawled evenly.

Dalton gulped and moved his hands only to the extent necessary for the rifle to slip from their sweat-greased palms and fingers and thud softly to the turf.

'Hey, you over there . . .' Murray began. And his voice rose and fell in volume to each listener's ear – so that it was apparent he wrenched his head one way and then another to search his immediate surroundings with suspicion-filled eyes.

'I hear you have a big mouth, Dal,' Steele said, and the flatness of his tone no doubt made him more menacing to his captive than a vicious snarl would have. 'Tell your partners to move out into the open with their guns high over their heads.'

'. . . let me hear all of you holler out or we'll come at you blasting!'

'Murray!' Luke pleaded in a quivering voice.

'Cut it out, boy!' Murray snarled.

'Mister, he won't take — ' Dalton started, and it sounded like there was something palpable in his throat over which his voice had to rasp to get out.

'No justice, is there?' Steele cut in. 'You haven't tried him and it's you who gets the death sentence. So long, feller.'

'Murray, Luke!' the man on his haunches suddenly shrieked powerfully, no longer trapped into immobility. Instead, shaking all over so that he had to lean against the base of the tree trunk to keep from toppling to the ground as his folded legs were drained of strength. 'One of them's got a gun in my neck! He says he's gonna blast me if you two don't surrender! Show yourselves with your rifles up over your heads! You hear me, you guys? I'm dead if you don't do it!'

'Goddamnit, Dalton, why's it always you that screws us up?' Murray roared.

'Murray?' Luke pleaded.

'Shut up!'

'But we gotta do it, Murray!'

'I said to shut up!'

There was another period of tense silence in which the early morning sun seemed to be unnaturally heated to some of those waiting in the timber.

'He ain't just talk, I know it!' Dalton urged.

'So how d'we know him and the others won't shoot all of us down then they got us where they want us, lamebrain?' Murray snarled.

'Shit, I'm throwin' in the friggin' towel!' Luke blurted, and made a lot of noise with his booted feet in the brush as he headed for the wire fence at the rear of the Sun place. 'Every lousy Injun in the territories could be closin' in on us and I'd rather take my chances with my own kind!'

'Mister, one of my buddies has done what you want,' Dalton pointed out weakly as Luke came into sight: the youngster careful to keep his rifle pressed into the air at the limit of his reach with one hand as he used the other to help him negotiate the fence behind the heap of rubble that had been the barn.

'So maybe I'll only have to half kill you, feller,' the Virginian replied as he eased the muzzle of the Colt Hartford away from its contact with the man's flesh.

'How the hell did I ever get myself mixed up with you two?' Murray groaned with forceful feeling as he pushed his Winchester into sight first above the tobacco plants, both his hands fisted around it, then rose and stepped into sight at the fence on the far side of the enclosed yard.

This as Dalton turned his head to look at his captor for the first time – and needed the support of the tree again as he responded to the gesture of the Colt Hartford and came awkwardly to his feet. The expression on his face was just beginning to alter from abject terror through relief to loathing. Then another motion with the rifle in the gloved hands directed Dalton to forsake the support of the tree and turn to join his partners in the open.

Steele stooped to retrieve the discarded Winchester as he followed its scowling owner, and kept Dalton covered with the Colt Hartford in a one-handed grip while he canted the confiscated rifle to a shoulder. This as he saw Edge rise into sight across the trail, the half-breed coldly impassive as he levelled his rifle in a double handed grip from the hip, aimed at a point midway between the advancing Luke and Murray.

'Shit, Murray, he looks a real mean and — '

'Cut it out, Luke!' Murrary hurried to interject on the frightened youngster, and was not so apprehensive himself that he was unable to shoot a recriminatory glance across the fire rubble at Dalton.

'Don't like having guns fired at me, fellers,' Edge said in a tone of voice that was a perfect match for the set of his features, as Sun got tentatively to his feet unaided and the two women helped one another – the widow in more need of assistance than Mrs Crawford.

'Mister, it weren't you Dal was — ' Luke started to explain, and was again interrupted.

'Or even pointed in my direction,' the dispassionate half-breed continued. 'Warn the most likely people to do it whenever I can. Like to have them know that I just give the one warning. Next time either of you has a gun in his hand aimed anywhere near me, he best shoot it fast and straight. He doesn't do that, he's dead.'

Edge was through with the warning as Murray reached one end of the dry stone wall, Luke stepped through the gateway and Dalton with Adam Steele behind him moved around the dead Indian at the other end. He let go of the barrel of his Winchester and sloped the rifle to his shoulder as he raked his glittering-eyed gaze over the face of each of the newcomers.

Murray and Luke stared incredulously and then mistrustfully at the half-breed while they kept their arms high in the air, hands fisted tightly around the rifles held aloft. Both of them had come to a halt and now Dalton did likewise, but turned from the waist to show a puzzled frown to Steele. He saw that the Virginian, although not looking so utterly lacking in warmth as Edge, was just as uncompromising in the brand of menacing silence that conveyed his indifference to the outcome of what was happening. And Dalton found that he jerked his right-hand away from the holstered revolver he had not been thinking of drawing anyway.

'Just what the frig is goin' on here?' he demanded in a half-angry, half-afraid tone as he shared a grimace of mounting incomprehension between the man who aimed a rifle at his back and the knot of four people who stood beside the tree across the trail – Edge at the front, the two women clinging together behind him and the half-Chinese in back of them.

'Nothing much until you and your two buddies showed up,' Steele answered.

'We just want Eddy Sun and — ' Luke tried again to contribute and was once more forced to abandon what he was saying.

'It sounds to me,' Edge said as he dug the makings from

his shirt pocket with his free hand, 'like that feller ought to be able to throw some light on the situation.'

'Mrs Crawford, Mrs Yancy,' the young man announced forcefully as he stepped out from behind the women, an expression of resolute determination on his unmatured face. 'If I'm going to be handed over to these killers, I want you to know — '

'Eddy Sun's known wherever he's been as a born liar!' Murray growled.

'Some might say he's just inventive,' Steele suggested evenly.

'Take it easy, kid,' Edge muttered to the youngster. 'Figure I need to know a lot more than I do now before I'd leave you to your own devices.'

The Virginian added sardonically: 'And I reckon I'm not going to be dictated to.'

CHAPTER SEVEN

DALTON ARLISS was a six feet tall, two hundred and fifty pounds man of something more than fifty years. He was still muscular but he was also starting to run to fat, most noticeably around his middle and from the neck up. If he had any hair none of it showed below the brim of his hat, outside of the grey curves of his eyebrows. His clean-shaven face was round and burnished and looked strangely smooth in contrast to the crinkled skin of his throat. He had grey eyes and teeth of a similar colour. It was the kind of face that would have an underlying sullenness quite easy to spot no matter what other expression masked it.

Murray Quinlan was about forty-five and a match for Arliss's height. But he was much less heavy and looked to be a good deal fitter. He still had a full head of only slightly greying black hair that was seen to be slicked down with greasy pomade when he removed his hat to greet the two women. He wore a neatly trimmed, very thin moustache as an adjunct to his lean and hungry good looks – his handsomeness enhanced when he showed his very white teeth and warmth in his green eyes when he smiled.

Luke Vicary was twenty-one or -two. No taller than five and a half feet and so skinny he probably weighed less than a hundred and twenty pounds. He was blond-haired and pale complexioned, except where freckles were thick on his forehead above his large, round, deep-blue eyes. He had jug ears and protruding teeth, an overly hooked nose and a nervous tic at the top of his right cheek that perhaps went away when times were less tense.

All three were dressed much like the dead man under the shade tree – and Edge. In Stetsons, riding boots, shirts and pants well suited to the country and climate. All wore gunbelts, too: the youngster packing a Remington while the other had Frontier Colts in their holsters. Arliss and Quinlan had on unfancy vests.

Quinlan made the introductions after he reached the side of the gateway where Vicary stood. He lowered his rifle gingerly to lean it against the gatepost and assayed the smile as he swept off his hat with one hand and gestured toward his partners with the other. This as Steele moved from around the back of Arliss and angled across the trail to halt on the other side of the doused camp fire from Edge. Arliss elected to remain beside the dead Ute.

'I think you may put down the rifle and rest your arms, boys,' Quinlan suggested, with a questioning glance at Edge and Steele after his introductions had drawn no response from anybody.

Luke Vicary's tic worked frantically and beads of sweat squeezed from every pore on his face as he brought his rifle down with his arms remaining ramrod straight – and lowered himself stiffly to his haunches to place the Winchester on the ground like it was an object of great fragility and value. His pent-up breath rasped noisily out of his pursed lips when he came erect and then he rubbed the sweat from his face with a shirt sleeve.

'It appears that you people have already experienced considerable trouble,' Murray Quinlan went on in a voice that sounded strained from the effort of maintaining its affectedly elegant accent. He encompassed his surroundings with a glance from which he learned nothing he did not already know. 'You were about to leave here when Dal Arliss allowed his enthusiasm to get the better of him. We apologise for—'

Arliss spat a stream of saliva and scored a direct hit on the genitals of the naked dead Ute. Amy Yancy uttered a low moan and the older woman held her in a tighter embrace. Edge said as he lodged his rifle in the crook of an elbow and began to roll a cigarette:

'It was your buddy with the bad taste shooting his rifle at us held us up, feller. You shooting off your mouth ain't nearly so good a reason for us to stay. Unless you want to talk about the Indian sign you said awhile back you saw on your way here?'

'Plenty, mister!' Luke said, fast and with an expression of determination on his youthful face that augmented his insistence on being heard this time. 'Smoke and lots of tracks left by unshod ponies. Seen a few parties ridin' here and there. Some that seen us back and some that maybe didn't. Never so many at a time, but all of them ridin' for some kinda meetin', looked like.'

'Boy's tellin' it like it was,' Arliss growled. He jerked a thumb over his shoulder to indicate the expanse of timber through which he and the other two had closed in on the unsuspecting group across from the burnt-out farmstead. 'All over a lot of country to the north of here.' Now he directed an ominous scowl over the fire-blackened wreckage as he went on: 'Never saw nothin' like this, but the way we came here didn't bring us through settled land in this neighbourhood. It's my opinion, though, that the Injuns are massin' to start in on raisin' a lot more of this kinda hell. And the sooner all of us make tracks outta here, better chance we got of not gettin' caught up in —'

Steele said, as Edge struck a match on the barrel of his Winchester to light the cigarette: 'Grateful to you for the information. I reckon you fellers have horses back in the timber somewhere?'

'Yeah,' Vicary answered eagerly. 'We hitched them back there when we saw the smoke of your cookin' fire and come on the rest of the way walkin'.'

'So you'll have to walk on back to them. Before you can start making fast tracks away from the Indian trouble.'

'Like hell we will, mister!' Arliss snarled. 'We come too many hard-ridin' miles to get this close to the Chink and not put the arm on him for Jerome Randell!'

'Dal, we ain't in position to call the tune!' Murray Quinlan rasped, and in his new state of perturbation again neglected to work on his grandiose accent.

'Sun?' Edge said.

'Yes, sir?'

'One of them mentioned a girl named Randell awhile back and now he's saying a man called Jerome Randell is real anxious for you not to —'

'The Randells got the idea I was going to marry Miranda!'

Sun explained anxiously. 'I never said I would and when I found out how important it was to them all I got out fast! I swear to you, mister! That's all there was to it! I knew Mr Randell thought a lot of his daughter, but I never thought he'd send gunslingers after me for just leaving her!'

'How much is on his head?' Steele asked evenly.

Luke Vicary was on the point of blurting out a response. But Arliss beat him to it, sending a censorious glance toward the youngster as he snarled:

'Five hundred bucks is all.'

'Where did you leave this Miranda Randell in the lurch, kid?' Steele asked of the half-Chinese.

'They live just outside of Wichita, Kansas. It's said that the Randell family own more land in Kansas than the state does.'

'Five hundred bucks apiece,' Arliss hurried to amend as he caught the drift of the exchange.

'Dal!' Quinlan groaned. 'These people aren't stupid. Kansas is a long way from here. They know that the likes of Andy Patterson and us don't take that kind of round trip for chickenfeed.'

'So tell them what the stakes really are, loudmouth!' Arliss challenged bitterly. 'Give them the figure and then figure to get your head shot off!'

'Five thousand is the price,' Quinlin said, meeting the bigger, older man's glowering gaze with one that matched its forcefulness. Then, as the youngest member of the trio nodded to confirm the veracity of this, Quinlin returned his attention to the group across the trail as he went on: 'So there you go! If you want to haul the Chink all the way back across the country to Wichita, dead or alive, you'll be in line to collect the five grand! But unless you shoot down my partners and me right here and now, you'll have to keep watching that we don't get him away from you. And we've got the right, since you didn't know what he was worth until we told you.'

'That's right!' Vicary put in quickly when Quinlan paused for breath and while Arliss continued to scowl his disgruntlement with the truth telling. 'And won't be just me and Murray and Dal, neither! Maybe Andy Patterson ain't around to take an interest no more since he got hisself mixed up with the Injun trouble here, but there's a whole bunch of other gunslingers and bounty hunters lookin' to collect that pot of Randell money. I can tell you that for sure!'

'What d'you reckon, Reb?' Edge asked into the brittle silence that came in the wake of Luke Vicary's frantic outburst.

'You're still wanted in Kansas, aren't you, Yank?' Steele countered.

'Not for a long time,' the half-breed answered. Sun groaned, then shook his head vigorously and became tacitly grim-featured – determined to face up to the inevitable without losing control of himself.

'Dear God, it's like one nightmare after another,' Amy Yancy said in a strangled tone as her shocked gaze raked over the scene and then became fixed upon the bloated face of Edith Crawford – begged for the older woman to tell her this was not happening or for her to do something to halt it if it was.

'You are simply in breach of promise to this Miranda Randell, young man?' the more self-controlled woman demanded emphatically, and needed to exert some force to extricate herself from the eager grasp of the one hovering close to the brink of breaking down.

Edward Sun, who had found himself relieved to switch his attention away from the men discussing him like a steer destined for slaughter, started to nod in response to Mrs Crawford's question. But suddenly thought better of this and muttered miserably with a shrug of his skinny shoulders: 'Well, ma'am, she told me she was going to have a baby, but I don't know if that's the truth.'

Free of Amy Yancy, the older woman placed her bulky frame between the youthful half-Chinese and all the other men. And emphasized her protective attitude by pushing out her arms to the sides as she proclaimed: 'Haven't liked him all along on account of him being a part Chinaman. Like him a whole lot less now I know he's impregnated a white woman and has left her in the lurch. But I will not allow him to be shot down in cold blood by anybody whose sole interest in the matter is financial. Particularly while the wretched boy's parents are newly dead from the Indian atrocity and are not yet decently buried in the ground.'

'I really appreciate what — ' Sun began.

'Don't you talk to me unless I ask you something, you despicable rapist!' Edith Crawford snarled.

'Hey, wasn't no rape to it,' Luke Vicary hurried to correct.

This as the younger woman seemed suddenly to draw strength from the demonstration of determination by the older one: and was able to suppress her own anguish as she stepped forward to add her slighter form to the protective shield in front of Sun.

'Was heading in the opposite direction to Kansas,' Edge said, after breaking off his apparently only casual watch on the three men across the trail for a fast glance at Steele. 'Pot would have to be a lot larger than five thousand to get me to turn around.'

'And run the gauntlet of massing Indians to boot, Yank.'

'So it's no skin off your noses if we take the Chink?' Quinlan asked eagerly, but there was a nervousness stirring just beneath the surface of the man's hope.

'Not so much a matter of skin off my nose as a bruise on my self-respect, feller,' Steele answered, and tightened his left gloved fist around the Colt Hartford canted to his shoulder as he pushed the other rifle out to the side, stock first.

'Might have left the kid to take care of himself,' Edge added, the cigarette bobbing at the corner of his mouth. He took a double-handed grip on the Winchester which he angled across the front of his body. 'But I figure it would be hard for me to live with myself if I allowed you to get at him through the women.'

Quinlan appeared suddenly to be very weary. Vicary at his side expressed a mix of disappointment and relief. At the end of the wall, Dalton Arliss spat again against the dead Ute brave sprawled at his feet, an ugly scowl of contempt for the world at large on his fleshy face.

'Pardon me, ladies,' Sun murmured politely as he eased his way carefully between the two women. Then, as he took a hold on the proffered Winchester and withdrew it from the

Virginian's grasp he said in the same mannered tone and with his neutral expression unchanged: 'I appreciate it, sir.'

'You're welcome,' Steele said.

'A man can't have others fight his battles for him, especially women,' the young man who took up a position between the half-breed and the Virginian announced, both his tone and his expression hardening – this after he had shown a moment of self-consciousness that indicated he was not familiar with the feel of a rifle in his hands.

Edith Crawford began a smile of admiration for Sun who she had moments ago claimed to despise. Amy Yancy showed surprise at this new turn of events. Edge drawled:

'Never too late for a feller to change his ways.'

The youngster raked the rifle jerkily from side to side and Steele eased his grip on the frame of the Colt Hartford as Edge started to cant the Winchester to his shoulder, freeing his right hand to take the cigarette from his mouth.

'I agree,' Sun said with a nod, and thumbed back the hammer of the Winchester. Then halted the sideways sweep of the rifle and pulled the trigger.

'Sonofabitch!'

'My God, Dal!'

'The bastard's — '

Quinlan, Vicary and Arliss yelled their shrill responses to the gunshot as the report resounded among the trees and against the bluff with the ravine in it across the fields of crops. This as the bullet went wide and low of its intended target, to ricochet off the base of the wall and bury itself in the hard-packed dirt of the trail six feet away from where Arliss stood. But the tall, heavily built man did not remain standing there for more than a half second – swung to the side and hurled himself head-first over the wall as he started the shouted curse. Which was ended with a snarl of disgust as he fell face down into the patch of Edward Sun's old vomit.

The man's two partners dived frantically into the cover of the same wall at either side of the gateway as the youngster with the rifle raked it toward them, thumb jerking back the hammer.

'Here we go again,' Steele rasped through clenched teeth

as he whirled and flung his arms to the sides, left hand still fisted around his rifle. Each arm curled around the front of a woman's waist as he went between them and his ears were pained by the shrillness of their screams at such close quarters as he went down face forward into the brush behind the tree root and dragged them down on their backs.

'But it can be too damn late to learn to fire a repeater rifle, kid!' Edge snarled as Sun pulled at the Winchester trigger a second time without pumping the action to eject the spent shellcase and lever a fresh round into the breech. The half-breed spoke as he curled just his right arm to the side – to capture the suddenly angry youngster, sweep him off his feet and then, with a fast turn and a shove of his hip, send the slightly built form crashing violently into the undergrowth close to where Steele had forced down the women and was still prone between them. Edge dove to the ground nearby as a revolver shot cracked out from the other side of the trail, its report and the thud of the bullet's impact with a tree masking Edward Sun's curse as he again failed to trigger an explosive response from the Winchester. The knowledge that they were being fired upon again served to silence the cries and still the struggles of Mrs Crawford and Mrs Yancy. And Edge growled: 'No use having two women fall for you if you can't aim better than that, Reb.'

The Virginian elected to wriggle out from between the women and turn around rather than to roll clear over one of them. He waited for a fusillade of fast revolver shots to subside before he rasped at the half-breed who was also turning around while he stayed as close as he could to the brush-covered ground: 'My way's to love them and leave them, Yank. Reckon you must have blinked. Twice.'

'Nightmare after nightmare!' the redheaded widow gasped, and clamped her palms to her ears again as she began to quake from head to toe.

'God in heaven, how can you two men act the jackass at a time like this?' the older woman demanded in a strangled tone of high tension.

Two rifles shots in quick succession exploded bullets across the trail and cracked them through the air above the group sprawled in the brush on this side: to signal that the surrendered Winchesters had been retrieved from the open ground at the gateway in the wall under cover of the volley of handgun fire. Edge struck a match on his rifle barrel to relight his cigarette that had gone out in the dive for cover, and growled:

'See, lady, you got ass on the mind at a time like this, too.'

Edith Crawford vented a snort of disgust as the trembling woman at her side began to moan in an animalistic key.

'On the subject of sex,' Steele murmured as he aligned himself alongside Edge, both their rifle barrels angled across the tree root, 'we going to just lay around here all day, or are we going to raise our ugly heads?'

More shots were sprayed across the trail – from rifles and a revolver. Chips of bark were exploded out of the root barricade and rained over the two men spread out prone behind it. Sun abruptly curtailed his string of curses when Edith Crawford snarled:

'Oh, give it here, you incompetent fool!'

The echo of the gunfire seemed to continue for much longer than before, and both the half-breed and the Virginian sensed that this was not an unreal effect created out of tension in imagination as they snapped their heads around from looking at where the fleshily large woman wrenched the Winchester of Dalton Arliss out of the grasp of the much shorter and lighter Edward Sun.

'Now?' Edge posed.

'Sure,' Steele answered.

'Go!'

They both raised their heads to put their eyes behind the sights of their rifles. And at that instant heard the distant gunfire clearly enough for the final vestige of the last chance that it might be an echo to be totally gone. They squeezed their triggers in perfect unison, and in such a situation as this there was no risk that they would both shoot at the same target. For Murray Quinlan was crouched at one side of the gateway, closest to Edge's line of fire. And Dalton Arliss showed his vomit-spattered head above the wall in such a position that Steele had to track the Colt Hartford even less distance than the half-breed to draw a bead on his man.

Both men at the wall had allowed themselves to be distracted by the gunfire from another source: and were peering out across the fields of growing crops when they took bullets in the head. Thus never knew the terrible danger they were in until the slugs drilled into their flesh, shattered their skulls and gained entry to their brains: all this happening so fast that perhaps they were dead before awareness of being shot was registered by nervous systems capable of transmitting sensations that could trigger thought.

The sullen-featured Arliss went immediately from sight behind the wall, dragging the rifle that had been resting on its top with him. While the classically handsome Quinlan let go of his Winchester which remained balanced across the top of the wall as he was sent sprawling on to his back, half hidden by the wall and half out in the open. If either of the men did have the opportunity to give voice to the agony and anguish of violent death, it was lost in the sudden tumult of exploding guns and galloping hooves as a group of frantically firing, headlong-racing riders emerged from the ravine in the bluff across the fields.

'Sonofabitch, it's the cavalry!' Adam Steele growled.

'My husband's men from Fort Hamilton!' Edith Crawford exclaimed in high excitement.

'Thank God, thank God, thank God!' Amy Yancy wailed.

'Edge, those fellers are — ' the Virginian began.

He had done a double-take out over the fields and the tense tone of his voice drew the half-breed's attention away from the farmstead gateway and caused him to peer long and hard at the fast-riding band of uniformed men.

'I see now!' Edward Sun exclaimed excitedly, and Mrs Crawford vented a cry that was partly of alarm and partly of pain as the youngster wrenched the Winchester from her grasp. Then he pumped the lever action of the rifle as he rose up on to his knees, thudded the stock to his shoulder and squeezed the trigger. And roared shrilly: 'Yeah, yeah, I got him! Hot damn, I got him! What about that?'

Edge and Steele and the two women now switched their concentrated attention away from the dozen or so troopers who were galloping their mounts hell for leather across the fields: to gaze with varying expressions at where Luke Vicary stood in the gateway of the wall, empty hands thrust high into the air and a crimson stain surrounding a dark hole in his shirt front left of centre. The pale-complexioned, freckle-foreheaded, jug-eared youngster was dead on his splayed feet at the moment he became the brief centre of attention for all five people on the other side of the trail. His round, deep-blue eyes directed embittered accusation at them all. Then he crashed stiffly forward to hide his death mask against the ground as his arms fell to his sides. There was a much larger exit wound in his back encircled by a more expansive stain of dark crimson.

Sun worked the lever action of the killing Winchester, the broad grin of unbridled pleasure in triumph still firmly fixed on his round and youthful face as he swept his shining-eyed gaze from Vicary's corpse to share his happiness with Steele and Edge and the two women. But then the brightness began to drain fast from his face when he saw the degree of earnestness with which they were all looking toward the fast-riding cavalrymen.

'What's wrong?' he asked huskily, as a brief interval in the gunfire seemed to mute the thudding of hooves. And actually the sounds of the gallop were dulled as the horses raced clear of the echoing confines of the ravine to spurt across the well-worked soil of the farmed fields.

'You mean apart from you shooting down a man who was surrendering?' the Virginian responded.

The gunfire started again, and the abruptly crestfallen Sun was able to see for himself that the uniformed riders were shooting back into the ravine.

'The soldiers are retreating!' the youngster blurted fearfully, and looked like he might get sick to his stomach again.

'And we got to shoot at the bunch that's chasing them!' Edge yelled sardonically against the mounting cacophony as he snatched the cigarette from his mouth and tossed it aside.

'Stay down!' Steele ordered the women as he and the half-breed powered up from the exposed root and sought the more secure cover of sturdy tree trunks now that there was a new danger from a different direction.

'It was just a lucky shot!' Edward Sun shrieked, and seemed transfixed to where he stood in the brush – perhaps more afraid of the responsibility for using the rifle in his shaking hands than of the large group of whooping Indian braves who came charging out of the ravine astride galloping ponies.

'More you practice, luckier you'll get, kid!' Edge growled.

He and Steele stood to their full heights, rifles aimed from their shoulders, each braced to his covering tree as he waited for a clear shot at the pursuing Indians who as yet were mostly obscured by their quarry.

'Plenty of scope for practice, Yank!' the Virginian yelled without looking toward the half-breed who was poised to open fire some ten feet away.

'I figure about twenty, Reb!'

'Sonofabitch!' the half-Chinese exclaimed as he was at last spurred into taking cover behind a tree. And his tone of voice and the expression on his face hardened once again as he yelled: 'You men leave them to me!' He shot a glance briefly across the trail at the fire-blackened wreckage of the farmstead where the brutalised corpses of his parents still lay. Then he returned his gleaming-eyed gaze toward the two groups of racing riders, and shouted loudly and shrilly enough for the two women and two men close to him to hear clearly what he said. 'They're the same kind of murdering bastards that tortured my folks!'

The crackle of gunfire, the thudding of hooves, the yelling and whooping of troopers and Indians, and the whinnying of horses rose to a crescendo that was deafening. And neither Steele nor Edge was able to hear his own voice as he commented wryly:

'Twenty isn't the kind of score just one feller can settle.'

And:

'Don't guess those troopers will mind too much about having a Chink in their army.'

CHAPTER EIGHT

THE CAVALRYMEN lost two of their number during the frantic race across the fields from the mouth of the ravine to the trail where it started to pass the front of the farmstead yard – no more than three seconds separating the near-identical incidents of uniformed figures hurling their arms in the air and then pitching sideways out of their saddles. To thud to the crop-covered ground and bounce and roll and then become inert as their own mounts galloped faster and other horses swerved to avoid the unseated and blood-stained soldiers.

Over the same distance just one of the braves was hit by a backward-aimed bullet – took the lead in the centre of his brow beneath his headband with a single feather in it, the impact of this tumbling him head over heels in a reverse somersault off his pony.

Then the three men in the timber across from the farmstead were given a clear sight of the Indians and they opened fire in spontaneous unison. And just one more figure in breechclout, waistcoat and feathered headband was plunged off his mount, trailing a spray of blood droplets.

The faster-to-fire Colt Hartford exploded a second shot and another Indian went down. Edge triggered another shot from his Winchester as soon as he had pumped the action and Sun was just a little slower squeezing off a bullet. Three braves were hit and two crashed to the ground while one continued to cling to his mount after dispensing with his rifle. Some of the troopers had cracked out shots at the same time and there was no reliable way for any man to claim a victim for certain. But Edward Sun shrieked his delight in the wake of each report sounded by his rifle and, sure enough an Indian was seen to fall. This as the half-breed and the Virginian remained silent, each with bared teeth between curled-back lips and gleaming eyes under lowered lids that formed expressions which might have been either smiles of pleasure or grimaces of hatred through the nebulous veil of drifting gunsmoke. In such a situation as this, there was no cynical competitive spirit between the two men as they directed shot after shot toward the charging Indians. For this was not at all like it had been yesterday at noon. There were too many braves posing too great a threat today: and no time nor inclination for either Edge or Adam Steele to take account of who shot well enough to score the greater number of hits. It mattered only that enough braves were blasted off the bare backs of their ponies to convince the survivors they should turn away from the deadly fusillade of gunfire.

For if that didn't happen – and happen soon – the survivors would be on the trail, across it and in the timber. And enough of them would live long enough to pay back in kind the men who had killed so many of their fellows. Or maybe all of those who made it across the open ground would live to take part in the imminent uprising after the civilian sharpshooters and the two women were dead . . .

This possibility caused the faces of Edge and Steele to display distinct scowls as they became aware of the troopers streaming past on the trail with no slackening of pace, and no longer firing at their pursuers. At the same time, the diminished but still-full-of-fight band of Utes became aware of the new element in the battle and altered the direction of their fire: seemingly prepared to allow the soldiers to flee unmolested while they dealt with the side issue.

Mrs Crawford pressed the screaming Amy Yancy to the ground while she vented a string of obscenities into the air that was suddenly menacingly full of cracking bullets and sprays of bark fragments.

The Virginian's six-shot rifle was emptied and, his scowl becoming more firmly fixed to his face, he drew the knife from his boot sheath – readied it for spinning end over end into a Ute brave if the situation got that critical.

Edge saw this on the periphery of his vision and his

expression was just for a split second close to being a gloating grin as he exploded another shot and levered a fresh round out of the repeater's magazine. Then, instantly, the mortal danger of the racing, firing, whooping, hate-filled Indians served to dismiss everything of no immediate consequence from his mind: and his demeanour was once more icily calm as he determined to take as many braves as he possibly could with him if he were to die here at the scene of so much other slaughter. And so, as he put from his consciousness even contempt for the troopers who were making good their escape under cover of the gunfire from the flank, the half-breed was poised to hurl down the Winchester and draw his revolver from the holster the moment the rifle's firing pin snapped into an empty breech.

Edward Sun squeezed his trigger and pumped his lever action and vented his shrill cries of delight. Apparently oblivious to all else as he experienced the intoxicating euphoria of triumph at wreaking vengeance for anguish still fresh in his mind.

Then the headlong speed of the attack faltered and the din of the running fight, which had become a potential pitch battle, diminished. The cadence of the rattling gunfire lessened and the whoops of excitement vented by the braves were changed to cries of dismay. There were just ten or maybe a dozen Utes still astride ponies now, and a number of these were unable to fire their rifles – needed to cling to the reins or to the manes of their mounts to keep their wounded bodies from sliding to the ground.

The leader of the war party signalled a swing away from the full frontal attack on the group of whites in the timber, and a final fusillade of shots cracked bullets across the trail before the veering move developed into a complete galloping turn and the Indians were in retreat.

Edge's Winchester was empty, but he checked the move to discard it and go for his holstered revolver. This as Steele stooped to push his knife back in the boot sheath and aimed the Colt Hartford skywards in one hand and with the other turned the cylinder to empty the chambers of spent shell-cases. There was still too much noise in the sunlit morning for the sound of the empty cartridges falling into the brush to be heard – and not only the thudding of unshod hooves against the already-trampled crops as the Utes rode back across the fields featured with their own and the army casualties of the battle of which they wanted no more part.

For the team in the traces of the Concord and Steele's black stallion hitched to the rear of the stage also contributed to the body of sound – snorting and whinnying and scraping at the ground as they calmed in the wake of the raucous din and tested with flared nostrils that the final traces of acrid gunsmoke were gone from the warming and brightening atmosphere. And, too, the clatter of shod hooves as the bunch of troopers' horses was walked uneasily back along the trail was another distinct sound that, unlike the others, grew louder. Loud enough, even, to cover the soft whimpering of Amy Yancy as she responded to the comforting stroking of Edith Crawford's hands in her hair and on her scabbed cheek.

Not loud enough, though, to mask the report of the final bullet in a dead man's Winchester as it left the muzzle, triggered by Edward Sun. And the eyes of all the whites switched from staring at the grinning youngster to peer out at where the withdrawing Utes suddenly reined their ponies to a halt.

It had been another lucky shot: that should have gone high or wide or short – or have tunnelled into the flesh of one of the Ute back markers or his pony. Whereas, as fortune would have it, Sun's bullet left the closer braves unharmed and sent the leader crashing to the ground.

'You crazy young fool, now we're for it!' Edith Crawford accused in a tone between a snarl and a groan as the Indians gathered around their chief and the troopers reined in their horses.

'Reload, men!' the troop's commander ordered. And carbines were drawn from boots as Edward Sun directed a glower of defiance at the older woman, worked the lever action of the Winchester and tried to send another shot cracking out across the fields. But there was not a live bullet in the magazine to replace the spent case that was ejected.

'Shit,' the youngster rasped.

And abruptly the Utes urged their ponies into a sudden

gallop from a standstill that was faster than before. And perhaps the surviving braves were carried back into the ravine at an even faster rate than the much larger force had emerged on the trail of the fleeing troopers.

A smile wreathed the unmistakably Oriental features of the youngster as he matched Edge's actions in canting the empty Winchester to his shoulder and straightened from the bullet-scarred tree. And inevitably there was mockery in back of his politeness as he said: 'You were saying, Mrs Crawford?'

'It's all right, my dear, they have gone now,' the older woman consoled the younger as she pretended not to hear what Sun had said to her.

'I did okay for a guy who needs to practice, wouldn't you say, Mr Edge?'

The half-breed went to squat beside his hurriedly discarded gear and delved inside a saddlebag to find a carton of cartridges for his rifle. He answered: 'A real Sun of a gun, kid.'

'I'm pleased I was given the chance to avenge the deaths of my parents,' the young man announced gravely. 'I consider myself particularly fortunate to have had an opportunity to do so at the very place where . . .'

'Something else you've learned very fast, feller,' Adam Steele muttered as he started out on to the trail across which Edward Sun was gazing – the young man unable to sustain in isolation his state of exhilaration and now suddenly disconsolate as he surveyed the razed farmstead.

'Excuse me, sir?'

'Revenge is sweet.'

'Sure is,' Sun answered absently and dully.

'But you don't get long to enjoy the taste of that kind of fruit before you reach the pits.'

CHAPTER NINE

THE CORPORAL who was the only man ranking above trooper among the nine uniformed riders to survive the chase across the fields issued a husky-toned order to dismount. Then ignored the men as they did so, leading his horse forward and halting below where Steele had climbed up on to the seat of the Concord.

'Like to thank you and your friends for your help in puttin' the hostiles to flight, sir,' he said after executing a sloppy salute and clearing his throat. 'We was in real bad shape already and looked to be done for when we seen the hostiles had already hit the Sun place. See, all the patrol that had experience of — '

'Glad to have lent a hand, Corporal,' Steele assured wearily as he began to reload his rifle with bullets taken from one of the bags on his saddle draped over a side of the seat.

'You folks off the stage sure look to have got here at a bad time, sir,' the corporal went on quickly as he made a hurried, wide-eyed survey of the fire-ravaged farmstead and the scattered bodies – the naked brave, the bullet-shattered Arliss, Quinlan and Vicary and the two men and a woman who had been roasted beneath the shade tree in the yard. 'Yes, sir, the riled-up sonsof . . . the Utes certainly gave the Sun couple — '

'Corporal!' Mrs Crawford cut in on the fast-talking young non-com as she came bustling out of the timber and on to the trail.

'Hey, McNally, that's old E.T.'s old lady,' one of the troopers rasped in a warning tone.

Corporal McNally was close to losing his self-control. He

had been using talk to keep a grip on himself. And now he seemed dumb-struck and dangerously close to the brink of an emotional delayed reaction to the recent slaughter as he stared at the heavily built, fleshy-faced woman bearing down on him and learned she was the wife of his commanding officer.

'You best detail some men to go check for wounded, feller,' Steele advised in low tones to the tall and skinny, hollow-eyed and blond-haired non-com who was about twenty-five – which looked to be the average age of the whole group of cavalrymen. Most of the others appeared to be exhausted by the events of the recent past and afraid of the immediate future. But none was in such an agitated state of nervousness as the man with the chevrons of responsibility on his tunic sleeves. 'Take care of your own, make prisoners of or finish off the Indians,' the Virginian concluded as he completed the move of climbing down from the Concord.

'I am Mrs Craw — '

'Yes, ma'am, I know who you are,' McNally told her in a less tremulous tone. And threw up a salute worthy of acknowledging her husband's rank. 'If you'll pardon me for just a moment, Mrs Crawford.' He swung away from the anxiously frowning woman to command: 'Saxon, Egan, Goldsmith! Get back out there and check the casualties! Bring in our own! Make the Ute wounded prisoners! Conran, Shackleton! Round up the loose mounts! Irvine, Jonas, Webber! Cover the rest! And don't just watch the ravine! None of you men need to be told you got to be on your guard against attack from every —'

'Sure, McNally, we got you,' the man who had reacted to the name Jonas growled. And spat noisily from his grimacing mouth as he swung up into his saddle. He was in his early thirties and the oldest of the survivors. He was short, but broadly built and had a square face on which a smile would look out of place. 'If you got no need to say it, why tell us?'

'Knock it off, Arnie!' the trooper named Goldsmith muttered. 'Phil ain't used to bein' — '

'I ain't used to havin' a no-account non-com passin' on the

orders of a no-account civilian, jerk,' Jonas rasped, only loud enough for those who made the effort to hear it against the sounds of all the soldiers save for McNally remounting.

Some of the cavalrymen were sufficiently recovered from their recent brush with violent death to look at the attractive and slender Amy Yancy with something more than idle curiosity as she emerged with Edward Sun from the timber when they rode on by to attend to their assigned duties. But she was too deeply withdrawn from the real world to be aware of anything that was not captured in her insulated mind behind eyes that looked without seeing.

'The Indian situation is obviously most serious, Corporal?' Edith Crawford asked, and it was patently not the question that had been uppermost in her mind since she had first seen the troopers racing across the fields.

'Certainly is, ma'am,' McNally answered and seemed relieved again now that he had the opportunity to talk. Then his peace of mind improved still more when the Virginian halted his move away from the side of the Concord. 'The Major's doin' his best with the men he has — '

'Ethan . . . that is Major Crawford, is well, Corporal?' the woman posed, and nodded and smiled fleetingly in anticipation of the confirmation she knew would be forthcoming.

'Yes, ma'am, he was in fine fettle last time I saw him. Which was just the day before yesterday when the patrol left the post.'

He was briefly glad to have been able to lighten the mood of his commanding officer's wife. But abruptly dejection of the worst kind hit him again as he looked away from Mrs Crawford's now grim set face to glance over the scene of carnage and destruction that was perhaps emphasised by the warmth and brightness of the early summer day.

Out in the fields the two uniformed men who had been blasted out of their saddles by the chasing braves were being shrouded in blankets before they were draped over the backs of their recaptured mounts. And just one of the fallen Indians was being roughly hauled to his feet, the two troopers who were manhandling him apparently making no allowances for the wound that had sheened a side of his face with blood. The mounted pickets seemed to be losing interest in their duty after failing to spot at first glance any sign of fresh danger: and they spent more time peering back at the area of the burnt-out farmstead and the trail where it ran past the yard wall than in watching any other potentially more dangerous piece of the surrounding country.

Within the walled and fenced confines of the fire-scorched and rubble-strewn yard, Edward Sun stood up after tenderly setting down his father's blackened corpse alongside that of his mother – having moved both of them several feet away from the body of Patterson who he now knew had come to his parent's place for no good reason. For stretched seconds the young half-Chinese merely stood peering stoically down at their heat-mutilated heads – as though he was unable to move but was adamantly determined not to look at their naked bodies. Then, with a grunt that seemed to signal enlightenment on some perplexing problem that had been bothering him, he turned and moved purposefully across the yard to the rear wire fence. He surmounted the fence less awkwardly than had Luke Vicary, but he was not encumbered with a rifle – had tossed aside the empty Winchester before he politely escorted Mrs Yancy out of the timber. Now Edward Sun went from sight into the trees that grew densely out back of the farmstead.

It was with a not dissimilar grunt that he had left the widow on the trail to go through the gateway and undertake the chore of separating his dead parents from the remains of the man who had come here to kill him. Probably, the disorientated Amy Yancy was not aware of the city-suited youngster bringing her out of the trees and then leaving her standing there as he stepped around the corpse of Vicary and past that of Quinlan to go about his business. For certainly she seemed oblivious to what was happening as Edge led his saddled gelding on to the trail and took a gentle hold of one of her upper arms – this action halting Adam Steele's move to leave the side of the Concord with the intention of tending to the younger woman now the older one was concerned with other things. Then, her pale-blue eyes devoid of expression and her finely sculptured mouth not even moving to form the shape of a word, she responded with robot-like compliance to the mild pressure the half-breed exerted to slightly turn her and guide her along the trail to where Corporal McNally was looking and sounding wretchedly demoralised again as he explained to Edith Crawford and Adam Steele:

'We were thirty strong when we left Fort Hamilton. Captain Mannin' was in command. Lieutenant Butler was along, too. And Sergeant Frank O'Reilly. I knew there was a good chance we was goin' to run into Ute trouble . . . but I never figured to be left in command with the officers dead and Frank O'Reilly, too!'

Talk on the wrong subject was worse for McNally's frayed nerves than no talk at all. He looked desperately around with a haunted expression in his deep-set eyes, seemed surprised to see Edge and Amy Yancy had joined the small group beside the Concord. Nothing about the impassive face of the half-breed acted to calm his churning emotions, but he suddenly pulled back from the brink of hysteria as he found his gaze trapped by the eyes of the pale-faced red-head. He stopped breathing so intensely and his hands ceased to knead the reins of his horse.

'Goodness, you look ill, Corporal,' the widow told him evenly, and there was concern in her previously empty eyes now. 'I most sincerely hope that you have not contracted the same sickness that claimed my beloved husband? Presumably, since you are in this part of the country, you are from Fort Hamilton and will have heard of Cole? Captain Cole Yancy?'

McNally's recovery from the effects of his traumatic experiences quickened in direct relation to his realisation that the younger of the two army wives was unbalanced – almost as if he saw in Amy Yancy an example of what could become of him if he did not strive to keep a grip on reason.

'Why . . . yes . . . yes, ma'am,' the corporal blurted and only half-completed a salute this time – as Edith Crawford directed a rancorous glare at the half-breed when she hooked an arm around the shoulders of Mrs Yancy to re-assert her responsibility for the widow's welfare. 'I knew Captain Yancy real well, ma'am. Well as one of my rank can know a commissioned officer, that is. He was well liked at Hamilton by all the men and we was all real sorry when he took the fever and . . . pas . . . when he died, ma'am.'

Mrs Crawford looked anxiously into the face of the younger woman. Saw just a smile of pride there as the perturbed young non-com stumblingly attempted to discharge what he obviously regarded as an additional duty. Then:

'Come, my dear. We'll be leaving this awful place soon, I'm sure. It will be best and more comfortable for us, I think, if we wait aboard the stage?'

Amy Yancy had retreated into the insulated world of imagination again – and responded without the slightest protest to Edith Crawford's guiding moves, the smile at what she had been told of her husband's reputation still on her face like something forgotten.

Steele opened the door with the broken window so that the women were able to enter the Concord. And as he closed it behind them, asked of McNally:

'You all right now, Corporal?'

'Thank you, sir, yes I am.'

'Lost two-thirds of the patrol strength, Edge,' the Virginian explained. 'Including two officers and a sergeant.'

'In that one running fight, feller?' the half-breed asked, jerking a thumb over his shoulder to indicate the unfenced fields from where the eight troopers were returning with two of their own dead and a lone wounded Ute.

McNally swallowed hard and shook his head. 'No, sir. How it was, we — '

'Corporal,' Mrs Crawford cut in, showing her grim set face in the glassless frame of the stagecoach door.

'Mrs Crawford, ma'am?'

'I realise that I am merely the wife of your commanding officer and as such have no standing in terms of . . . but I really do think we should make all haste to be on our way from this awful place.'

'Goin' to fix to do that right now, ma'am,' McNally assured her, as she treated Edge and Steele to a rancorous glower that seemed to blame them for much else besides the delay in leaving. Then, after she had withdrawn into the Concord and could be heard speaking in soothing tones to

Mrs Yancy, the non-com said: 'The major's wife is right. The bunch that just took off could take it into their heads to hit us again. Or there's rumours that a whole lot of others are taking the warpath. Sooner we get you civilians to Oro City and get back to Hamilton with a report of what's happened, better I'll like it.'

'Not rumours, Corporal,' Steele told him as Edward Sun emerged from the timber in the area where Dalton Arliss had been hidden. The young half-Chinese was leading the three travel-stained horses of the bounty hunters by the reins. 'Stage was hit by a group some way east of here. And I saw a lot of Ute activity further to the east.'

'There are bands roaming the country to the north of here, too,' Edith Crawford added as she abandoned her seemingly doomed attempts to unlock the younger woman's mind. This as the troopers reined in their mounts at the side of the Concord, two of them leading horses with blanket-shrouded corpses draped over the saddles and the scowling Arnie Jonas holding a length of rope that was noosed around the neck of the wounded prisoner. 'We were told so by men who quite obviously were in no mood for idle gossip and scaremongering.'

McNally looked like a man who longed to be left alone in peace and quiet to think out a plan of action. And there was a not too distant relation of panic in his deep-set dark eyes as he raked his gaze from the stage to the troopers, then to the prisoner, to Edge, to Steele and to Edward Sun.

'What are you doin'?' he demanded harshly of the young half-Chinese.

Sun, still clutching the reins of the three horses, had halted on his way toward the gateway in the wall. And he was gazing with expanding hatred at the Ute with blood on his face and a noose around his neck, the expression that seemed to be such a bad fit on his own face making him look briefly much older. The Indian was unable to hold the powerful stare and dropped his face against the rope, just before Sun's distorted features returned to normal.

'Excuse me, sir, but it is my intention to bring my parents to Oro City for burial,' the city-suited youngster answered deferentially. 'Their bodies are naked and there are blankets in the bedrolls on these — '

'Yeah, sure,' McNally cut in, regretful for his attitude. 'I should have figured you were a relative or a friend or somethin' – you bein' a Chinaman, too. Do what you gotta. But quit messin' with the prisoner.'

'His kind were responsible for all this,' Sun reminded, gesturing with his free hand to encompass the farmstead as he led the horses into the yard. 'I was just thinking it was a pity that the only Indian I can be sure I personally shot was no more than wounded.'

Both Edge and Steele looked longer and harder at the Ute – bending their knees so they were able to better see his tipped-forward face. Jonas saw this and gave a vicious jerk on the rope to force the brave to bring up his head.

'Trooper, take that rope from around his neck and tie him to your saddle!' McNally snapped, and it was obvious he would not have any delayed qualms about venting his spleen on the recalcitrant Arnie Jonas. 'Then take the reins of the stage! Are they bodies up there on the roof?'

'Driver and guard who were killed by the Indians yesterday, Corporal,' Edith Crawford confirmed to the non-com who once again seemed confident of command.

'Obliged, ma'am. Be further obliged if you and Mrs Yancy — '

'Hey, is the redhead Captain Yancy's widow, Phil?' a trooper with a broken nose and some livid scar tissue above his right eye asked in surprise. And it was apparent he voiced a query that had occurred to several of the other men.

'Yeah, she is, Saxon,' McNally supplied, needing to control an urge to make the retort an angry one. He shot a glare at every trooper and nodded his satisfaction with the disconcerted expressions most of them showed. 'It's good that you all know that, so you'll be able to treat the lady with the respect due her. As I was saying, Mrs Crawford, it will be a considerable help to me if you and Mrs Yancy will ride up on the outside seat with Trooper Jonas.'

'Corporal?' the older woman posed uneasily.

'I don't intend to concern myself with the Indian dead,

ma'am, but I feel duty-bound to bring the remains of all the whites to Oro City and — '

'Yes, yes, of course. Mrs Yancy and I will most certainly ride outside so that the bodies may be transported in here.'

'Thank you, ma'am. Do as I told you with the prisoner, Jonas. Saxon, Egan: I'm assignin' you two to ride close escort on him. Goldsmith, Conran: soon as the ladies are out of the stage, take those corpses off the horses and load them aboard. Then switch the driver and guard from the roof to the inside. Rest of you men, go give the Chinaman a hand with his folks and collect up the other civilian dead.'

While the troopers swung out of their saddles and went dolefully to attend to their assigned tasks, Edge led his gelding to the rear of the Concord which placed him out of everybody's way. He was joined there by Steele who had retrieved his saddle and other gear from the seat as McNally held the door and helped the women out.

'It's the brave the kid's last bullet brought down sure enough,' the half-breed said as the Virginian began to saddle the black stallion.

'No doubt about it. If I'd seen him stretched out in the field with that much blood on his head, reckon I'd have thought he was more than just creased.'

'Sub-chief of some kind.'

'He was the head man, sure enough.'

'Not at the start of it, he wasn't,' McNally said as he and Edith Crawford escorted the still serenely smiling Amy Yancy around to the rear of the Concord: where the women were shielded from the sight although not the sound of the macabre work being done by the troopers and Edward Sun. The older woman acknowledged with a nod the tacit enquiry expressed by the corporal, then placed a fat arm around Mrs Yancy's thin shoulders and the both of them gazed along the trail between the trees in back of the stage become a mobile charnel house: neither of them, for different reasons, seeing the rustic vista spread peacefully before them.

The cavalryman disassociated himself from the females by moving around to the other side of the black stallion where Edge and Steele stood. He amplified: 'When they hit us as we were starting to break up the night camp, another Ute was leadin' them.' He nodded to where Jonas finished tying the hands of the prisoner, then shoved the hapless brave viciously toward the two troopers McNally had detailed to guard him on the ride ahead. 'A taller and older brave was head man. A real smart sonofabitch . . .' He glanced anxiously over the back of the newly saddled stallion as Steele stooped to tighten the cinch, relieved that the women seemed unaware of his bad language. 'Timed the attack for after Captain Mannin' had called in the perimeter pickets and before the call to mount. The captain and Sergeant Frank O'Reilly went down right off. Along with half a dozen or more men. It was all such a Godawful mess right there at the start, guess no one'll be certain of the damn details until the site of that camp is looked over.'

Now McNally, absently massaging the nape of his neck like the skin there had developed an irritation, gazed out into the same middle distance as the women. And from his horrified expression it was plain to see that he was visualising the events of which he spoke.

'Figure your officers didn't bed down the patrol in the best place, feller?' Edge prodded evenly.

'They sure as hell didn't, mister!' McNally shot back, bitterly angry. And it was impossible to guess the target of his rancour until he moderated his tone and looked from one to the other of the men he stood with. 'But it wasn't nobody's fault and ain't a man that survived can in truth lay the blame. We were thirty strong and didn't know of any bad Indian trouble. Patrol that big was sent out after word reached Fort Hamilton that a couple of bands of renegades was cuttin' loose and raisin' a little hell here and there. Major Crawford and the rest of the top brass at the post figured it wouldn't do no harm for the army to swing through the country and show the Utes who it is runs things these days. Just in case some more of them sonsofbitches figured to get ornery like the ones already caused the trouble.'

'What kind of trouble, Corporal?' the Virginian asked as he completed fixing his bedroll in place behind his saddle on the black stallion.

'Stealin' was all. And some rustlin' of cattle. Some shootin' when the braves were spotted in the act. One farmer got a bullet in the hand, but no one was killed. Indians included, far as anyone could tell.'

'No sign of any trouble on the patrol until the Utes attacked, feller?' Edge asked, starting to roll a cigarette as the task of loading the several corpses into the Concord neared completion.

'No, sir,' McNally answered, tone even but the expression in his hollow eyes and the set of his mouth revealing a hardening of his attitude as he was urged to recall again the carnage of early morning. 'No sign of any kind of Indian activity. Which I guess some will say should have made the officers suspicious, sir. On account of usually a patrol out of the post sees somthin' of the Utes. But the men figured – and I guess the captain and the lieutenant didn't think any different – that they was keepin' outta sight because we was scarin' the hell out of them like we was intended to.' He sucked in a deep breath, ballooned out his cheeks with it and then let it rush out through clenched teeth before he growled: 'Man, was we as wrong as anybody can get.'

Edge struck a match on a Concord wheelrim and lit his cigarette. Then swung up into the saddle. Seeing this, and then that Adam Steele was on the point of mounting, too, the corporal spoke faster – as if he felt it essential that the two civilians should know everything before they left, so there would be less chance of them drawing the wrong conclusion about the conduct of the two officers he had quite obviously held in high regard. And perhaps, too, he was eager that his own actions in command should be seen in a good light.

'There was maybe more than twice as many braves as you saw in back of us just now, Mr Edge, Mr Steele. As many as three times, I don't know. It sure looked like one hell of a lot. Hit us hard and fast like I told you, and the captain and Frank O'Reilly was among the first of our men to go down. Right after the Utes stopped sneakin' up on us and came at us firin' and yellin' and scarin' all kinds of hell out of a lot of us.'

McNally was standing between the two horses, head

tilted back to look up at the men astride them. The brightness of the sky above the half-breed and the Virginian caused him to squint and this served to emphasise the expression of intense fervour on his thin face. He gulped a lot and he kept clenching and opening his hands like he was preparing to snatch at the bridles of the stallion and the gelding if the riders should try to leave before he was through with what he had to get said.

'We was a long way from any cover except for what the Indians had used to get in close to us. Lieutenant Butler done the only thing he could. Ordered a mount and a retreat. But we done for a whole lot of them Indians while we was runnin'. Dropped more of them than they did us. First when the lieutenant was in command and then when I took over.'

'There's ever a chance for men to go out and count the dead, Phil, the truth of that will be seen,' the broken-nosed, scar-faced Saxon assured.

Jonas sat in a hunched shoulder attitude up on the seat of the Concord. The Ute prisoner was even more round-shouldered as he sat astride a cavalry mount, bound wrists tied to the saddle horn and his chin resting down on his chest. All the other men, including Edward Sun, had gathered into a group beside the stage, holding their horses by the reins or bridles as they listened to what McNally was telling Edge and Steele. Silent and unmoving until one trooper spoke, when several others nodded or made vocal sounds of agreement.

'Lieutenant Butler was givin' me my orders when he was hit,' the corporal continued after sparing an absent glance for the group of troopers and then nodding in brief acknowledgement of something he had perhaps already forgotten. 'Yellin' at me as we were movin' at a full gallop. Told me I'd be in command of the men if he went down. Told me I should bring them here to the Sun place and make a stand if there was enough of us left. Then he took the bullet in the head and he was gone. A good ways off from the other end of the ravine that you saw us come out of. And we kept on givin' a good account of ourselves, way I saw it. But when I saw the Sun place wasn't there no more . . . well, I was almost sick to my stomach right off. Then I saw the stage and when you people started to shoot out of the timber . . . well, it was a couple of real bad seconds while I figured I was leadin' the men away from one bunch of hostiles toward another bunch.'

The young non-com ceased to open and close his hands all the time and the ramrod stiffness of high tension drained out of his slender frame. This as his face gradually took on the expression of a man close to total exhaustion but who is fully satisfied that the task which so wearied him has been well done.

'Ain't one of us didn't figure it the same way as you, Phil,' a trooper growled.

'We was runnin' scared and would've run our horses into the friggin' ground if — '

'Watch your language, Webber!' McNally cut in imperiously as he firmed his stance and hardened his expression. 'There are ladies present.'

'That there are,' Arnie Jonas growled as he turned to direct a sneer of contempt at his fellow troopers and McNally as the corporal moved to speak with Edith Crawford and Amy Yancy. 'And at least one real man, Webber! Who wasn't runnin' scared – so I don't want you or anyone else in this bunch of bleedin' hearts to talk about how I was when you got no idea — '

'All right, Trooper, you've made your point!' McNally cut across what he was saying as he shepherded the women around the far side of the stage from where the men were grouped. 'Help the officers' wives aboard and see to it they are as comfortable as possible during the trip. Rest of you men, mount up.' He emerged from around the rear of the stage after leaving the grimacing Jonas to do his bidding. And, still looking gaunt but with a light in his eyes that suggested he was drawing on a previously unknown store of inner strength, he went on: 'You civilians are free agents, of course. Since we have the bodies of his parents aboard the wagon, I presume Mr Sun will be travellin' with us to Oro City. In view of the Indian situation which is now irrefutably serious, I would advise you, Mr Steele and Mr Edge, to come along with us.'

The troopers completed their mount and Edward Sun decided between the horses he had brought in from the timber, climbed awkwardly into the saddle of the bay gelding with a white flash. From somewhere he had scavenged another Winchester, which he thrust into the rear-slung boot.

'You're going my way, Corporal,' Edge said as he slowly wheeled his horse.

'From what I've seen, the Utes are massing back that way,' Steele added, hooking a gloved thumb to indicate the trail curving away behind the stage as he urged his mount to face in the opposite direction. Then nodded at Edge as he added: 'So I reckon I'm with him.'

'I surely will be riding along with you,' Sun hurried to confirm.

'And I'm surely glad to know we have three men with your kind of gun skills to augment the patrol,' McNally countered, and was even able to grin as he swung up into his saddle, so hard and fast was his grip on recovered composure.

'You ain't the only one, Phil,' Jonas was quick to add, as he began to wind the team reins around the brake lever. 'Though I ain't never bothered to use all them five dollar words that officers use to say it like you.'

'What d'you think you're doin', *Trooper* Jonas?' McNally demanded harshly, placing heavy stress on the cavalryman's lowly ranking.

'Seems to me, *Corporal*!' the man shot back with a mocking emphasis on McNally's title, 'that if the civilians that brought the stage here are movin' right along with us, then they oughta handle the rig and let a horsesoldier do what he's supposed to.'

Arnie Jonas had made to start to climb down from the stage. But the glare directed at him by McNally held him where he was. And, after a moment, he felt compelled to look away from the powerful glower of the corporal and found himself trapped into meeting the steady gaze of Edge, who told him through the drifting haze of smoke from his cigarette:

'It's not my scene, being on the stage.'

Steele drew the trooper's scowling attention to himself

when he drawled: 'And I reckoned I played my part up there already.'

'I'm sorry, but I don't think I could drive such a —' Sun started.

'Nobody's askin'!' McNally snapped, his anger with Jonas expanding. 'The trooper will attend to his assigned duty or he will answer to the consequences when we return — '

'All right, all right!' Jonas snarled as he slammed down on to the seat again and snatched up the reins. 'I get all the lousy duties around the post so I oughta be used — '

He lowered his voice and then allowed it to fade away altogether as he saw he was being ignored by the men who were jostling into position ahead and to the rear of the Concord in response to tacit but emphatic commands indicated by the non-com's gesturing hand and pointed index finger. Then McNally said in a tone backed up by his expression that implied he would not tolerate any argument:

'Havin' told you civilians I'm pleased you are ridin' with us, I have to tell you now that I consider you are bounded by cavalry regulations. And that I am in command of this detail.'

'Where do you want me to ride?' Edge asked.

'I'll give you fair warning when I'm getting ready to leave this man's army, Corporal,' Adam Steele assured.

Edward Sun, eager to say something, added: 'Whatever you say, sir.'

'The three of you will bring up the rear,' McNally rapped out, and tugged on his reins to turn and ride his horse out to the head of the knot of troopers who sat their unmoving mounts at the front of the stage and team. The Virginian, the half-breed and the half-Chinese youngster moved into line abreast at the rear, behind Troopers Saxon and Egan who were flanking the Ute prisoner. Then the lowly ranked cavalryman in command called: 'Forward!'

'Or in terms of the stage, let's get the show on the road,' Steele murmured as the Concord and its complement of escorting riders started to move.

'Or in a word,' Edge said as he took the cigarette from his mouth and arced it over the wall where everything that could be burnt had been: 'Role.'

CHAPTER TEN

FOR SEVERAL minutes, during which time the slow-moving stagecoach of the Central Western line and its mixed escort of military and civilian riders covered the best part of a mile, there was no talk. In this time and over such a distance, the country which surrounded the Concord and riders was considerably changed, for the rolling foothills of the mountains with their contours softened by grass and timber gave way to dust and rock on a landscape where harsh angles were much more in evidence than gentle curves: and where little grew, that which did looking almost as dry and bleached and scorched as the element-punished ground from which it struggled to survive.

But the trail followed a route that carried it in a sweeping curve to the south of the majestic grandeur of the canyonlands which the half-breed and then the Virginian and the others aboard the stage had yesterday seen in the far distance from the high ground at the head of the valley. And the section of scrub desert which they all now traversed was a lot safer from potential Indian ambush than would have been the timber left behind and the vast tract of canyons and mesas and buttes and outcrops and ridges that they were detouring around.

Those who recognised this because they were experienced in watching out for trouble, and knowledgeable in when the high points of danger are past, became noticeably less tense. Others were not long in sensing and then seeing that the easing of tension around them meant the immediate threat was gone.

'You heading anywhere in particular, Reb?' Edge asked when they were moving across a piece of country where it would have been impossible for more than a handful of Utes to be concealed within effective rifle range. 'When you decided to turn around back there?'

'Had the decision made for me, Yank.'

'Whatever.'

'A time after we parted company at that outlaw bolt-hole in Colorado I was shot up pretty bad.'

'I know the feeling and it's never good, feller.'

'Almost died. From the bullet or a lynchrope. Could have been either.'

'Hard man to kill, uh?'

'Reckoned I was until that time, Edge,' the Virginian replied with a slow shake of his head while his dark eyes seemed to peer into a middle distance playing host to images from the past that were no longer painful to recall. 'Known for a long time that the only certain thing about life is that nobody ever gets out of it alive. But I never before was reminded so painfully of my own mortality.'

Steele suddenly sat stiffer in the saddle and for part of a second seemed disconcerted – before he shot a sidelong glance at Edge who rode on his right, and saw the half-breed was not looking at him. Sardonically or in any other way. But then the taller and leaner man, with whom he always felt he was in competition whenever they met up, said:

'So you figured to start riding around with your eyes closed every now and then to see if — '

'Decided to call a halt to riding around in any way, Yank!' the Virginian cut in harshly, and knew for certain Edge had spotted his brief lapse of alertness just now and guessed he had been caught in a similar state of wool-gathering when he was first seen yesterday morning.

'But you ain't found where yet, uh?' the half-breed asked, neither perturbed by the other man's consternation nor showing any sign that he considered he had scored a point off him by riling Steele.

'No, I haven't found where. So it's just as likely to be in this direction as over beyond where the Utes are massing.'

'You have something particular in mind to do when you find it, Reb?'

'Raise thoroughbred horses, Yank. Didn't I tell you that way back?'

'I don't remember. Sounds good. Lot of stuff people talk about sounds good. You ever noticed that, Reb?'

'I don't listen much to what other people talk about, Yank.'

Edge nodded. 'Yeah, most of the time they don't mean what they say. Either that, or what they say doesn't mean anything. Right?'

He showed a faint grin that drew back his lips but did not add warmth to the glittering light in his slitted blue eyes as he looked at Adam Steele as part of his constant scanning of the distant country and his immediate surroundings.

'Some people some of the time, Yank,' the Virginian answered. 'I've been raising the wherewithal since that time I almost got killed for something I didn't care about.'

And now it was his turn to spread a faint smile across his time-lined and element-burnished features. His dark eyes did not remain cold, though: held a glimmer of far less than icy triumph as the half-breed completed a double-take at him and nodded in acknowledgement that he knew it was the truth he had heard.

'That's good, feller,' Edge said after the moment of tacit understanding between two men with violence-forged rapport had passed. 'Maybe one day I'll get me the inclination and the dollars to live under something more permanent than my hat.'

'Again.'

'Uh?'

'Seem to recall you told me you were married and settled up in the Dakotas way back?'

Edge nodded and if he felt any modicum of pain at the ancient memory he did not allow it to alter the set of his impassive expression as he continued to scan their barren, sun-baked surroundings. He said: 'For you it was down in Texas, wasn't it?'

'Right. But this time it's going to be different. Just be me.'

The half-breed nodded again. 'Way it has to be for the likes of me and you, Reb. But when my turn comes I figure I'll know right off.'

'Maybe you will, Yank. It just didn't happen for me like that.'

'When the going gets tough, the smart get all the way out, Reb.'

'If that's how it happens for you,' Steele allowed evenly, but stole a surreptitious glance at Edge while the other man was doubly engaged in making a cigarette and unnecessarily keeping too close a watch over the corner of the scrub desert they were crossing. But the Virginian saw nothing in the lean, dark-skinned profile to confirm his suspicion that the half-breed was attempting to needle him out of an uncharacteristic feeling of envy. 'In my case, I don't reckon the going got any tougher. I just started to realise that it wasn't going to get any easier.'

'Like it's supposed to as a man gets older – if he's lucky?'

'I reckon.'

Edge lit his newly made cigarette with a match struck on the butt of the Colt jutting from his shoulder.

'Pardon me,' Sun said tentatively.

'You do something, kid?' the half-breed asked.

'I cannot but help overhear what you are saying to each other.' In the few hours of this new day, the youngster had endured the shock of finding his horrifically murdered parents, seen that his home had been destroyed beyond rebuilding, discovered a man had hired other men to hunt him down and kill him, and had himself faced up to what it was like to kill a fellow human being.

And now as they eyed the half-Chinese expectantly, both Steele and Edge were struck by the notion that he had seemed to age many years since they had last paid any particular attention to him. His round face seemed to have developed angles, his complexion appeared less sallow and there were previously unnoticed lines in his otherwise smooth skin at either side of his mouth and eyes. Instead of looking to be about eighteen years old, it would have been easy to mistake him for close to thirty. Or maybe it was the bright clarity of the light out here in the desert, or perhaps just that they had not looked at him so long and hard before.

'Reckon the Yank and I have nothing to say to each other that we'd be ashamed to have overheard,' Steele said.

'You are talking, I think, of getting older,' Sun went on, and both men riding to his right experienced a slightly unreal feeling, but held back from asking wryly if the fast-aged young man could read minds. 'I simply wished to repeat a saying of my late father which he pronounced quite often. It was that there is at least one good thing about a man growing old – that it takes his past longer to catch up with him.'

In much the same way that Adam Steele tended to drop years from his appearance when he displayed an infrequent warm smile, so Edward Sun looked youthful again as he grinned – at first happily and then wistfully as he reflected on the fact that he would never again hear his father say this or anything else.

'I bet he stole that off Confucius,' Edge growled.

'How does a farm boy from Iowa get to know about an ancient Oriental philosopher, Yank?' Steele asked.

'Same way as a rich man's son from Virginia I guess, Reb. First I learned to read, then I read to learn. And some real strange stuff stayed put in my head.'

'All your book learning will serve no purpose, white eyes,' the captured Ute who was tied to the horse moving directly ahead of Steele's stallion announced in a threatening tone, without turning to look back. 'And if you wish to repent your past lives, you should do so soon. As you should do anything that you have left undone.'

Saxon, who rode in front of Edge and to the right of the prisoner, vented a low grunt as he jerked the Spencer carbine from his boot and thumbed back the hammer as he pressed the muzzle into the yielding flesh at the side of the Ute's neck.

The brave gulped and sat suddenly upright in the unfamiliar saddle, terrified of dying but ready to die if that was how it had to be.

'What the frig, Earl?' the short and overweight, red-complexioned and animal-eyed Trooper Egan squeezed from his alarm-constricted throat as Arnie Jonas and the two women up on the outside seat of the stage snapped their heads around to see the cause of the harshly spoken words.

But Egan's voice had not been raised to the extent that would have carried it to the ears of McNally and the other front riders against the clopping of so many hooves and the clattering of the Concord's wheels.

'I ain't gonna just ride along here listenin' to some stinkin' Injun sonofabitch tryin' to scare the shit outta me, Roy!' Saxon growled, the crimson of his risen temper making the livid scar tissue stand out more starkly above his eye.

'Looks to me that he scored better than just trying, Trooper,' Steele drawled.

'You ain't gonna blow his head off, Earl,' Egan said and both his expression and his no-longer-constrained voice made this a statement rather than a question.

'I friggin' oughta!' Saxon countered bitterly as Jonas displayed a scornful smile and Edith Crawford looked in bewilderment into the face of Amy Yancy – the redheaded widow showing an eager smile on her attractive face as her lips moved in a soft-toned or perhaps even soundless entreaty that was incomprehensible to anyone who did not pay her close attention.

'I go along with what your buddy Roy says, feller,' Edge said.

'I don't give a shit about what you or your buddy Steele says, mister!' Saxon rasped.

'Usually we don't say much at all,' Steele replied in the same even tone as Edge. This while the attention of everyone aware of the situation was focussed upon the brave with blood crusted on his face or the scowling trooper who was the squeeze of a trigger away from causing a fresh flow to erupt.

'Just now we happened to be catching up on what's been what since him and me last got together to kill a bunch of people,' Edge went on. 'Sort of killing time between the times of killing.'

'But we were running out of agreeable subjects to talk about.'

'And we'd much rather listen to the Indian shoot his mouth off.'

'Which he was doing real well before you pretended you were going to blow his head off, Trooper.'

'Well I wouldn't!' Earl Saxon retorted vehemently, and thrust the carbine muzzle harder into the side of the brave's neck. 'The murderin' sonofabitch is my prisoner and I don't have to put up with the kinda shit he was startin' to spout — '

'Earl, don't get so mad you won't be able to — ' Roy Egan started to cut in.

'Hey, Saxon,' Edge said, his tone not loud but definitely compelling. Sufficiently so for Egan to curtail his anxious plea and join all the others except for the Ute in peering at the half-breed with glittering slits for eyes and lips, with a cigarette angled from the side, that hardly moved when he continued: 'Maybe it was Confucius again or maybe it was just me. But somebody said you can get more with a kind word and a gun than you can with a kind word.'

'You lost me, mister!' Saxon snorted, and tried to tear his gaze away from the trap of Edge's stare – but failed.

'The Indian was beginning to speak freely and perhaps give us information of great use to us before you stopped him with your gun, sir,' Edward Sun suggested, switching his slant-eyed gaze rapidly back and forth between the trooper and the half-breed.

'That's right, kid,' Edge allowed without unlocking his gaze from Saxon's face as he shifted his right hand from the reins of the gelding to drape the butt of the Frontier Colt in his holster. 'And you, Trooper, will be lost to the whole damn world if you don't put that carbine back in the boot. On account of it's just sometimes I draw this revolver without giving much of a shit if I use it to kill somebody or not. This is not one of those times, Trooper. That's a lot of kind words, I'd say?'

'I'm with you, Earl!' Jonas yelled back from the stage. 'Do what you figure you have to and if the hard nose tries to stop you I'll — '

'*Detail, halt!*' McNally roared against the voice of the other man, and the troopers reining in their mounts forced the cursing Jonas to swing around and attend to bringing the stage to a stop.

'Just one other thing,' Edge went on as he and the rest of the riders in back of the Concord had to halt their horses.

'I ain't going to waste the time with that count-of-three stuff. Just say to you, do it now.'

'Just what the — ' the Corporal began as he made to wheel his mount from the head of the column.

Edge fisted his right hand around the revolver butt.

'Civilian's — 'Arnie Jonas started.

'Don't!' Mrs Crawford shrieked.

'Yes, yes, yes!' the widow blurted as she found her voice at last.

'Earl, he ain't — ' Roy Egan managed to warn.

Trooper Earl Saxon jerked the carbine away from the neck of the Ute and then wrenched his glinting-with-rage gaze away from the face of the half-breed: just for long enough so that he could see he was pushing the Spencer firmly into the boot – then he stared back at the man who had moved his right hand from the revolver butt to take hold of the reins again.

The actions of the two men directly involved in the confrontation served to make those in a position to see them cut short what they were shouting. Then McNally and Jonas were silenced by Saxon's snarling:

'All right, you crazy bastard! All right! Have it your friggin' way! You wanna listen to the friggin' Injun runnin' off at the mouth like it's all of us that's *his* prisoner instead of the other way around, you come ride with the stink of him up your friggin' nose and McNally can put me on as many friggin' reports as he likes!'

'Trooper!' the glowering corporal roared with sufficient force to hold Saxon fixed where he was as he made to jerk his mount away. This as McNally wheeled and reined his own horse to a halt at the rear of the Concord. 'Just what the hell is all this ruckus about?'

There was nothing to choose between the extent of the near-trembling rage that had taken a grip on McNally and Saxon as they seemed to be trying to outstare each other. And both appeared to have been temporarily robbed of the ability to speak by the effort of will it required to bring themselves under control.

'The prisoner was actin' up, Phil, and Earl was showin' him who has the upper hand here,' Jonas announced in a composed tone as he raked a supercilious gaze over the group of men seated in their saddles amid the settling dust of the abrupt halt. 'Civilians seemed to think Earl was out of line.'

'Hey, come on, Arnie, it wasn't so much like that and you know it!' the doleful and nervous Egan argued.

'I despise the kind of man who makes trouble out of trouble!' Edith Crawford put in vehemently, staring across the stooped shoulders of the widow she was embracing at the almost-smiling Jonas: her fleshy face set in a mask of hatred. 'And whatever is reported officially to my husband the major I intend to add my views on certain aspects of this affair!'

'Mrs Crawford, ma'am?' McNally interjected apprehensively as he at last suppressed his anger and became wary of offending the wife of his commanding officer. He seemed on the point of saluting, then decided against it. He had to clear his throat. 'With all due respect, this is a military matter and — '

The actions of Edge and Steele caused him to curtail what he was saying: as the two men heeled their horses forward with resolute purpose but no haste, to force wider and move into the gaps between the Ute and Saxon on one side and Egan on the other.

The half-breed growled to the still angry Saxon: 'Since you made the offer, feller.'

And Steele drawled to the perplexed Egan: 'Pardon me, Trooper.'

Then, as everyone with the exception of the prisoner gazed at them, they both did a double-take at the Ute brave. Saw him with more than merely passing interest for the first time. He was a man of thirty-five or so with a squat build – not much taller than five feet but weighing close to a muscular one hundred and seventy-five pounds: the powerful development of his frame clear to see since he was naked above the waist of his rawhide breechclouts except for a dull-hued choker around his neck and bands of a similar pattern encircling his upper arms. His face, beneath the headband with a single feather at the rear and between the thick black hair that reached almost to his shoulders, was strong featured, and displayed a bone structure that was too jutting and thrusting to lend him the handsomeness that might otherwise have been suggested by his dark eyes, flared nostrils and finely shaped mouth. Even without the fan of dried and flaking blood that marred one side of his face and the scabbed scar of the shallow bullet wound at his temple, this very Indian-featured Ute would have looked belligerently ugly. For, Edge and Steele now saw – as did the others who felt drawn to look at him – a quiet smile on such a face detracted not at all from the inbred aggressiveness that was latent within him. Then, as the compulsion to kill the brave that had gripped Earl Saxon began to infect others, the Indian dispensed with the smile and his abruptly pragmatic attitude and tone took his audience completely by surprise when he said:

'So you are the woman of Major Ethan Theodore Crawford?'

Mrs Crawford had found her shocked attention held a secure prisoner by the smile on the face of the Indian. And now she seemed unable to stop herself from confirming: 'Yes, yes I am married to the major.'

'Ma'am?' McNally said huskily.

The older woman abandoned her ministrations to the wretchedly distressed younger one as she shook her head as if to physically clear her mind of emotional shackles. And then she became grim-faced and her tone was harsh as she ignored the agitated corporal to demand of the Indian: 'What of it, you murdering savage?'

'You will call me what you think is right or what you think will insult me, woman,' the brave replied in his most stylised English. 'As the helpless captive of Ethan Theodore Crawford's band of women and children killers I will be wasting what little breath I have left to me to — '

'Shut your lyin' mouth, Indian!' McNally roared, his right hand fumbling with the flap of the holster on his right hip.

The troopers who had been riding with McNally at the front of the stage had drifted toward the rear. Some of them looked to be as close to the brink of shattering violence as were McNally and Saxon. While others shared in the same brand of almost trembling uneasiness as Roy Egan. Only Arnie Jonas derived quiet pleasure from the highly charged situation – as the two civilians flanking the unruffled Ute went for a rifle and a revolver. But left the weapons in the boot and holster with their hands draped loosely around stock and butt when Edith Crawford leapt to her feet. Then the woman whirled to glower across the length of the Concord's roof as she commanded:

'Corporal, in the name of my husband, I demand an end to this stupidity! If it does not end immediately there will surely be further bloodshed! And whatever the outcome, this troublemaking Indian and the rest of his savage tribe will be the winners.'

'The lady's talking sense, Corporal,' Steele rasped, his dark eyes settling their unblinking gaze on McNally after he had raked it over the other dangerously angered uniformed men. And had seen that they were staying their moves to draw their firearms as they looked for orders from the non-com.

'Goddammit to hell, I want no more part of this whole lousy mess!' McNally groaned, his hand dropping away from the unfastened holster as his dark eyes seemed to sink deeper into their sockets while his entire face got gaunter. 'I was never supposed to be in this kinda command!'

While Steele had divided his attention among several of the troopers, Edge had kept apparently indifferent watch on just Jonas. And now he tightened his hand into a fist around the butt of his Colt and began to ease it out of the holster, thumbing back the hammer. Matched his moves to those made by the trooper on the stage as he readied himself to blast a bullet into the broad chest of this man with a cunning smirk on his square-featured face.

But Edith Crawford was also alert to the danger of the man's intentions and, with a shriek of rage, she hurled herself across the still-hunched-up form of Amy Yancy, to crash her not inconsiderable bulk into the seated, half-turned Arnie Jonas. He grunted a forceful bellow of mixed pain and alarm as the woman's impact sent him toppling over the side of the seat, the Army Colt he had drawn arcing away from his hand as he flailed both his arms in an effort to balance his fall and then break it against the rock-hard trail.

The big-built woman almost went in his wake: and probably would have had not Mrs Yancy returned to awareness of what was happening around her – and, with a shriek of alarm that was far more strident than that of Jonas, she flung her arms around Edith Crawford. And hugged her with far more force than was necessary to keep this woman who had cared for her from plunging off the high seat.

This as the trooper failed to adjust the attitude of his fall and crashed heavily to the ground with sufficient power to knock the wind from his body and the consciousness from his mind. And, for stretched seconds while he lay prone with his legs splayed and his arms sprawled out above his head, he could not be heard breathing while everyone else remained utterly silent. But then the involuntary functions and reflexes of Arnie Jonas resumed command of his physical being and his lungs began to fill with and expel air with accompanying rasping sounds in his throat.

Then, as if this concluding part of the final act to this violent drama served to remind everyone who witnessed it of how much worse it could have been, there was an almost palpable easing of tension. Pent up breath was vented by many with almost as much harsh noise as that which had signalled the unconscious man's continued survival. And hands shifted from some guns to draw sleeves across foreheads or run kerchiefs over cheeks and down the sides of necks to mop off the sweat of fear.

Then Edith Crawford extricated herself from the grip of Amy Yancy and rose to her feet with a remarkable degree of dignity. And smiled down at the upturned face of the other woman as she smoothed the skirt of her dress and patted her dishevelled hair.

'It sometimes surprised menfolk, my dear,' she said evenly, and transferred her smiling-eyed attention to the mounted men at the side and rear of the stage, 'that we members of the certainly gentler sex can lash out to good purpose when the occasion demands it.'

There was a triumph that came close to arrogance on her

puffy face as she looked at each of the men in turn, as if inviting him to take issue with her.

'It is truly said that we should never underestimate the power of a woman,' Edward Sun said with seemingly sincere admiration audible in his tone and seen on his face.

Edge eyed the sprawled form of the raggedly breathing Arnie Jonas and said in an even tenor as he returned his gaze to the jubilant Edith Crawford: 'Fine piece of man-handling, lady.'

Steele tipped his hat to the no-longer-smiling woman as he shifted his dark-eyed gaze from the unconscious trooper and showed her a warm but brief smile before he drawled: 'There's no denying some women can get some men to fall real hard for them, ma'am.'

CHAPTER ELEVEN

IT WAS not a camp as such. Just a stopover by common consent rather than by choice at the place where the intitial pause had been enforced. But the place where the Ute had unwittingly triggered the series of events that might well have led to his own death and the violent ending of the lives of several of the whites was as good a spot as any for the ill-assorted and uneasy group to pause and rest and talk. In the present circumstances, at least, it was agreed. The present circumstances being that it was more important to be on guard against a sneak attack by vengeance-fired Ute Indians than for the travellers to enjoy better shade than the Concord could provide.

The team and saddle horses had no kind of shade from the glaring sun of mid-morning and nothing to crop on, but at least they were rested from hauling the stage with its grisly freight or from being burdened with disgruntled, bewildered, frightened or angry riders.

Trooper Arnie Jonas had the best of it without being aware of the fact – was given full benefit of the available shade as he was bedded down, still blissfully unconscious, beneath the stalled Concord. Where, without anyone being asked, Amy Yancy volunteered to attend to him: her care perforce comprised of little more than sitting so that his head rested in her lap while she pressed a damp rag to the discoloured swelling on his right temple.

After a few moments the initial relief of climbing down from saddles and realising the narrow escape they had had was gone. And as the feel of tepid canteen water in their throats lost its appeal, some of the troopers became disconcertingly aware of the sweet smell of old death that emanated from the stage.

'Might help if we hung our blankets over that busted window in the door, Phil,' the baby-faced Roy Egan said diffidently to the non-com who was squatting down with his back against a rear wheel as he sipped from a canteen.

For a moment it seemed that as he continued to peer into the sun-bright middle distance where the desert gave way to the more broken landscape of the canyon lands, Phil McNally had not heard the trooper's suggestion – was even as far withdrawn into that insulated private world of mindlessness that had detached the redheaded widow from reality for many hours. But then, as the uniformed men of lesser rank began to exchange apprehensive glances and even a few whispered suspicions about the corporal, the gaunt-faced man stoppered his canteen with a deliberate action and allowed, as he glanced up at the side of the stage:

'Sure, Roy. And why don't you hang some more blankets all the way around the other windows. Seein' what's inside the stage likely makes the corpses seem to smell higher than just knowing they're in there, wouldn't you say?'

'Yeah, Phil.'

'We'll get right to it, Corp,' the broken-nosed Earl Saxon hurried to assure, then moved quickly with the other troopers to carry out the chore: as if in response to a snarled command from a far higher ranking authority than a corporal who had obviously on few occasions considered himself, or been treated, as any different from these enlisted men until this morning's costly attack by the Utes. Then McNally rose wearily to his feet and was watched with curiosity by the civilians and uneasiness by the prisoner as he went toward the brave: who was seated, hands still bound at the wrists, against the front wheel on this shaded side of the stage.

'If I'd have figured you might speak our language, Indian, I'd have ordered you put out of your misery,' he said evenly, then shot a challenging glance at where the half-breed and the Virginian and Edith Crawford stood in a group after stepping back from where the men were draping blankets over the sides of the Concord. 'And not given too much of a damn what these folks thought about it.' He sighed as he drew the stopper out of the neck and held the canteen for the Ute to reach up and take it from him. 'Hell, I might have done it anyways. If I'd been thinkin' straight instead of bein' all nerved up from bein' in command.' He pushed the canteen forcefully toward the thirsty but reluctant Indian. 'Go ahead, now you're alive, ain't no point in you sufferin' when it ain't necessary.'

The brave took the canteen between the palms and fingers of his bound hands, made to drink, but then paused in the act to stare into the hollow-eyed face of McNally and acknowledge: 'Black Hawk who is the grandson of Chief Red Eagle and the son of Chief Straight Arrow and is a sub-chief himself thanks you for your kindness, horsesoldier. But he tells you there can be no more than such simple giving and receiving under terms of truce until the slaughter of my people has been avenged.'

'He certainly seems to think he has a genuine grievance, you know,' Edward Sun said with a sage expression on his Oriental face and a pensive shaking of his head as he joined the group after inexperience had caused him to take longer than anybody else in attending to the needs of the bounty hunter's horse he had commandeered. 'From what he said before and the way in which some of the soldiers have — '

'I do not doubt it, young man,' Mrs Crawford told him with a brief, bleak-eyed glance before she swept her attention back to McNally. 'And whatever it is, the savage seems to attach considerable importance to the fact that I am Major Crawford's wife and — '

'I think it better if the corporal tells us about it?' Sun suggested. 'Instead of us asking questions all the time. Is that not a good idea, Mr Steele, Mr Edge?'

'I'm a man of few words and I even prefer them to come from other people, feller,' the Virginian answered.

'If there's one thing I'm better at than listening, it's thinking,' the half-breed added. 'And right now I think I'm ready to listen to just why I could get my ass shot off by any Ute Indian that happens to catch me unawares.'

'Not just you, Edge,' McNally said bitterly and inattentively. 'Any white man, woman or child in this whole piece of country.' He gestured with an arm to encompass the terrain to every horizon and then added wryly as his gaze lingered briefly on Edward Sun. 'Or yellow. Black, too, I guess.'

'Yes, yes, Corporal!' Mrs Crawford said impatiently. 'Please ignore the apparent selfishness of these two gentlemen. Who, I should remind, would not be here with us now had they not proved from the start that they care about the welfare of others as well as for their own safety. But that is neither here nor there for the moment. Please do as the young man suggested – or allow the savage to tell us?'

'I am pleased that you no longer call me a *murdering* savage, woman of Ethan Theodore Crawford,' the Indian said with feeling as he held the canteen between his knees while he replaced the stopper. 'I am a sub-chief of the Ute nation which is the most fiercely warlike of the Shoshone nation. But we make war only against those who rouse us to treat them as our enemies.'

'It's hot and uncomfortable and entirely disagreeable out here in open country, Indian,' Edith Crawford complained as she fanned her fleshy face with both flapping hands. 'I don't think any of us is in the mood to listen to speech-making.'

'Sure ain't,' the stockily built and squint-eyed Conran agreed as he and the other troopers came to squat in the restricted patch of uncool, mid-morning shade. All of them wore some form of grimace from the chore they had just completed. A cigar and four cigarettes were lit.

'It was all a terrible mistake, ma'am,' McNally said as he turned his back on the group that gazed at him expectantly, while Black Hawk seemed to be readying himself to refute what the woman had claimed. 'On the whole, the Indians and whites – the civilians and the military both – get along without too much trouble around here. Twenty-three days ago, though, a routine patrol out of Hamilton reached a Ute camp north of the post at a place called Arroyo Bend. A bunch of the braves there were drunk on rotgut – pardon me, ma'am – on cheap whiskey. The questionin' got a little heated and a little out of hand while the captain was tryin' to find out where the whiskey came from. A shot was fired outta one of the lodges and one of our men took it in the stomach. Then all hell – then it got really ugly, ma'am. Our men started in to fire and before they came to their senses a whole bunch of Indians was dead.'

'Ten braves, six squaws and five of the young not yet twelve years of age. One of these a baby in the arms of its mother.' Black Hawk spoke the tally in a flat tone of voice as McNally paused, the soldier not needing to catch his breath – rather to reflect on the events of which he was telling.

'That was the final count at Arroyo Bend,' the non-com confirmed with his back still to the attentive group of civilians and the brave and the men in blue and yellow uniforms who were anxious for the tale to be told and done with. 'There were no wounded except for the one trooper, who died on the way back to Fort Hamilton. The patrol killed anythin' that moved in the camp. The wounded were finished off like they was sick livestock. All the stock was killed. Them Indians that run away were let go. Idea at the time was what they'd tell other Indians – warn them against breakin' the law. Especially against shootin' at the United States Cavalry.'

'Crazy idea,' Edge growled.

'And I reckon that must have been realised by somebody?' Steele added.

'I never thought my husband could be such a fool as to countenance such a — '

'Major Crawford didn't, ma'am,' McNally told her as he turned around and showed the expression of remorse that was carved firmly into his wan face. 'When the patrol returned to the post and the officer in command gave his report, the major ordered that a search be made for the runaways. And near enough every man on the post except for them in the hospital and a handful left to guard the fort was sent out after the Indians.'

'With what intention, Corporal?' Mrs Crawford asked in the manner of one who uneasily suspects the question is superfluous. This as Arnie Jonas grunted and groaned his way back toward consciousness.

'To kill them, ma'am,' McNally replied in a dull tone and with lifeless eyes.

'You tell how you know my numbers for dead at the camp are right, horsesoldier,' Black Hawk intoned.

There was a stirring of anger for the prisoner's arrogance in using such a demanding tone. But others eyed him with pity and even some remorse.

'A special detail was sent to Arroyo Bend,' the corporal supplied, and tilted his head to squint up into the brightness of the morning sky instead of peering across the desert now. 'To remove all traces of what had happened there. To make it look like there never even was an Indian camp there, let alone . . . let alone the killing.'

'The massacre, horsesoldier,' Black Hawk corrected. 'The Arroyo Bend Massacre. It already has the name for the history of the Ute nation. Given by my grandfather Chief Red Eagle when he was told of what the horsesoldiers from Fort Hamilton did. Told by the three braves who survived the massacre and then escaped from the bands of Crawford's killers sent to finish those who escaped.'

McNally nodded several times as the Ute made his contribution – and then was prevented from confirming verbally what had been said when Arnie Jonas rose up on to an elbow and growled with thick-toned bitterness through teeth gritted against pain:

'We done all right, didn't we? Right, Phil? All them stinkin' braves and their lousy squaws and yellin' papooses at Arroy Bend. And only missed but the three outta the seventeen that took it on the run.'

Amy Yancy stared in horror at the bruise-faced man for whom she had recently been so tenderly caring. Then she caught her breath as if to check a scream as he scrambled up from where she had been sitting half under the Concord. This as the prisoner said over his shoulder and through the spokes of the wheel to Jonas:

'Seventeen braves, squaws and children of an age to move unaided, horsesoldier. Three more babies in the arms of their —'

'Well, we sure as hell wasn't about to burden ourselves with a mess of yellin' Injun orphan kids, was we?' Jonas countered. 'And especially since the major give us the orders that we was to see to it so it'd look like there never was any of them Injuns ever existed?'

Edith Crawford's new-found strength of purpose in the wake of McNally's seeming abandonment of duty was seriously depleted as she listened to the events of the massacre and its aftermath: told in bald terms by the corporal, with increasing fervour by Black Hawk and with something close to blustering pride by Jonas. But then she found herself able to draw upon previously untapped reserves when she saw that the younger woman had been able to suppress a new urge to panic.

'My husband is a career military man of considerable experience who doubtless did what he considered his rightful duty to secure the safety of those he is charged to protect,' she argued in an overly haughty tone.

'Tell me,' the redheaded widow asked anxiously before anyone could take issue with the older woman, and dry-washed her hands as she scanned the frowning face of every soldier except for Jonas who continued to lay beneath the Concord, indulging his discomforts as he cautiously explored his injured parts. 'Was my husband . . . was he involved in. . . ?'

'Not in the trouble that set off this whole mess, Mrs Yancy,' the ginger-moustached and prematurely balding Goldsmith answered apologetically. 'But he was given command of the special clean-up detail sent to Arroyo Bend aferwards.'

'Captain Yancy was following his orders, my dear,' Edith Crawford told her, speaking in a more natural tone now. 'Doing his duty.'

'Yes,' the younger woman answered simply, with a sigh. And succeeded in keeping the tears from spilling down her cheeks at least until she turned to peer out across the desert. Then, if she wept for her dead husband, she did it silently.

'We all were, ma'am,' Earl Saxon said to the back of the woman as he absently massaged the scar tissue above his right eye with a hand that clutched a dead and forgotten cigar.

'Was all we was doin' at that Injun camp at the start of it!'

Jonas proclaimed adamantly and perhaps defensively as he winced and interspersed what he was saying with grunts of pain as he dragged himself out from under the stage. Nobody felt moved to argue his point while he struggled awkwardly to his feet and dusted off his uniform as he got his breath back and glowered maliciously down at the wooden-faced Black Hawk. 'Sellin' whiskey to the Injuns is against the law hereabouts and Captain Mannin' and the rest of us on that patrol was doin' the right thing questionin' them drunken braves about who sold them the rotgut hooch.'

The prisoner had been gazing across the same stretch of sun-baked desert as Amy Yancy, but now he turned and tilted his head to stare up at Jonas with dark and glittering eyes that seemed to be emanating a palpable force – so deep was the hatred they held for this man who had confessed to being at Arroyo Bend on the fateful day.

'Leave it, Trooper!' McNally snapped as he recognised the signs that Arnie Jonas was preparing to retaliate with more than a mere look and further vehement words.

For a stretched second, as he inched a booted foot back and forth just a few inches away from where Black Hawk sat, the square-faced trooper with the dark swelling on his temple seemed like he might not be able to hold back from launching a vicious kick at the helpless Ute. And Black Hawk nodded in a brand of triumphant understanding of the kind of uncontrollable temperament that could result in the ill-treatment of one bound captive or the wholesale slaughter of a camp of defenceless Indians.

Then: 'Sure, Phil,' Jonas allowed at last, the two syllables rasping out through clenched teeth that were gritted in rage rather than pain now. And he dragged his gaze away from the almost sneeringly scornful sub-chief and got an expression of something close to atonement on his features as he scanned his audience of fellow soldiers and strangers before he growled: 'It shouldn't have happened and nine hundred and ninety-nine times outta a thousand it wouldn't have . . . it doesn't. It was the first anybody at Hamilton had found out about whiskey being sold to the Injun hereabouts. Guess the captain was maybe a little too hard in the way he questioned the head man at the camp. He was over anxious to get to the truth and maybe he shouldn't have held his sabre across the throat of that squaw while he was doin' the askin' of the head man. And if most of the braves hadn't been liquored up the way they was, I guess one of them wouldn't have blasted the bullet into Charlie White's guts.'

Now Arnie Jonas swept his intense gaze around the face of everyone, including Black Hawk and Amy Yancy – the woman drawn to turn around again by the degree of contrition in the voice of the tough trooper as he endeavoured to elicit understanding and perhaps even sympathy from the group beside the stalled stage coach on this desert trail.

'One of the young braves – a boy, I guess – laughed when he saw Charlie go down with blood all over his tunic at the belly. If that hadn't happened . . .' Jonas shrugged and for a moment chewed on the inside of a cheek. 'And as he swung around to see what was happenin', the captain's sabre made a cut in the squaw's neck. Nothin' much. Not deep. But she yelled and she ran around with blood all over her hands. Charlie grabbed his carbine as he fell down and he blasted a shot at the kid that was laughin' at him. But his aim was way off on account of him takin' the tumble and the bullet went into the back of the squaw with the little nick in her throat. Then the whole mess of Injuns started in to high-tail it outta the camp. And Captain Mannin', he give the order to open up and cut down them scatterin' Injuns.

'Like I say, it never should have happened, but it sure as hell did happen. And while it was goin' on, I swear wasn't one of us didn't get a charge outta seein' them Injuns go down. On account of seein' Charlie White get it like he did, and on account of it just seems plain natural for troopers out here in the middle of nowhere to hate Injuns worse than they hate anythin' else. Out at Hamilton things have been pretty quiet for a long time, but ain't many of us there now who ain't served on some other posts where hardly a day went by we didn't lose men or heard about civilian settlers gettin' done in real bad by Injuns.'

As he reached the climax of his account of the massacre and began to try to justify the slaughter, Arnie Jonas altered his tone of voice and the expression on his face while he scanned his attentive audience: gradually strengthened his tacit challenge for anybody to take issue with his opinions. From his fellow cavalrymen he drew several grim-faced nods and a couple of shamed refusals to hold his questioning gaze. Edge smoked a cigarette and continued to search the blood-crusted face of Black Hawk for useful sign. Steele kept up his casual surveillance of the far distant horizons. Edward Sun nodded more enthusiastically than any of the uniformed men while he obviously recalled what the raiding Indians had done to his parents. And the two women seemed only part intent upon what Jonas was saying as in the back of their minds they struggled to come to terms with images of their husbands being involved in such an atrocity.

After a few moments of tense silence, Edge asked: 'Matches up with what you know, I figure, Black Hawk?'

'I know nothing of killings by Indians of other nations in other parts of — '

'That's understood.'

The Ute sub-chief inclined his head and vented an affirmative grunt, then said: 'It is as they have told it, perhaps. I hear by way of many tongues that a brave did fire the first shot while his senses were blurred by liquor. I know nothing of what followed except that many other Utes die at Arroyo Bend and those who escape are hunted down. But three outwit Crawford's killers and tell the tales that anger to the warpath every Ute who hears it.'

'Major Crawford knew the Utes were stirred up by the massacre, Corporal?' Steele asked. 'That some braves survived and what they told about — '

'You don't have to answer his questions, Phil!' Earl Saxon claimed quickly, with a scowl. And the resentment that he felt in the wake of shame – or perhaps it was merely overlaying the more disconcerting feeling – was immediately caught by other uniformed men.

'Yeah, what's it to you, mister?' Arnie Jonas asked. 'The army does what it has to the best way it knows how and right or wrong the way the major called it ain't nobody's business except his own and the top brass at Department of Utah headquarters, Camp Floyd.'

'I know what I can and can't do, Trooper Saxon!' McNally

growled. 'And Jonas, you've had your say and now you can shut up for awhile.' His voice was low but commanding, and then he made a hard-eyed survey of all the troopers before he went on. 'These people are as likely as us to get their heads shot off by hostile Indians. Same as all the civilians at Oro City and them folks that are settled outside of town. Now they all know how this mess got started and some of them have seen somethin' of how the hostiles plan to end it, it's only right they should know the rest of it. On account of if any of us got a chance of gettin' outta this thing alive, we need their help much as they need the help of the United States Cavalry.'

'And did not we here prove what a help we can be to the United States Cavalry at what was left of my home, sir?' Edward Sun asked eagerly.

McNally had no intention of waiting for the approval of his men. And showed irritable impatience while he waited for the young half-Chinese to finish the boast, then admitted:

'I'm sorry, but I lied about the reason for the patrol Captain Mannin' took out of Hamilton. There's sickness there. Real bad.' He glanced fleetingly at the widow. 'Captain Yancy was the first to die from it. Six more were dead and a dozen were in the post hospital when we pulled out.'

'You said the major . . . ?' Edith Crawford began anxiously.

McNally nodded. 'I didn't lie about that, ma'am. Major Crawford was healthy enough. And so were thirty or so others.'

'Thank God,' the older woman murmured and looked briefly skywards, as if to stress that she meant the spontaneous remark as an actual prayer of thanksgiving.

'Were you fellers deserting when the Utes hit you?' Edge asked.

McNally glowered at him and the troopers powered to their feet with matching expressions and a menacing rumble of angry talk.

'You just said you weren't out on a show of strength detail, Corporal,' Steele put in.

This as the half-breed rose up off his haunches after

placing his cigarette butt on the ground. And now he stepped on it and waited impassively for a reply to his own and the Virginian's questions.

'We were ordered to head for Camp Floyd. Or to get to Fort Bridger if we couldn't make department headquarters. To bring more men to reinforce Hamilton.' McNally enunciated his words with great emphasis as the troopers struggled as hard as he did to keep a grip on his temper.

'Thirty men, feller?' Edge posed with glittering eyes and a hard-set mouth, the lips of which moved not at all to rasp the implied query. 'That's more like a relief column of reinforcements being sent — '

'All right, all right!' McNally said sharply into a silence tense with resentment emanating from the tight-knit group of cavalrymen. 'You asked if we was desertin'? Well, we sure as hell weren't, mister!' An expression that was a plea for understanding not dissimilar to that which Jonas had worn now became fixed to the non-com's haggard face as he looked at each of the civilians in turn. 'But a lot of men might have. There was damn near a mutiny at Fort Hamilton the day before yesterday. After the major detailed just six men to ride to Floyd or Bridger. Not on account of anyone bein' too scared to stay and face up to whatever the Utes could throw at us, though. It was the smallpox . . .'

'Oh, my God,' Amy Yancy gasped.

'A sickness that bad?' Edith Crawford muttered rhetorically.

Black Hawk's mouth remained compressed but there was the glimmer of a smile in his eyes. Edward Sun caught his breath and Edge and Steele exchanged a glance of comprehension.

'That's what got so many of us scared fit to take it on the run from Hamilton and shoot down any officer who tried to stop us,' the non-com finished on a low note after the civilians had reacted to his naming of the disease that had struck Fort Hamilton.

'When Phil says *us*, he don't mean himself,' Roy Egan was anxious to point out. 'He was assigned to go with Captain Mannin'.'

'It don't matter now who wanted out of the post and who

was detailed,' Saxon growled. 'All that needs to be told has been. And some that didn't need to be, seems to me.' And he glowered at the civilians, daring them to question this proposition.

'I'm easy,' Edge allowed, and this signalled an initially silent and unmoving but very discernible slackening of the high tension that he had triggered when he made mention of desertion.

'But it will soon get harder for every white eyes!' Black Hawk snarled with a menacing scowl for all his captors as some of them nodded and others made sounds of agreement with what the half-breed had said. 'Already you have tasted something of what is in store for all white eyes who do not run faster before us than did the horsesoldiers – before me and my brothers were so treacherously ambushed by — '

He abruptly finished his vehement diatribe against the group who were once again allies after a period when dissension among them had come close to exploding into violence. Chose to interrupt his heated words as he became aware that nobody was any longer paying him more than disdainful passing attention as, without the giving of an instruction, preparations were made to leave this place on the burning floor of the rim of the desert. Horses were mounted and the two women and Jonas took their places up on the outside seat of the blanket-draped Concord again.

Then, for a stretched second after he realised he was being virtually ignored as he boastfully predicted the doom that awaited them and their like, the Ute sub-chief seemed poised to explode into a burst of anger that would need more forceful outlet than mere words – until he saw that he had one attentive listener still. This was the youthful Edward Sun who stood beside his horse with a serene expression on his smooth, immature face as he looked down at the prisoner against the wheel. To Black Hawk this not quite white eyes seemed to be little more than a child and Sun's unafraid demeanour served to emphasise how futile rage would be in his present predicament. And he moderated his tone as he went on against the bustle of noise and movement:

'Until now, the attacks have been as nothing. Just diversions to gather weapons and horses and food and to sharpen the battle teeth of the Ute braves as they gather for the council where my grandfather Chief Red Eagle will set us upon the path to the great war which will end white eyes' occupation of our lands and their mistreatment of our people.'

Then, as Edward Sun continued to be the sole overt listener – the youngster chewing on the nails of one hand while he constantly clenched and unclenched the other – the brave elected to shift into his native language as he gazed straight ahead into the middle distance of the sun-parched desert: where first Amy Yancy and then Corporal McNally had found some brand of solace for as long as their minds had been able to sustain the state of detachment from reality.

'It will be a war you will have no part of, Indian!' Sun broke in on Black Hawk after the Ute had intoned no more than two dozen words that were incomprehensible to the whites.

Black Hawk was jerked out of his short-lived reverie and for a stretched second did not know who had spoken the half-heard threat. He looked in the wrong direction first, along the side of the team in the traces, and it seemed as if he were to be abandoned here on the open trail across the desert floor. For all the soldiers except for Jonas were mounted in a double-file column out front of the stage. And McNally appeared to be on the point of giving the command to move forward.

Instinctively, the Ute leaned forward: to bring his bare back away from the spokes of the wheel he was certain would begin to turn at any moment. But then, as he snapped his head around to look toward the rear of the Concord, his perplexed mind was freed of the final vestige of unreality and he saw he was about to be killed. For the youthful Edward Sun, after he rasped the warning words that ended the short period of withdrawal for the Ute, had slid the Winchester from the boot on the saddle of the horse at his side: and now he started to swing the rifle to the aim. There was a quiet smile of confidence in triumph on the round face with its ochre tint complexion and slightly slanted eyes. And, despite the sub-chief's resolve to die bravely, he was unable to prevent his own features contorting into a grimace of disillusionment that his end was to be so inglorious.

Then there was a flurry of movement on the periphery of the Indian's vision: blurred to him because he saw only the tracking rifle barrel in perfect clarity that made everything outside of this indistinct . . . and it shamed him to think this effect was caused by tears of despondency on the brink of spilling. There was no time to ponder anxiously on why his hearing was also impaired as he heard voices.

Steele snarled: 'Don't be a fool!' as he lunged at the half-Chinese from the side and lashed up at the underneath of the rifle barrel with both gloved hands interlocked into a single fist. So that the tracking Winchester was forced violently upwards before it could cover the intended target. And the bullet that was exploded out of the muzzle amid a pungent cloud of black-powder smoke went harmlessly into the sun-bright sky to fall wastefully to the arid ground many hundreds of yards along the trail ahead of the Concord.

By which time Edge had sidestepped to be within arms' reach of Sun from the back. Had his Frontier Colt held out at the limit of his reach, angled slightly downward so that the muzzle of the revolver in the rock-steady fist rested lightly against the nape of the young man's neck. Only now did he thumb back the hammer with a series of metallic sounds that were disproportionately loud in the hard silence that followed the final echo of the rifle shot across the vastness of the desert. Then the half-breed said:

'We need him a lot more than we need you, kid. Let go of the rifle or it'll be Sun down a little early today.'

The half-Chinese was standing in a frozen attitude, the Winchester still aimed high into the air and with a shocked expression aging his youthful face as he felt the muzzle of Edge's Colt pressing harder into his hair-bristled flesh. He had to swallow hard several times before he was able to whisper:

'I am most sorry, sir, but I am not able to do as you ask.'

'I'll do what I can to see you're buried along with your folks, kid.'

'Hold it, Edge!' Steele snapped, and plucked the rifle easily from the slack grip of Sun, who then was unable to keep his arms from falling slackly to his sides, and would have collapsed to the ground had he not had his horse to lean against.

'It was not that I did not wish to obey, sir,' the close-to-fainting young man assured in stronger tones than before. 'But I was unable to move any part of me, I was so afraid.'

Edge eased forward the hammer of his revolver and slid it back into the holster, his slitted eyes glittering dangerously as he looked into the contrite face of the youngster who was beginning to tremble to the dictates of delayed shock. Then Steele reached between the half-breed and Sun to slide the Winchester back in the boot as Arnie Jonas peered bleakly down at the men beside the Concord's rear corner, to growl:

'We're ready to roll, you civilians. And I don't guess Phil McNally or anyone else gives much of a damn whether it's with that Injun or without him. Right, Corporal?'

'You men want to get mounted up now, or you want to catch us up later?' the non-com responded in dull tones and with a weary-eyed glance that implied he was in total agreement with what the trooper on the stage had said about the prisoner.

'All that talking you did in English?' Steele said to the Ute, gesturing for him to get up from against the wheel where he had sagged again after his latest close call with ignominious death. 'Was it just talk, or do you know for certain there's going to be a war council for the whole nation? With Red Eagle the top chief there?'

It was difficult for Black Hawk to get to his feet unaided while his wrists were bound. But he succeeded and after the series of awkward moves was completed he stood to his full height and surveyed all his captors with a defiant scowl as he answered: 'I not lie, white eyes. My grandfather is chief of all the Utes and I am one of his messengers sent to tell our people to come to the great council and — '

'Reckon we called it right, Yank. Best to keep him alive.'

'Right, Reb. No telling what the chief of the whole nation will give to have his grandson returned without any bullet holes in him.'

'Yes, yes!' Edward Sun blurted, able to stand without support now and showing an expression of self-disgust in place of sweating fear. 'He is a most valuable hostage, of course. I was thinking selfishly only of what his kind did to my mother and my father and of my desire to avenge them. You will pardon me, please?'

'I already did, kid,' the half-breed growled as the young man swept his apologetic gaze over the faces of the soldiers and the women who responded with indifference.

'Or at least a stay of execution until one of Jerome Randell's hired guns gets lucky,' Steele drawled, and this reminder caused a different brand of fear to take a hold on the Oriental features of the youngster.

The Virginian spoke as he gave the still-scowling Indian a boost into the saddle. Now, as he tied the prisoner's bound hands to the horn, Black Hawk accused scornfully: 'If you think a great chief of the Ute nation will enter into trade for the life of one of his kin while the burning need for vengeance is ablaze in all our hearts, you are even more stupid than you are ugly, white eyes!'

The Indian raked his dark-eyed gaze over every one of his captors as Steele hitched the reins of the cavalry mount to which he was bound to the rear of the Concord. But the two women and Jonas up on the seat had their backs to him, and of the soldiers out front of the stage, only McNally was looking back to check when all would be ready to leave. Then the Virginian and the half-breed swung up into their saddles and Edward Sun hurried to mount, still keeping self-anger with the past off his face while he indulged in anxiety about the future.

McNally called: 'Forward at a walk, forward!'

Hooves clopped, a number of horses whinnied softly and the wheels and springs of the Concord clattered and creaked. As Edge and Steele moved in to flank Black Hawk, and Edward Sun inexpertly manoeuvred his mount into position behind the prisoner, the half-breed cast a glance around at his immediate surroundings and with an expression of disapproving appraisal, growled:

'You're right, Black Hawk. Guess we ain't so good-looking. But I figure we're looking better for having you along with us in one piece.'

'Even pretty good,' Steele added.

The Ute stared fixedly at the rear of the slow-rolling Concord – perhaps in the hope of concealing from the men at either side of him the clearly discernible lack of confidence that his bluster failed to mask. And growled with a tone of finality: 'Ugly, and fools, too!'

Edge delved into a shirt pocket for the makings and said with an easy grin: 'I guess there are times when we are a couple of jokers, uh Reb?'

The Virginian rasped the back of a gloved hand over the bristles on his jawline as he answered: 'Reckon so, Yank. When we crack wise.'

CHAPTER TWELVE

THE BLANKET-DRAPED Concord coach of the Central Western Stageline Company with its decomposing cargo of corpses and its escorting riders at front and rear rolled past the town-limits marker of Oro City as the short desert evening gave way to full night. The strangers to this part of the country came upon the community unexpectedly, because those who were familiar with the place made no mention that it was close by as the group of time- and tension-wearied travellers moved slowly up a long, pine-clad incline beyond the ridge of which the town was spread out over the north-west-facing slope of the low hill.

It was seen, in the light of a bright moon augmented by the glow of several kerosene lamps that were mostly clustered at the foot of the hill, to be a town of one main street that snaked across the hillside in a series of gentle curves: from the marker close to the crest to where it became again an open trail heading west beyond the railroad station out of which a single track ran due north.

Here and there along the main thoroughfare that veered to left or right to swing around areas of high ground or avoid depressions on the far from naturally featureless slope, side roads cut off. None of these were seen to be very long before they went from sight into timbered valleys or behind rugged outcrops of bare, element-eroded rock. Or perhaps the trail did not become a town street proper until it had meandered the best part of a mile and a half beyond the marker to reach the well-lit section of Oro City at the base of the hill?

If anyone contemplated this point, they did not do so for very long before they lost the inclination to care about something so inconsequential. For everyone was too wearied by the journey and drained by its violent events to be concerned with much else outside of the prospect this town provided of rest and food and, to an extent, safety. But, as they started to move along the first curve of street beyond the leaning over and almost bleached out marker, the new arrivals to Oro City began to sense and then see that all was not as it should be in this town.

On this first stretch the buildings were widely spaced and faced each other across a distance that seemed too wide to be termed, yet again, a street. These were large private houses set in extensive gardens bordered by fences. There were both single and two-storied houses, constructed of timber or stone or a mixture of the two in a number of different and not always identifiable styles. Here and there a house was in a good state of repair and its surrounding garden was well-tended. Most, though, were neglected and stood in weed-choked surroundings enclosed by leaning or fallen-down fences.

Just two of the houses not yet started toward becoming derelict showed cracks of light at draped windows and had woodsmoke rising from cooking fires below their chimneys. The rancid odour of decay masked the acrid taint of the smoke. There were no sounds from the occupied houses that were loud enough to be heard above the clop of hooves and clatter of wheelrims. The more perceptive of those passing by had the distinct impression that people were watching them surreptitiously from in back of windows in rooms purposely not lit.

Further down the snaking and slightly undulating street it narrowed and the buildings were sited closer together – a mixture of smaller, less flamboyant houses and business premises. Almost all of them single story and frame built. None of the houses seemed to have more than four rooms and they had yards rather than gardens, most with at least one shade tree. The commercial establishments were stores and a few craftsmen's and repairers' workshops. Nearly all the more modest houses of the poorer citizens of Oro City were lit and had smoking chimneys. Cooking food could be smelt through the stink of smoke and the rotting dead. Many men and women and some children were silhouetted at open doorways and at undraped windows making candid examinations of the newcomers – and were patently not impressed with what they saw, until the truncated column had past.

Then, in the wake of the stage and the riders passing, there erupted a considerable amount of whispering back and forth within some of the houses. And it was obvious to any of the new arrivals in Oro City who did not totally ignore the rasping voices and silent watchers that the attitudes of the local citizens underwent a radical change. Suddenly the people in the houses were host to a burning curiosity: but this was allied with a fear of hearing the worst that checked the urgent desire to call a first question that would undoubtedly signal a whole plethora of others.

Some men stepped out of their houses to follow the sluggishly moving stage, but kept their distance from it. Other men who wanted to follow submitted to the wishes of their women and remained inside their homes.

Then the column crossed the intersection of the final side street, where a Protestant church stood on the corner, and rounded the last curve to enter what was literally downtown Oro City. Here the street was at its narrowest and straightest as it ran down a gentle incline at the foot of the hill between the premises occupied by the more essential or most prosperous civic and commercial enterprises of the community. Many with appellations that referred to the reason for the town's existence.

On the same, north, side of the street as the spired church was the Paydirt Cafe, the Ingot Hotel and a saloon called The Golden Place. Across a vacant lot from the saloon was the Oro City Railroad Station. On the other side of the street was the law office, Livesey's Livery Stables, the Miner's Rest Boarding House and the Central Western Stageline Company depot. All these buildings were stone-walled and all of them except for the law office had two stories – the saloon even had dormer windows in the steeply pitched roof to give it a third floor. There was an awninged sidewalk in front of the saloon and the hotel and the cafe. Except for the livery all the other premises had roofed stoops.

Because most of the buildings were brightly lit in many of their windows, the impression had been created from a distance that this part of town was bustling. At close quarters this was seen to be false. There was a group of perhaps two dozen people who had moved out of the railroad station to watch the new arrivals reach the foot of the hill. While the places of entertainment and succour that had obviously prospered from high spending customers in the past were tonight only lightly patronised with people who stepped into doorways, the better to see what was happening on the evening of what had seemingly been a day of so far unfulfilled expectation.

Some hundred yards short of where the law office and church faced each other at the intersection with the side street, Edward Sun apprehensively broke the vocal silence that had clamped over the travellers since long before they came over the top of the hill and saw the widely scattered town below.

'Pardon me, gentlemen?'

'You're excused, kid,' Edge told him without turning around as he swung his glinting-eyed gaze slowly to left and right in cautious surveillance over the shortening length of street in front of the cavalrymen.

'Please, no more humour,' the young half-Chinese urged, and now sounded almost gulpingly afraid as he interrupted the chewing of his nails. 'There are so many strangers to me here. Any of them could have been sent by Mr Jerome Randell to — '

'He means it's all right for you to leave us, feller,' Steele explained. 'Personally, I'd have ducked out of sight before this.'

Sun did gulp now, and the sound of it drew the attention of both men who flanked the ramrod stiff Black Hawk: as they grimaced at the prospect of the youngster getting sick to his stomach again. But he was able to retain a firm hold on that aspect of his fear and looked close to being pathetically pitiable as he rode astride the horse that was too big for him: while even on his slight frame the once stylish and now dirtied and dishevelled and fire-scorched city suit looked to be too short and too tight in its fit. He had long ago lost his derby hat, which in the present circumstances would perhaps have made him too ridiculous.

'I thank you, sirs,' he said stiffly, making an attempt at dignity that acted only to emphasise his pathetic quality that stopped just short of the comical. 'For this and all that has gone before. Especially for not attempting to earn the reward that Mr Jerome Randell has placed upon — '

'I don't need to earn money that way anymore, feller,' the Virginian said.

'And I just couldn't see myself having the gall to collect five grand for your hide, kid,' the half-breed added.

A train whistle howled mournfully in the distant north and Edward Sun suddenly displayed a broad smile of relief, then hurried to get said:

'I give to you both my horse to sell, my very good friends in difficult times. I take my rifle in case of need in times that are still difficult?'

His intonation and a quizzical arching of his eyebrows changed the final comment from a statement to a query. And he accepted the way in which Edge and Steele turned their backs on him as an affirmative response. Then, as the two men resumed their careful watch on the street ahead, the youngster quickly swung down from his saddle, walked alongside the horse for a few paces as he struggled clumsily to draw the Winchester from the boot, finally veered away and quickened his pace to go from sight across a tree-shadowed vacant lot between the totally darkened law office and the dimly lit livery stable. This as McNally veered to the same side, to lead the column toward the front of the Central Western depot which was the last building on this side, diagonally across from the railroad station. The townspeople following on foot at a distance doubtless saw Edward Sun take his leave of the group of new arrivals, but his actions did not trigger any shouts of perturbation.

Steele said evenly to Edge across the front of the wooden faced Ute: 'Do you sense that it's not just Black Hawk here who isn't welcome in this town, Yank?'

'In one, Reb. I also get the impression that after that train leaves, it's not going to be half the town it used to be.'

Even as this exchange was taking place, the majority of

people at this end of town who had been watching the arrival of the newcomers began to abandon their unfriendly and even hostile interest in them: this caused by a second blast of the train whistle, which stimulated those at the front of the station to turn and pass through the building and go out on to the platform that stretched away at right angles at the rear.

Those would-be passengers who had chosen to wait in the saloon, the hotel, the cafe and the boarding house bustled toward the station, hauling suitcases, carpetbags and trunks. And several couples had to deal in addition with fretfully complaining children. Here and there, a wailing baby refused to be placated in the surge to be on the platform for when the approaching train pulled in. Almost without exception the people who thronged into the train station had a look of wealth and well-being about them which suggested they came from the higher placed, better part of town. But there were more of them than could have lived in the dozen or so houses that flanked the broad stretch of street up there at the top of the hill.

'They run like frightened rabbits from the vengeance of the Ute nation,' Black Hawk murmured in a tone that suggested he was merely stating aloud a premise in which he had implicit belief: and cared nothing for what response it might draw.

It drew none from Edge and Steele who were the only ones close enough to the Indian to hear what he said.

The crowd of local people flocked into the station, seemingly spurred to greater urgency by each intermittent call of the rising in volume whistle. They became new targets of tacit and soft-spoken animosity by those Oro City citizens who were not planning to board the train. But then, as the last of those intent upon leaving town went from sight through the pillared station entrance, those who were to stay switched their hostile attention back to the Concord and its escorting riders. This as the column came to a halt out front of the stage-line depot which was dimly lit and where a fat man with melancholic eyes and a ragged grey moustache stood in the open doorway – seemingly the only watcher who viewed the new arrivals with anything less than enmity.

'Detail, prepare to dismount . . . dismount!' McNally commanded with weary-sounding officiousness.

With the blanket-draped Concord stopped directly outside the stage depot, the three men at the rear were directly opposite the front of The Golden Place saloon on the other side of the street. All the patrons who had moved out through the batwings to stand on the sidewalk were men. Most of them strong-looking and hard-eyed – like those who had followed the column down the snaking street and now enlarged the group out front of the saloon. Work-wearied men dressed in hard-wearing, much laundered and often repaired clothing. Few of them young, none old and most about forty to fifty. None armed in a manner that was at once obvious. Intermingled with these were a sprinkling of merchants and professional men. Most of these in the older age group, softer looking and a little better dressed. Perhaps thirty in all, who Edge watched without failing to be aware of what was taking place elsewhere in the immediate area while Steele reached across to free the prisoner's hands from the saddlehorn.

'You tend to the horses while I take care of the Indian?' the Virginian suggested.

'No sweat,' the half-breed answered as the both of them climbed out of their saddles.

'Troopers Egan and Goldsmith – help the ladies down from the stage and into the depot!' McNally ordered, barking out the command louder than was necessary, even though the rattle and clatter and roar of the approaching train was becoming the most obtrusive sound in Oro City. The lacking in confidence non-com was obviously seeking to stamp his authority on the situation in face of the increasing hostility emanating from the men aligned along the sidewalk before the saloon. 'Saxon, Shackleton, Webber – go with Jonas and the coach back up the street. Just want the two troopers still aboard when you return. Check with the local preacher about what to do with the rest.'

'Hey, Corporal!' one of the men on the saloon sidewalk yelled. 'McNally, ain't it? From out at Hamilton?'

'Yes, sir. Yes, it is.'

The question and response, yelled against the rising

volume of clamorous noise from the train, acted to halt all movement in the area of the Concord.

'How come the dude and the guy with the tied-down six-shooter got a stinkin' Injun prisoner when the army's around?' He was one of the tougher looking of the less prosperous citizens.

'And what the frig you got him as a prisoner for when he oughta be buzzard meat?' another of Oro City's manual workers wanted to know.

'Stinkin' is right!' a clerk or a storekeeper snarled. 'I've got the powerful smell of him up my nose from right across the street!'

There was a raucous chorus of agreement with this, curtailed when Arnie Jonas countered: 'That's a coachful of dead men you can smell, civilians!' And as he made the snarling response he leapt to the street and yanked aside one of the blankets draping the Concord's windows on the side facing the saloon. This just as the sound of the train stridently braking toward a halt at the station platform rendered useless for several seconds any more attempts at across-the-street conversation. At the same time the powerful headlamp of the locomotive penetrated far enough through the night and splayed its beam wide enough to augment the moon and kerosene light on the street, illuminating more brightly the interior of the Concord. Where, clearly displayed among a mass of booted feet, was the death-masked face of one of the corpses whose head had been jolted free of its blanket shroud during the ride from the Sun farm.

Horror, nausea, fear and even terror showed on the faces of all except for one man in front of the saloon as they stared at the grisly cargo carried to town by the stage. And, because his expression was so different from the others, the man who had advanced from deep inside the saloon to pause at the batwinged entrance stood out starkly from the rest. For he eyed the pile of dead in the Concord with total dispassion at first. Then did a double-take and stepped across the threshold of The Golden Place, pushing the batwings aside. And, just for a second, he was mildly intrigued by what he saw.

There was about this man, who was tall and lean and had a face that was almost cadaverous, a demeanour and a style of dress that would have set him apart from those about him – even had he shared their initial reaction to the many dead. And Edge felt sufficiently intrigued himself to step to the rear corner of the stage and glance in through the window a moment before a withering stare from Edith Crawford and a pleading one from Amy Yancy caused Jonas to drape the blanket back into place. Was able to see that it was the pale-skinned, partially freckled face of the young gunman – Luke Vicary – that had struck such a chord in the man from the saloon. A man, almost twice the age of the dead one, and who – from the way he looked and dressed and carried an ivory-butted revolver in a tied-down holster on the left side – might well be a more polished bounty-hunting gunslinger.

The locomotive and line of four passenger cars with a caboose hitched at the rear screeched and clattered and clanked to a halt at the station. And most of the troopers, along with Edge, had to take the time to placate the travel-weary saddle and team horses spooked by the unfamiliar sounds and scents of the raucous and acrid arrival. Then, with an abrupt release of unused steam through the safety valve – that began deafening and quickly diminished – the coming of another period of tension-taut quiet in Oro City was signalled. During which, as the agitated horses were calmed, a man broke from the group at the saloon and was joined by four others.

The man who was first to move was short and fat and round-faced with thinning grey hair. He was near sixty years old and if he had done a day's heavy work in his life it no longer showed. He was dressed in a threadbare, dark-coloured suit, grubby white shirt and bootlace tie. Of the quartet who came across the street with him, three looked like they were merchants or clerks and the fourth was obviously a manual worker. All between forty and fifty. Emnity was not so evident in their eyes and the set of their mouths now, as they struggled to keep a check on different emotions that they felt it would be shameful to display.

A few of their fellow citizens – and the thin-faced man

who had recognised the dead Luke Vicary – went through the batwing doors into the saloon while a dozen or so remained on the sidewalk, to eavesdrop over a distance of several yards from the corpse-laden Concord on what was told to the deputation.

'More Injun trouble, I've no doubt?' the fat little man asked, waving a pudgy hand at the stage. He addressed the query to McNally who had come to stand between and slightly in front of the two women, in an almost protective attitude.

'That's right, Mayor DeWitt. A bunch of Utes attacked the stage down from Wolf Creek Pass. And — '

'Elroy and young Tod Carmody?' the man with the ragged moustache in the depot doorway groaned.

'They went down fighting to protect the passengers,' Amy Yancy said across the backs of two of the team horses.

'Guess they'd do that all right,' the close-to-tears man murmured.

The jittery state of McNally's nerves could be seen most clearly in the tic that worked the flesh beneath his right eye as he waited impatiently for what he considered this irrelevant exchange to be finished. Then: 'And a troop of thirty men from Fort Hamilton were ambushed at Fletcher Flats. Those that survived made a run for the Sun place. That had already been hit. Mr and Mrs Sun were dead, their place burned.'

From across the street, a red-haired, ruddy-faced, barrel-chested and paunchy man who looked on the point of bursting out of his shirt and pants demanded: 'I surely hope that you soldier boys done more to the friggin' Injuns than took just the one prisoner!'

There was vehement recrimination in the man's tone, and then hatred filled his gleaming eyes as he glared toward the rear of the stage where Edge continued to hold the reins of his own and Steele's horse as the Virginian started to steer Black Hawk back up the slope – the Colt Hartford canted to his left shoulder while his right gloved hand grasped the Ute's upper arm.

'We gave a good account of ourselves in the circumstances, Mr Monk,' McNally answered as he tightened a grip on his self-control – while most of the troopers made no secret of their scorn for the manner in which he was submitting himself to the cross-examination by civilians. 'The Suns or the stranger that was there with them did for just one brave.'

'But the guard and driver on the stage made some of the savages pay for their crimes before these gentlemen finished off all the rest of them,' Mrs Yancy assured, speaking over her shoulder at the stage depot man and then brushing a hand in the direction of Edge and the departing Steele.

While the widow was a brief centre of attention, McNally shot an anxious glance at the troopers. And for a moment he looked like he was about to bawl them out as he saw the reproach in their faces. But then he faced the town mayor and his companions and raised his voice to ensure that the men on the sidewalk across the street were able to hear him.

'It looks certain that the Utes are massin' for an uprisin'!' He jerked a hand to indicate the station. 'And it seems that a lot of Oro City people are just as sure! I gotta tell you that them that are leaven' are doin' the wisest thing, Mayor DeWitt . . . all of you!'

'Runnin' scared, them that are plain yellow!' Monk snarled. 'And got the money or valuable goods or whatever, that means they won't lose all they got if the friggin' Injuns wipe this lousy town off the face of the friggin' earth!'

McNally continued as if there had been no embittered interruption: 'You'd need a thousand men, maybe twice that many, to defend a town like this spread out all over this hill! Against the number of Utes that are massin' in the east! And I gotta warn you that you can't expect much help from the men at Fort — '

'Where you takin' that Injun, mister?' Monk demanded to know, and there was a latent threat in the tone that caused Steele and Black Hawk to halt as one man. And then the Virginian glanced back down the slightly curving grade while the Indian continued to stand erect and unmoving beside him.

'Law office is back up there, beyond the livery, across from the church?' Edge replied as he stopped in the process of turning the gelding and the stallion away from the rear of the Concord.

'Sheriff Rafferty was murdered by a band of Utes out at the Grainger place yesterday morning,' DeWitt growled sourly.

'Don't want Black Hawk arrested by a peace officer, feller,' the half-breed said, and stood where he was while Adam Steele urged the sub-chief forward again. 'Just put behind bars for awhile. Guess there's a gaolhouse out back of the law office?'

'Yeah, there is,' one of the softer men with the mayor supplied.

The tallest and broadest and youngest of the group asked coldly: 'What the hell you wanna lock up a lone Injun for, mister?'

Monk, his strength of feeling threatening to burst his muscular torso out of his shirt in several places, snarled: 'Yeah, what you want with one Injun? When any time now we'll have a whole mess of the bastards ridin' through town? With hardly anyone to stop them? Not even any soldier boy who was the ones got the Injuns riled up at the start?'

The volume and tone of his voice acted to rekindle the old animosity among the smaller group of men out front of the saloon. And as these angry citizens were reminded of the army's responsibility for the Indian trouble, McNally and the troopers became the centre of hostile attention.

DeWitt gestured for the men to quell their noisily rising tempers. But Edith Crawford's voice had more effect, as she spoke before McNally had time to issue an order.

'Mr Edge and Mr Steele have a notion that particular savage might be used to bargain with the rest of them, sir. You see, he claims he is the grandson of the chief of the Utes.'

The slow clop of hooves as Edge resumed leading his own and Steele's mount up the street ended the brief pause which followed the woman's explanation. Then Monk growled scornfully:

'Injuns ain't like real people, lady. They don't give nothin' for nothin' if they take it into their crazy heads they won't.

Guess a fine lady like you appear to be can't be expected to know about Injuns. That down-at-heels dude neither, maybe. But the gunslinger looks like he's been around out West for awhile. And McNally and the rest of the soldier boys could've set straight anyone that needed the settin'. Am I right, or am I right?'

He glared to left and right, his angry eyes demanding agreement from his fellow citizens. And when it came, he nodded and came close to grinning in satisfaction. Then spoke across the affirmative murmuring.

'Utes that are startin' to run wild hereabouts got just the one thought in their crazy heads – which is to kill every white person they can for what the army done to that bunch over to Arroyo Bend.'

'Ain't seen nothing that goes against what you say, feller,' Edge called evenly to capture the puzzled attention of the Oro City citizens who had been about to direct their antagonism toward the soldiers again. 'But it just seems to me that when people don't have much to fight with, they'd be crazy in their heads not to hold on to what they do have.'

There was another short pause. Not a silence, for there had never been even a half second of silence in this part of town since the train pulled into the station. The locomotive hissed and its cooling metals cracked. The people who were getting aboard the cars contributed to a constant body of noise in which few sounds could be separated and identified.

Then the man with the cadaverous face and the fancy gun in a holster tied down to his left thigh showed his head and shoulders above the batwings of The Golden Place, and draped his hands over the tops of the doors as he said in a husky voice:

'A guy that ain't having his insides chewed at by fear and don't waste time hating anything and everything that it don't help to hate . . . that's the kind of guy most likely to talk the most sense.'

After which, he turned from the doorway and went back into the depths of the saloon: but in making the move locked his gaze on that of the half-breed – and in a split second was able to convey that he was positive they were kindred spirits in a situation that placed them on a far higher plane than those whom circumstances forced to share in it. And Edge thought he was probably just another part of a second too late in directing a globule of saliva at the street – so that the turning man failed to see his tacitly eloquent reaction to his arrogance.

Then, just as the half-breed was about to turn around himself and go about his self-imposed chore of attending to the horses – Steele had already shepherded the Ute sub-chief out of sight in the area of the law office – three figures appeared at the pillared entrance of the railroad station and caught his attention. A white man with a woman clinging to his arm and a black man in railroad company livery who had a bag in each hand and another tucked under each arm. The Negro was nervously anxious to have done with his current task while the elderly white man and the beanpole-thin woman who was half his age and a great deal uglier were, respectively, irritable and concerned as they surveyed the fraught-with-tension scene that greeted them at journey's end.

Edge had time to see that the tall and broad and upright man of sixty plus and the thirty years old woman without, at first glance, a single attractive feature in her appearance were well and expensively dressed. Then Adam Steele's fine black stallion gave an impatient toss of his head which acted as a signal to start some more back-and-forth yelling between the men at the front of the saloon and those newcomers who had stayed with the Concord. And the half-breed spat again, less forcefully, before he continued on toward Livesey's Livery Stable. Growled to the eager horse:

'Yeah, you and me both, feller. Comes a time when a jaw needs to work on something more satisfying than words.'

The stallion tossed his head again, and vented a low whinny, as Edge ambled to a halt out front of the livery with faint light glimmering through the cracks around the double doors.

'Okay, maybe you horses don't talk,' he allowed against a rising tide of angry voices down the street.

'That's the reason they're good to talk to, mister,' a woman said in a sad voice through the crack where the two doors of the stable met. Then she pushed open one of the doors to show herself to be a tall, fine figured girl of little more than twenty: with green eyes, jet-black hair and a flawless complexion that was probably not so drained of colour as it appeared to be in contrast with her hair and the vivid red rims of her eyes that looked to have been squeezed dry of tears. 'They make noises sure enough, but long as you know one end from the other you can tell what's horseshit or not.'

'You're Livesey?' Edge asked after taking a half-step backwards to glance up at the faded paint lettering on the board between the tops of the doors and the hayloft hatchway. And now with a degree of puzzlement he eyed the beautiful brunette in the long buckskin skirt and oversize man's shirt that failed to conceal her generous form.

'Dolly Livesey,' she replied in a more dispirited tone than before, her voice a good match for the numbed look on her face. 'Pa knew all there was to know about caring for horses and he taught me most of it before he died. Fifty cents a day an animal for the stall and feed, mister. Currying and veterinary service extra if it's needed.'

She had trouble with the word veterinary and only just managed to get it out at the first attempt. And only after he realised this did the half-breed catch the smell of liquor on her breath against the more pungent aromas that emanated from the dimly lit stable in back of her.

'Just need them bedded and boarded, miss,' he said. 'Unless you find they need doctoring. But keep in mind they're animals and if they need any alcohol it's only to be rubbed in.'

For a moment she looked angry that he had seen through her attempt to hide the fact that she was drunk. But then she shrugged her wide shoulders in a gesture of unconcern that caused a lot of jouncing movement inside the too-large shirt, and invited with something close to an ingenuous expression:

'If you want to bring in the horses and stay awhile to check on how I bed them down, there's a whole pint of Pa's best sipping whiskey not yet opened?'

'You got anything back in there more substantial than

oats, Miss Dolly Livesey?' he asked as, from down at the end of the final gentle curve of the street, a voice called urgently for any latecoming passengers to get aboard the train.

The railroadman's shout was countered with a raucous and scornful roar from the throats of many of the Oro City citizens who had elected to remain in town. And the girl on the threshold of the stable waited until this vocal sound was masked by the growl of the whistle and the rush of steam as the locomotive started to move in reverse out of the station, pushing the cars into motion with a clanking of coupling chains and a crashing of buffers on buffers; then she swung the door wider and stood sideways on with her back to it, to allow space for Edge to bring the two horses inside.

'Sure, mister, but I ought to warn you that Pa always used to say my cooking would be the death of him,' she replied after pulling the door closed behind the swishing tails and swaying rumps of the two horses. 'But a hot roll in the hay never did anybody any harm, did it?'

The closing of the door acted to mute the sounds of the train's departure. And the girl's sharp intake of breath was plainly heard within the livery as the half-breed abruptly whirled and directed a glittering, narrow-eyed scowl across the backs of the horses at her, while what might have been a still-born obscenity vented through his clenched teeth as an inarticulate exhalation of his own breath. His tone was ice-cold when he said:

'Did your Pa teach you to talk dirty, Dolly, or did you dirty-talk him to death, maybe?'

She recovered from her moment of terror of him as quickly as he had brought his impulse to anger under control – and matched his chill tone when she countered:

'You can go to hell, mister. My Pa was — '

'A man who didn't understand your animal instincts, seems to me,' the half-breed cut in on her. 'Taught you a whole lot about horses. But you talk like you'd work better in a cat house.'

CHAPTER THIRTEEN

SHE PRESSED herself hard against the inside of the door and looked by turns shocked, dismayed and then abjectly depressed. Edge thought that if she had not been cried out she would then have collapsed into a weeping jag. But, after perhaps five seconds of failure to find more tears to spill, Dolly Livesey straightened from leaning on the door and spread a hard expression across her lovely face as she told the half-breed in a monotone:

'My Pa was killed by Indians yesterday morning, mister. Out at the Grainger place. Him and Sheriff Rafferty and Mr and Mrs Grainger and their little daughter Kate. Pa went out there to check on a sick cow and Sheriff Rafferty was out there from spending the night after celebrating little Kate's birthday. She was seven the day before yesterday and the sheriff was her uncle – Jenny Grainger and him being sister and brother. It was some people coming into town to get the train who found Pa and the rest of the dead. Pa and the sheriff and Mr Grainger were badly cut up and nailed to trees in the yard. Jenny Grainger was staked out on the ground. They'd cut her, too. Little Kate was hanging by her arms from a tree limb and there were eleven arrows in — '

'All right, Dolly,' Edge said as the girl's dry, red-rimmed eyes developed a glassy glitter in the soft glow of the single lit lamp that hung from the ceiling. And her voice began to crack with the strain of sustaining the monotone. 'Figure we got off on the wrong foot. You're Dolly Livesey. I'm Edge. I'd be obliged if you'd take care of these horses for me and a feller named Adam Steele. Or, if you don't feel up to it, like to bed them down and feed and water them myself in here while you — '

She gave a vigorous shake of her head and anger blazed in her eyes and compressed her full lips into an almost-thin line. But although she swung around the horses and advanced purposefully toward Edge, he was not the object of her outrage.

'Excuse me, but this is my place and I'm the only one who is going to take care of animals left here. It's nice to meet you, sir. If you want to go and get yourself bed and board there's nothing to choose between Mayor DeWitt's Ingot Hotel and Mrs Harper's boarding house. The saloon's cheaper but the rooms are dirtier. Mabel Joy who used to be an extra attraction at The Golden Place is one of those who just left on that train. Or if you want to take a drink of good sipping whiskey first, you're welcome, sir. I'm real sorry we got off on the wrong foot and I really appreciate it that you straightened me out before I did too much that I would be sure to regret.'

She had taken the reins that he had surrendered easily as she began to speak. And kept her back to him as she led the gelding and stallion deeper into the livery where just one other horse was enstalled. Then, as she began to unsaddle the animals, she seemed to be trying to give the impression she was ignoring Edge. But he sensed that she shot several surreptitious glances at him as he surveyed the well-kept interior of the redolent stable and doubtless appeared to her to be undecided until she finished what she was saying. When he said:

'No sweat, Dolly. Be happy to take that drink. Maybe drown a regret of my own.'

Now they looked openly at each other for a moment as he moved to where she had been doing her solitary drinking – across the livery from where she was now tending to the horses. He showed her a smile that had a glimmer of unusual warmth in the low level of light. And she responded with a brighter smile of her own that was filled with relief.

'Just imagine if it had been a less . . . a different kind of man who came in and — '

'But it wasn't anybody except me, Dolly,' Edge cut across what she was saying as he stepped into the office section of the stable that had been formed by removing the centre divider between two stalls. Into this alcove between the flanking stalls had been pushed a table and chair, two bureaus and a free-standing closet. There were two shelves to either side of the window in the wall at the back of the alcove, lined with bottles, jars, cans and some books. The area within the alcove was on the very fringe of the cone of light from the ceiling lamp and it was possible for Edge to see that the books were concerned with the veterinary care of livestock and that the containers were of medicines, ointments, pills and powders for the treatment of animal ailments.

On the table was a darkened lamp, an empty glass and an unlabelled bottle with a shot or so of rye whiskey left in it. After he had lowered himself gratefully into the hard, polished-by-use Windsor chair, Edge emptied the bottle into the tumbler glass.

'I'll finish that later, Mr Edge,' the girl hurried to tell him. 'The good stuff's in the bottom drawer of the bureau to your right. Be a clean glass on the top shelf in the closet. And it will be clean, you can be sure of that. Been said by a lot of folks in and around Oro City that though he was just a veterinarian, he could teach doctors a few home truths about how important it is to have the place and his instruments clean and — '

'Fine for now, Dolly,' Edge said, holding up the glass in the manner of a toast as he took off his hat and set it on the table. He swallowed half the drink and then rolled the glass between his palms as he relished the feel of the liquor heading from his throat into his stomach. Had to make a conscious effort not to yawn as he listened to the small sounds the girl made as she ran her expert hands and eyes over the horses. This while the horses became as lethargic as the half-breed within the peaceful shelter of the livery stable: into which not a single sound intruded now that the clatter of the departing train had faded from earshot and the commotion on the street between the saloon and the stage-line depot had been reduced or maybe ended. 'You and your Pa make much of a living here?'

'What you see is more of less what he left me, Mr Edge,' she answered as she finished her cursory examination of the stallion and started on the gelding. 'We had rooms at Mrs Harper's place. Just never did get around to setting up house. Just too comfortable there, I guess. And apart from that, there was always the prospect of me getting married – and Pa wasn't much of one for housekeeping chores. Either that, or we'd be moving on.'

'Before the town finally died?'

She straightened up with a small sigh, and pronounced: 'The gelding is going to need a set of new shoes pretty soon. The stallion has the start of caries in the fourth upper molar. Apart from that, there's nothing wrong with either of them that won't be fixed by good feed and a night's rest in the warm and dry.'

'Obliged.'

He finished the drink at a second swallow and then watched Dolly Livesey coax the horses into neighbouring stalls. Then he saw she was as strong as a woman of her age and build had a right to be as she swung each saddle and bedroll up off the dirt floor to hang the gear on pegs at the front of the stalls. He had to make a conscious effort not to think carnal thoughts as he watched her body's curves shift and become by turns emphasised and concealed by the fit of her clothes as she stooped and stretched and turned.

'But a man like you would know those kind of things about his horse, I'd say,' she told him as she moved to attend to feed and water for her charges. 'And would be sure to see they got attention early enough.'

'Was planning to have the gelding shod next town I reach with a blacksmith, Dolly. The Reb maybe knows as much about horseflesh as you do, so I guess it won't be news to him that his mount has a decaying tooth.'

'That's good. Yes, there was always a better chance of Pa and me upstaking and moving on from Oro City than of me getting married and settling down here.'

'Figure it was almost a boom town, one time?'

'Sure was, Mr Edge. Ten years ago, when Pa and me moved out here from Denver after Ma died. I was just a little girl then, but I remember new strikes and new claims were still being made. But further and further from town. And never anything really rich. But there was still a lot of hope. And the men that had exhausted their claims were making good money from working for those who were luckier.'

She had finished her chores now, but remained in the stall with the gelding for a few more moments – splashing water and then making other, less clearly indentifiable sounds. She continued with her story.

'But it was the beginning of the end when we got here. And already a couple of the richer seams were worked out and the people who owned them had left or were starting to try to farm. Which meant there was more work for Pa, of course. Farmers having more stock than gold miners, of course. But the soil around here isn't good for growing and the climate is all wrong.'

She emerged from the stall and it was apparent she had spent the past few moments doing as much as she could in the circumstances to eradicate the ravages of grief and liquor and loneliness from her appearance – she had doused her face with water and hand-rubbed it dry, in the process brought colour to her cheeks, had finger-combed some of the tangles from her hair and had tightened the waistband of her skirt after tucking in her shirt more firmly to stretch the fabric free of wrinkles.

'But you aren't really interested in any of that, are you, Mr Edge?' she asked as she crossed the livery, raising her head from looking down at herself.

'If it helps, Dolly.'

'Helps?' She stopped short of entering the alcove, and seemed genuinely perplexed by his comment.

'You've had a bad time. I made you feel worse without intending to. My horse needs to rest up and maybe I do, too. Figure there are worse places than this for a man to take the weight off in this town. And worse company to be in. If talking helps you with what ails you . . .' He shrugged. 'Hell, I don't usually talk this much without saying anything. Bottom drawer of the bureau on the left, you said?'

'The right. And don't bother with another glass. I think I've had enough for one day.' She pressed fingers to an area above her right eye and moved them gently in a circular motion. The eye that was not obscured by her hand was now dull as the first symptoms of an unfamiliar hangover began to make themselves felt.

'I expect that's what makes it even harder to bear,' she said as Edge rose from the chair and opened the correct drawer – to find the pint of bourbon wrapped in a towel among some papers. He sat down again and took the cap off the bottle when he saw she was heading back toward the double doors. She opened one until there was a foot-wide gap and breathed deeply of the air that was still cool when it reached into the alcove where the half-breed poured himself a double shot of the good whiskey. When she had taken her fill of deep breathing, the tall and full-bodied, green-eyed brunette chose to remain at the part-opened door, just half-turned to face the man she was talking to.

'For months we'd been thinking about upstaking and leaving Oro City. Once a week a train comes into town with mail and freight and leaves with a family or two or three. It's gotten to be a big event when even a drummer gets off the stage. Most times, somebody leaves town for Denver or Virginia City or beyond. A year from now, maybe less, if there was anybody left here at all it would be Calvin Brownlow at the stage-line depot, Pa said.'

Edge relished the taste of the sipping whiskey rather than welcomed the effect of its warmth penetrating through his frame. Then he dug the makings from his shirt pocket after he set down the glass and resealed the bottle.

'Pa never allowed smoking in the livery, Mr Edge. On account of all the fodder and straw and the fact that horses are never addicted to tobacco.'

'I'll go so far, Dolly,' he said evenly without interrupting the cigarette-making. 'Your Pa was a wise man who spoke a lot of sense, from what you've said. He's dead now. And I'll be careful.'

She gave the slightest of shrugs before she resumed her indifferent survey of a probably empty street that perhaps personified her mood and the prediction her father had made. 'Pa was not going to be driven away by Indians, though. Like a lot of other people hereabouts. The stubborn kind. Others can't go unless they're willing to lose everything they have. I doubt there's a person in town or around who doesn't think it was horrible and disgusting what those soldiers did at Arroyo Bend. There was a lot of bad feeling for the soldiers when the news of what happened first reached town. But then we began to hear about the Indians getting their own back on whites who were just decent and honest farmers and gold grubbers and travellers.'

She breathed in noisily through her nose and shook her head slowly. 'Well, Mr Edge, people fast ran out of sympathy for the Indians then. Not just because they were killing innocent white people. But the way we heard they were killing them.'

Edge struck a match on his Colt butt and lit the cigarette. Then tossed back the rest of his drink in one swallow, rose from the chair and swept his hat off the table and on to his head.

'I say something wrong?' the girl asked anxiously.

He shook his head as he halted short of where she stood on the livery threshold, and now he took a couple of deep breaths from the chill, fresh air of the Utah night. 'I've heard enough and I guess you won't ever say enough to talk the way your Pa died out of your mind – not while you're talking about Indians and the way they kill for vengeance.'

'You're right,' she agreed miserably.

'It happens sometimes. Something of which I'm even more sure is that I'm hungry.'

She nodded and moved back into the livery, to unhitch a length of rope from a peg and lower the lamp to the floor: went to it and crouched to extinguish the glow. Moonlight shafted in through the doorway and three windows to keep the darkness far from pitch.

'If you want to take a chance with my cooking, Mrs Harper allows me to use the kitchen since Pa and I lived in her boarding house for so long. Or Annie Austin at the cafe cooks good and plain food at reasonable prices.'

From where he had assumed the place on the livery threshold vacated by Dolly Livesey, Edge had been able to watch Adam Steele amble down the street after he first reappeared at the mouth of the alley on the far side of the law office.

'I like the sound of good and plain at reasonable prices,'

the Virginian drawled. And pulled up short when he saw the beautiful young woman who emerged from the livery after Edge pushed the door open wider for her to pass outside ahead of him. Then Steele hurried to tip his hat as the near scowl he had been directing at the half-breed became an appreciative smile as he added: 'Although I reckon I'd be willing to risk your cooking if this feller wants to eat at the cafe, Miss . . . ?'

'Miss Dolly Livesey, feller,' Edge introduced. 'And this is Adam Steele.'

'I'm glad to know you, Mr Steele,' she said inattentively as she securely fastened the livery doors, unaware of how the Virginian's dark eyes shifted from her face to appraise her form and then expressed approval.

'How's Black Hawk, Reb?' the half-breed asked evenly.

'He doesn't say much, but I reckon he's as hungry as I am. How are the horses?'

'Your stallion has caries.'

'I know, Yank. If it doesn't wear down, I'll see about getting treatment for that tooth.'

'What did I tell you, Dolly?' Edge growled.

'Mr Edge said you knew about horses,' the girl put in quickly as she detected the hardening in the Virginian's attitude after he learned he had been spoken about in his absence. 'My Pa was the vet — '

'Her Pa was killed by Utes yesterday, feller,' the half-breed cut in flatly as all three of them found their attention drawn to the strip of street between the stage-line depot and the saloon. 'Liquor was helping her some with her grief. We decided that a man right now would leave her with something a whole lot worse to live with than a hangover.'

Steele spared the time to tacitly convey his thanks to Edge and to receive an indifferent response before the two men matched the girl's degree of curiosity in watching what was taking place at the foot of the sloping curve of the street.

A flatbed wagon was now standing where the Concord had earlier come to rest. Arnie Jonas was up on the driver's seat and two blanket-shrouded forms were tied down in the back. The rest of the troopers stood beside their horses out front or at the rear of the wagon. Just a small group of men watched from the sidewalk before the saloon, while the only two passengers to get off the evening train stood in the doorway of the neighbouring Ingot Hotel. The uniformed men all seemed to be impatient to leave, most of them glancing nervously around as if they expected something to happen that would prevent their departure. The townspeople who watched openly were mostly either disgruntled or disgusted by what they witnessed. The tall, elderly man and the skinny and ugly woman beside him seemed no more than mildly curious.

It was the opening of the door of the stage-line depot that had caused a stir of activity which had captured the attention of the trio out front of the livery stable. And now they remained where they were to watch as the cadaverous-faced man with a fancy gun in a tied-down holster emerged from the building, moved along the stoop and went around the front of the troopers and wagon to cross the street and enter, with the stylishly dressed man and woman, the hotel. The interest generated by the man's sudden appearance was quickly dissipated as far as the troopers and the by-standers on the saloon sidewalk were concerned.

Edge said, as he dropped his cigarette butt into the dust of the street and stepped on it: 'If that feller is the gunslinger he looks to be, Reb . . . ?'

'His name's Harve Baker and Sheriff Rafferty told Pa that's what he is sure enough,' Dolly supplied. 'Wanted in Texas and Kansas and Missouri. All for murder.'

'Obliged.'

'Grateful to you, Miss Livesey. I just caught a glimpse of that couple, Yank, but I reckon I know what you're driving at. Dollar to a wooden nickel they're Jerome Randell and his daughter Miranda. And Baker's here looking to collect on young Sun's hide.'

The girl was between the two men as the three of them started down the street, and she glanced quizzically from one thickly bristled profile to the other. Dolly said grimly:

'I've no idea what you are talking about, but I don't think anybody should be concerned with personal differences until the Indian trouble has been dealt with.'

'About that Indian trouble, Reb?'

'Black Hawk's locked up tight, feller.'

'After McNally takes his men out of town,' Edge replied evenly, 'some of the other local citizens might start to dwell on the thought that the army only started to stir the . . . the mess.'

'Don't mind me,' Dolly said grumpily as she massaged the area above her right eye again. 'I'll stop my ears if you want.'

Steele had looked curiously at Edge as the half-breed altered what he had planned to say in deference to the girl. Now he glanced at Dolly as he realised that she was suffering from an attack of ill humour that did not arise entirely out of the discomfort of liqour turning sour in her stomach and thudding in her head. And had nothing whatever to do with her recent bereavement.

'Ain't you I'm concerned with,' Edge growled as he came to a halt alongside the vacant lot between the livery and the Miner's Rest Boarding House. And Dolly and Steele stopped, too – all their attentions focussed upon the facade of the stage-line depot again, which was where everyone on and across the street was looking. The half-breed went on: 'You're not drunk enough anymore to do anything stupid, I figure. But there could be some other people in this town who maybe won't need to take even a snort to set them thinking that there's just one thing better than an Indian in a cell.'

It was Mrs Edith Crawford who appeared first in the doorway of the stage-line depot and drew all eyes to peer in this direction again. Close behind the fleshily built, puffy-faced, aging woman came the younger, shorter, slimmer and more attractive Amy Yancy. Both dressed as they had been earlier, they had taken the opportunity to wash up and neaten their appearance while they waited in the depot for the Concord to be replaced by the flatbed – and presumably for just the bodies of the two troopers killed on the Sun farmstead to be switched from one rig to another. But past brushes with violent death, present tensions and forebodings of what the future held counteracted much of what the women had done to themselves and they both looked taut and weary and older than their years.

Corporal Phil McNally who followed close behind them and lent Arnie Jonas a hand in getting the women up on the seat of the wagon – where they draped blankets over their shoulders and around their legs – appeared to be as near exhaustion as they were. But his voice was harshly strong when he stepped down off the stoop, accepted the reins of his horse from Trooper Webber and commanded:

'Detail, prepare to mount – mount!'

The rest of the soldiers in front of and behind the wagon aped the non-com's moves to attain their saddles as Jonas retrieved the reins of the two-horse team after the women were settled on the seat beside him.

'The local preacher can't do much of anything for the dead until they're ready for burying, Edge,' Steele drawled. 'And I reckon he's sick and tired of praying in an empty church for the deliverance of the people who should be filling the pews.'

'You left the preacher guarding the Indian?'

'Nobody from Oro City would ever raise a hand against the Reverend Rice,' Dolly assured.

From down the street, McNally's commanding voice rang out again: 'Detail, forward at a walk – forward walk!'

Unobtrusive sounds and small eddies of dust rose from the wagon and team and the mounts of the escorting soldiers as hooves were lifted and set down, wheels turned, harness metals jangled and springs creaked. And an atmosphere of sweet relief seemed to be a palpable emanation from all those who were leaving town. Until a more potent combination of hopelessness and acrimony was exuded by the silent and unmoving group of Oro City citizens who continued to watch from in front of the saloon.

'Black Hawk's a converted Christian, Yank,' the Virginian drawled. 'It was seeing him take Communion through the cell bars that reminded me how hungry I was.'

Almost as if he had felt dutybound to move the column at a sedate pace while it was inside of the town limits, McNally hand-signalled the order to trot just as soon as the two back markers were past the marker at the end of the street and on the open trail. After which, the fat, moustached, melancholic-eyed Calvin Brownlow doused the light in the stage depot and emerged to head across the street to the saloon: where the group of men on the sidewalk were suddenly no longer silent as they dispersed – just a few going ahead of the stage-depot manager through the batwings while the majority headed up the sloping curve to go to their homes beyond the boarding house out front of which Dolly Livesey and Edge and Steele stood.

Those men with hats on tipped them to the girl and the others muttered brief goodnights. The two travel-stained, gun-toting strangers to town who were with her were pointedly ignored or subjected to fleeting scowls of distrust. Even when they were not scowling and even when they spoke with outward kindness and sympathy to the girl, the men were quite obviously harbouring deeply felt grievances: that were perhaps made harder to endure because of the frustration of having no clearcut target on which to vent their hatred and worse.

'Well, do you want to try my cooking or eat at the cafe?' Dolly asked, several seconds after the last of the homegoers had gone on by. It had taken her that long to shake free of the unnerving sensation that had affected her as the street emptied yet seemed eerily still occupied. Her voice sounded too husky from the strain of trying to seem unconcerned. And as she became aware of this, and also realised that the half-breed and the Virginian were no longer so nonchalant as they had been moments before, apprehensiveness flooded back through her.

But Steele spoke before she was able to pose the question formed in her uneasy mind. 'Another time perhaps, Miss Livesey.' His left gloved hand fisted around the frame of the Colt Hartford canted to his shoulder as he raked his dark-eyed gaze up and down the moon- and lamp-lit length of street that was visible from in front of the boarding house. 'You want to bring Black Hawk and me something from the cafe, Edge?'

'No sweat, feller,' the half-breed answered as he turned one way and the Virginian the other, so that their backs were toward the beautiful young girl. 'Hungry enough to eat anything, I guess?'

'I reckon. Just coffee to drink, though. I'm still off liquor.'

'I got enough problems without listening to your hard-luck stories, Reb,' Edge growled with just a hint of good humour discernible in his tone as the two men started along the street in opposite directions: Steele striding out at much the faster rate.

For a stretched second Dolly remained rooted to the spot, perplexity displacing anxiety on her beautiful face as she shared a glance between the men moving away from her. Then she caught her breath and elected to swing to the right as she raised the hem of her skirt and hurried to catch up with Edge.

'You're right, of course,' she told him breathlessly, and surveyed the street in both directions with mounting uneasiness as she massaged her brow above the right eye again. 'It's not like it ever was before in this town and anything might happen. Even to the Reverend Rice. I'll bring you and your friend and the Indian some food if you want to go — '

'Much obliged, Dolly,' the half-breed said as he came to a sluggish halt and moved into an unhurried about-face – the torpidness of his actions at odds with the vigilance that she could see at this close range in the glittering slits of his ice-cold eyes as he surveyed the menacing darkness beyond the reach of the moon and the lamp light. 'Tell the lady at the Paydirt Cafe that the Reb and me will settle the check later.'

'Goodness, I don't think Annie –' Dolly started to protest. But abandoned it and moved out to cross the street when she saw that Edge had turned his back on her again – but this time was heading in the same direction as Adam Steele. And was moving with fluid speed in long strides that did not quite qualify as a run.

Then a man bellowed into the short silence that followed the girl's unfinished sentence: 'Hey, you!'

And Edge came to an instant halt, when he was directly opposite the steps below the boarding-house doorway again. Further down the street, Adam Steele stopped with the same abruptness. He was at the furthest front corner of the law office.

'Mr Randell would like to talk to you!' the rangy, thin-faced, hard-eyed Harve Baker announced from the threshold of the Ingot Hotel. His voice was not so loud now that he had succeeded in getting the attention he required. And there was a faintly amused tone underlying it as he enjoyed the effect that his initial shout had caused. 'Just one of you will do. Whichever one is in need of a couple of bucks.'

Both Edge and Steele had turned slowly from the waist as Baker was talking. And as the man in the hotel doorway finished, first the half-breed and then the Virginian swung into a full turn, bringing one booted foot from around behind the other. They were too far away on the opposite side of the street to see if there was any change of expression on the skeletal face of the gunslinger who moments earlier had been indulging in enjoyable self-confidence. But as Edge moved his right hand to drape it loosely over the butt of his holster revolver, and Adam Steele moved his rifle a few inches forward from his shoulder and thumbed back the hammer, they both saw Baker stiffen into a more upright stance.

'Hey, Yank!' Steele called.

'Yeah, Reb?'

'I don't need a couple of bucks!'

'Me, neither!'

'You need any help?'

'No sweat.'

'That's fine.'

'Listen!' Dolly Livesey shouted, and her voice perhaps sounded more fraught with concern because of its contrast with the even-toned exchange called back and forth between Edge and Steele.

But now the half-breed was emphatically grim as he growled: 'Get your butt off the street and your nose out of my business, young lady.'

'You don't — '

'Do like he told you, miss!' Harve Baker urged, and moved off the hotel threshold, across the sidewalk and down on to the street. The moonlight out from under the sidewalk roof was more revealing than had been the light of the hotel lobby lamps that spilled from the doorway and flanking windows. And before the gunslinger placed his hat on his head after turning it a complete circuit through the thumbs and forefingers of both hands, his eyes were seen to sparkle and his teeth to gleam in a dangerous smile of pleasure that anticipated a greater enjoyment to come. And then, in response to a command rasped at him from within the lobby: 'No, sir, this ain't nothing to do with that.'

'Listen, you fools!' Dolly shrieked to what could have been the limit of her capability. 'The train's coming back, for God's sake!'

Footfalls had started to thud on floorboarding inside the saloon. And some voices had been raised to shout questions. The girl's shrill words carried into the building as clearly as they rang along the street. And brought a brittle silence to the entire town. That remained intact for varying lengths of time to various people. And perhaps the more hard of hearing never, in fact, detected the muted-by-distance clatter of the locomotive and cars racing southward toward Oro City again. But only the stone deaf could fail to hear the mighty crash of the explosion that reached town in the immediate wake of the flash that was the first awesome sign the train would never reach the end of the line at the station.

'No it ain't, Dolly,' Edge said tonelessly to the girl who stared fixedly at him with shock cutting deep lines into her face as her eyes widened until there seemed to be an impossible amount of white around the green irises: aging her and taking away her beauty while her mouth hung open like she had forgotten to close it.

Then people spilled out from between the saloon bat-wings. The upright old man and his skinny, homely woman companion who had come to town on the train ran from the hotel. A less conspicuous couple appeared in the doorway of the Paydirt Cafe. And a lone middle-aged woman wrenched open the door and stood on the threshold of the boarding house. All of them expressed some degree of shock and all of them made a contribution to the tumult of shouting that masked any sounds of the train wreck's aftermath that might otherwise have reached town. And then running footfalls and high-pitched voices sounded from the mid-town area of Oro City: swelling in volume by the moment as people recovered from the stupefying effect of their initial shock and came dashing and staggering down the snaking, curving street.

All this in less than five seconds, while Edge and Baker swung their heads this way and that – perhaps more deeply affected by the trauma of the distant detonation than the panicked people all around them. Because, during the tense second before the massive crash so totally shattered the peace of the surrounding night, each man had known he could be teetering on the brink of sudden death. And now it was difficult to reconcile themselves to this abrupt change in circumstances that quite obviously caused their confrontation to pall into insignificance.

'Dear God, what could have happened?' Dolly forced from her constricted throat after she had fought her mouth and eyes back to their normal proportions. And she swung around to come toward Edge, her arms thrust out in front of her. Terror had replaced shock on her face and this acted to make her look beautiful in a far different way than before – asexually appealing.

This image she presented to Edge as she sought him for comfort and protection served to plunge him back into the reality of this fear-filled night that held dangers far greater than one man with a fancy handgun who had been intent upon killing him.

'Indians for sure,' he rasped, and did not speak it as an aside while his mind was engaged elsewhere: and neither was there anything less than calculated caution in his mien as he started to rake his gaze in every direction again. Searching for a first sign that the wrecking of the train had been a diversion.

Then, as the frightened girl came up hard against him and he instinctively reached an arm around her, he saw with a jolting sensation of rage and fear that the Ute uprising was unlikely to be of any further concern to him. For Harve Baker was coming toward him, the gunslinger seemingly oblivious to the noise and movement all around him as he moved on an even paced, unwavering diagonal line between the hotel and the boarding house. His gun was out of the holster, his left hand fisted tightly around the fancy butt. The smile that had been on his emaciated face before Dolly's shrieking words signalled the train wreck was back there again: but had a fixed quality, like the man was working harder to maintain this aspect of his appearance than any other.

The shouting died down and the pounding of running feet lessened. A whispering and a shuffling noise filled the night as the once intensely bright glow that had dimmed the moonlight to the north of town was reduced to a faint luminescence. If anybody had ever been on the street between Edge and Baker, except for Dolly, they were now well clear. And nobody inched closer in at the sides while those behind the adversaries scurried to get out of the line of fire. The boarding-house door slammed closed.

Dolly Livesey gasped, as she became perhaps the last person with a view of the downtown curve of street to realise the wrecking of the train had not ended the showdown.

'Ain't no one calls me and walks away, Edge!' Baker said as he came to an easy halt some twenty-five feet away from where Edge dropped his left arm from around the girl's waist and tried to side-step clear of her.

'Baker!' Jerome Randell snarled. 'It was never supposed to — '

'I told you, this is personal!' the gunslinger said coldly, still talking through his teeth clenched in the line of a smile while his gleaming eyes never shifted from their level stare at Edge's impassive face above the shoulder of the girl. And the Remington with the ivory butt plates maintained an unshaking aim from his hip on the base of Dolly Livesey's spine.

'Move out of the way,' Edge rasped in her ear.

'But he's got his gun out and pointed at you,' the girl groaned huskily, still with her head craned around to look at Baker as she clung on tightly to the half-breed's waist with both her hands.

'He had equal chance with me before you started to yell about the train,' Baker reminded as he took a step forward.

his smile becoming brighter as he relished the anticipated taste of triumph that would soon be his.

People began to shout again. All of them speaking out against Harve Baker, as far as Edge could tell. Except for Adam Steele, who simply made an offer to abandon his neutrality if that was what was needed. Most of those who attempted to out-shout each other never got said what they wanted to before their voices were drowned or they realised they were wasting their breath.

'Baker, I'm warning . . .'

'You gotta be crazy to — '

'We're all gonna get killed by In — '

'Still no sweat, Yank?'

'Frig you, Baker!'

'You sonofabitch, you — '

'Dear God, why . . . ?'

'As mayor of this town I . . .'

'I said to move, Dolly!' Edge spat out the words viciously as he brought up his left knee to slam it into the girl's crotch. Then moved both his hands in blurs of speed as she screamed and wrenched her hands away from him to claw them at the source of her agony, freeing his arms from her terrified embrace. His left hand he brought up and chopped her with the side of it across her throat – to snap her into an upright attitude as she was starting to fold double. His right hand grasped the butt of his Frontier Colt and slid the revolver smoothly out of the holster, his thumb cocking the hammer as part of the same fluid action. His ears were filled with the uproar of screams of horror and shrieked, incoherent words. And then a gunshot cracked, sounding almost inconsequential against the tumult of human voices.

Edge was flinging himself to the ground then, eyes and then the muzzle of his gun fixed upon the grinning Harve Baker – as the gunslinger's Remington wisped smoke to show he had fired that single shot. The half-breed had been wounded by bullets a half dozen times in the long-ago past. And knew that if there was no pain to provoke a scream from an injured man there was at least the thud of an impact of lead through flesh: that more often than not forced a shriek of fear from him as he failed at the moment of being hit to know if the shot had drilled into a vital organ. Tonight he felt nothing outside of continued fear and rage for another part of a second, before there was the double jolt of his hip and elbow crashing to the street. But, an immeasurably short space of time before he hit the ground, he squeezed off a shot.

And it was like the report was echoed countless times across endless night as he saw Harve Baker hurl both arms high in the air – his fancy gun flung high and wide from his jerked open hand. He wore dark clothes and Edge was unable to see any blood against their backdrop to show where the man was hit.

Not so Dolly Livesey. The man's shirt she wore – her Pa's, more than likely – was cream-coloured. Until the bright stain of crimson had started to form on it at the back, halfway up and left of centre. She lay curled up on her side, close to the foetal position, with both hands trapped in the folds of her skirt at her crotch. He could not see her face because her head was hung low. He was able to see that she was held in the utter stillness of unmistakable death.

The gunfire he had imagined to be the echo of the shot from his Colt was suddenly much louder. So was the shouting and the thudding of running feet. He felt himself very much caught up in the reality of what was happening all around him as he rose unsteadily to his feet. He knew that the army was in retreat again – McNally and the troopers racing at the gallop back along the trail by which they had left town earlier. But the wagon was ahead of them to slow them down as they exploded a constant barrage of gunfire back at their pursuers – protecting Edith Crawford and Amy Yancy as the two women clung to each other on the seat while Arnie Jonas demanded the utmost speed from the two horses in the traces. He did not know for certain, but he could guess that it was a band of Utes that had the cavalrymen on the run again. He knew that he and Harve Baker and Dolly Livesey were now being ignored by almost everyone in Oro City as the tide of people swept past them and did not falter until it came to a disorderly halt out front of the railroad station.

He knew that a woman had emerged from the boarding

house and stepped down off the stoop to go and squat beside the dead girl. He heard her tell him: 'I'm Amelia Harper who took care of her and her father – now they're both dead.' He knew he offered the woman no word nor even a gesture of condolence. He knew the man who had tried to kill him and killed her instead was still alive. He knew that two men were watching him down what was now a deserted stretch of moon-lighted street as he took the ten strides that brought him to a position standing over Baker.

'Five grand I came all the way out to this lousy town to collect, mister,' the gunslinger said, his Adam's apple rising and falling rapidly. 'And then that moneybags of a Randell comes to tell me his pig of a daughter wants to give the Chink another shot.'

Harve Baker lay on his back, legs splayed and both hands pressed to his belly, holding the bullet hole from which the blood seemed to have stopped seeping. His hat had fallen off and his gaunt, prominently boned face could be clearly seen as it expressed a grimace of bitter disappointment rather than pain. His teeth gleamed still, but his eyes were dull now. The expression had not changed by a single line since the half-breed moved into his range of vision, to tower over him at his side, Frontier Colt aimed down at him. While he was catching his breath and struggling to control the frenetically bobbing Adam's apple, the crackle of gunfire reached a crescendo and then was curtailed. Edge knew this and the man he had at his mercy must have been aware of the noise diminishing to the thunder of hooves and clatter of wheels.

'Bastard told me he'd make it worth my while if I found the Chink for her. Alive. That ain't my business, mister. Made me mad, that worth-my-while crap. I get top dollar for killin' men, or I don't work. Sometimes kill men just for the hell of it. When I'm mad. Couldn't let you get away with talkin' to me the way you did. Made me madder still. Tell me somethin'?'

'I don't owe you a thing, feller,' Edge answered, and extended the revolver downward at the limit of his reach. Thumbed back the hammer.

'Accidents happen, mister. Accident that I shot the girl

instead of you. Accident that a man who I guess ain't a pro put a bullet into me. Luke Vicary ran with a couple of real fast guns called Dalton Arliss and Murray Quinlan. And there was a better man with a gun still, name of Andy Patterson, who I was told came out this way lookin' to — '

Baker did not alter his expression as the Frontier Colt was tracked up his body while he spoke. And then, as the muzzle came into line with his right eye, both his eyes seemed to express a brand of doleful understanding about what must inevitably happen to him. Like an animal that has wilfully been recalcitrant despite repeated warnings of the consequences.

Edge blasted a bullet into the right eye to end the expression, the talk and the life. Then the hammer was thumbed back as the muzzle was moved to cover a new target – to drill another bullet into the other eye that was already glazed by death. One into the mouth and then two that all but tore the nose off the face after Edge had used his booted foot to tip the head into profile. This emptied the revolver of live bullets and went some way toward relieving the half-breed of the unfamiliar burden of anger and fear that Harve Baker had laden him with a few seconds before.

Down at the end of the street, as Edge tilted the Colt, thumbed aside the loading gate and rotated the cylinder to allow the expended shellcases to drop out, the wagon and army horses had been brought to a skidding, rearing, creaking, snorting halt. The Utes who had chased the cavalrymen and their female charges back to town had withdrawn into the moon shadowed country. Most people gathered around the stationary wagon and the dismounting soldiers, calling questions and yelling the news about the train wreck.

The Randell father and daughter, who had never moved too far away from the hotel, suddenly scuttled back inside as Amelia Harper rose from beside the dead Dolly to rebuke the half-breed:

'A person can only die the once, young man!'

'It's an imperfect world, lady,' Edge replied as he began to reload the chambers of the revolver with fresh bullets from the loops on his gunbelt.

From in front of the livery stable, where he stood with Adam Steele beside him, a short and round man with a sixty-year-old face above a grubby cleric's collar countered: 'The world is as the Lord intended it should be, and only mankind has —'

'With all the funerals you've got to officiate at, preacher, best you save your breath?' Edge interrupted the man evenly as he turned toward him, and became aware of the Virginian's presence for the first time since Steele had called out the offer of help before Dolly was shot. 'How's it going, Reb?'

'Not so far and so fast as Eddy Sun and Black Hawk, Yank,' the man in the worse for wear dudish style of garb answered, with a soured sidelong glance at the preacher.

'He told me,' the abruptly more perturbed Reverend Rice blurted, 'that is, the young man of an Oriental cast, that he had been requested to bring the Indian . . .' He looked quickly from Steele to Edge and back again, his anxiety expanding as he failed to draw any comforting sign or word from either of them. Then swallowed hard and moved along the street in a wide arc that took him around the half-breed and the two corpses with plenty of space between them and himself. He felt the need to keep talking and blurted: 'You men are quite obviously non-believers and I feel I will be better able to serve . . . to fulfil my ecclesiastic . . . to do my duty among those of my flock who . . .'

Now he gave it up and moved as fast as his cassock would allow him toward the large gathering of less agitated people at the end of the curving, gently sloping street. This as Edge completed the reloading of his revolver and slid it back into the holster. Then, as the half-breed ambled toward the livery stable where the Virginian continued to stand with the rifle canted to his shoulder, he said:

'I ain't a non-believer, Reb.'

'Me neither, Yank. You know what I believe?'

'You're going to tell me, I guess?'

'I believe there could have been something between you and the girl.'

'There was.'

'Uh?'

'About twenty years.' Edge began to unfasten the door latch on Livesey's Livery Stable as he added: 'I didn't tell you what I believe.'

'No, you didn't.'

'I believe I'll have another shot of her Pa's best sipping whiskey.'

CHAPTER FOURTEEN

FEAR NOW had an almost palpable presence in the chill night air of Oro City as Adam Steele crossed the street toward the Paydirt Cafe and the cluster of people around the wagon and soldiers began to break up.

Some of them were in a great hurry and spared no glances to left or right – and deviated off the straight line shortest distance between two points only to swing around the area of the street where Harve Baker lay in lonely death and the boarding-house keeper knelt beside the dead girl, gently stroking the jet-black hair of the corpse. Others made far less haste and were more intent upon peering into the moon-shadowed night to the north and west and up at countless pockets of darkness spread throughout the town on the hill slope than they were on getting where they were going.

Everyone expressed some degree of fear. Including the couple who had clung to each other's arms as they slow-footed it to the cafe. They were both in their mid-forties, both of medium height and build, both had brown hair and undistinguished features. They looked nervously in every direction except the one in which they were going, and vented gasps of alarm when the Virginian straightened up from leaning against the wall beside the closed door of the cafe.

'Can I get something hot to eat here tonight?' he asked of the couple who had come to an abrupt halt with their leading feet up on the sidewalk.

'I'm sorry . . .' the woman managed to force out and pressed a hand to her left breast.

'I asked if I could — ' Steele started to repeat as he lowered his hand from tipping his hat.

'She heard, mister,' the man cut in, letting go of her arm and working hard to mask his anxiety behind an expression of aggressive enmity that was obviously not characteristic of the man and did not fit his face well. 'What the wife was goin' to say is that we're about to close up the place. Get ready like everyone else for the Injuns to hit us.'

'We truly are sorry, sir,' the woman assured as her husband urged her across the sidewalk and then pushed open the door to usher her into the cafe, which was still brightly lit and was invitingly clean and warm to the senses of the travel wearied Virginian. But he was resigned to eating out of his saddlebags in the less comfortable surroundings of the livery – until the woman stopped and turned and prevented the man from closing the door. And the determination she expressed was almost as forceful as the ill-fitting look on the face of her husband when she said: 'Goodness, all we can do is load the guns and wait to use them? And waitin's always the worst part. Whether it's good or bad that's expected. Help's if a body keeps busy, I've always found. Come along inside, sir. And I'll fix you up somethin' to make you loosen your belt a notch while Milton dusts off the guns and whatever.'

'But, Annie . . .' Milton began to protest, then recognised from years of marriage to her that her look meant her mind was made up. And he shrugged and got something close to a smile on his nondescript face as he beckoned for Steele to enter. Said: 'Well, if those riled up Utes do hit us pretty soon, the way you tote that rifle around with you all the time means you can use it real good?'

'Grateful to you, ma'am,' the Virginian said as he came through the doorway and took off his hat. 'Rifle's important to me, Milton. Because it was important to my Pa and it was the only thing he left me when he died. And, oh yeah, I can fire it pretty well when I have to.'

There were ten tables in the square-shaped room, all with four chairs at them and four place settings on pink and white patterned linen cloths. Light was from a central ceiling-hung lamp and four others on the rear and side walls. Heat came from a stove in a corner at the other end of the rear wall from a doorway through which the woman went. Steele chose a table close to the stove and a chair from which he could look without turning across the cafe to the glass panelled door and the large window at one side of it. Lace curtains were hung at both panes of glass and other homely touches were given by a half dozen pastoral water colours hung on the walls and small vases of artificial flowers on some of the tables.

The table linen and curtains were much darned and had some tears and holes that needed more repairs, there was a great deal of mismatched cutlery, most of the vases were chipped and their contents were faded, and one of the pictures was curling out of its frame. But the couple were obviously doing their best to keep up appearances in their failing business in a dying town. And the place was clean: and its warmth and the aroma of earlier cooked food that had wafted out of the doorway when Annie went through was a combination that caused Steele to care not at all about anything else at the moment. But Milton wanted to talk and said as he stood with his back and spread hands toward the stove:

'Got out my old Henry repeater rifle and Navy Colt when we folks here in Oro City first heard that the local Injuns had got stirred up by what happened out at Arroyo Bend.' He directed a surreptitious glance at the closed door at the end of the wall. 'Never told Annie what I'd done. Didn't want to alarm her. But she got plenty alarmed when we started to hear about what some of the Injuns had done to some of the folks on the scattered homesteads way out in the country. Some folks we kinda knew from feedin' them here at the Paydirt now and then when they used to come to town.

'Hell of a thing, what the army done to that bunch of Utes. But that's water under the bridge now, ain't it? If the Injuns had to have revenge, they oughta have just hit the army at Hamilton. Not gone rampagin' all over everywhere killin' innocent workin' folks. And not just killin' them. The Utes ain't content to do just that. They gotta torture and mutilate and . . .' His voice trailed away and he shook his head and sighed. 'But I don't guess too many of us townsfolk ever thought all them Injuns would get together and hit us here in Oro City. But it sure looks like that's what theyr'e fixin' to do, don't it?'

'I reckon that could be, feller,' the Virginian allowed as he continued to gaze levelly at the glass panelled door as he eased the buckskin gloves off his hands – waiting for it to open and for the two people loitering outside to come in.

'Sure does. That young McNally already told us about all them Utes that are massin' in the east. Well, you know about them, don't you? Seein' as how you and your buddy come in from that direction with the stage? Well, there was two dozen Injuns that jumped them soldiers and the women again out on the west trail.' He shook his head ruefully again.

'Killed that young Shackleton that was payin' court to Ernie Monk's daughter and used to bring her in here sometimes. And George Webber, too, who could never hold his liquor when him and some of the other soldiers from Hamilton come into town to blow their pay in The Golden Place. On liquor and on Mabel Joy that left town with so many others on the train. Had to be more than just a handful of Utes north of town to fix the train is the opinion, mister.'

He continued to speak in a melancholy tone and to peer into an image-filled middle distance as the door was now pushed open and Jerome Randell stepped into the cafe, his daughter following very closely behind. 'Needed quite a sizeable bunch of them to stop the train and send it steaming back here. Not so many, I guess, to set the dynamite or whatever they used to blow it sky high. McNally is gonna take some men out along the track. See if there's any of them folks aboard that . . .'

The ramrod-stiff, clear-blue-eyed, darkly complexioned and silver-haired Jerome Randell cleared his throat noisily and the cafe owner only now seemed to become aware of the newcomers. Certainly he did a double-take at the elderly man and the skinny-framed, mousy-haired, pale and plain-faced Miranda before he hurried to explain as he turned from the stove: 'This here's a special customer the wife invited in to supper. I'll have to check with Annie about servin' other folks tonight when — '

'We ate from a hamper on the train,' the father cut in.

'I just couldn't have eaten a thing even if we hadn't done that,' the daughter added, clinging as tightly to her father as Annie and Milton had held on, one to the other, after they heard the worst about a possible imminent attack by the Utes.

'Just like to talk with this gentlemen, here, if that's all right?' Randell asked, darting his bright-eyed gaze between the Virginian and the other man, who had paused at the door to the rear of the premises. 'It's Mr Steele, isn't it?'

'Okay by me,' Milton allowed and went out to join his wife.

'Adam Steele,' the Virginian confirmed and half rose from his chair as he nodded a tacit greeting to the woman who seemed to make no attempt to improve on unkind nature with cosmetics or clothing or the art of hair styling. And who, from the way in which she clasped her father's arm in both hands and spent more time studying the floor than with her eyes raised, looked to be as lacking in character and personality as she was unlovely of face and form. Then he shifted his rifle, hat and gloves from off the chair to his right and placed them on the floor. With a hand gesture invited the Randells to sit at his table as he told them: 'But I can't tell you where Edward Sun is.'

'Is he well?' Miranda blurted, flicking her gaze up from the floor and briefly fixing it intently upon Steele's impassive face.

'When I last saw him he was fine, Miss Randell,' the Virginian answered. 'Except that he was very afraid some of your father's hired guns might be here in town waiting — '

'Yes, I can understand how that would be so,' Randell cut in, having made to move toward the table where Steele sat before he decided to remain where he was, just inside the doorway. The door was still open but Steele was close enough to the stove not to be bothered by the cold night air that encroached against the warmth of the cafe. With the chillness, sounds entered, also. Distant voices, not shouting. Footfalls, not running. Hoofbeats as horses were ridden at a canter northwards, alongside the railroad track. There was an underlying nervousness behind all the sounds, but the frenzied fear of earlier had been dissipated or was under control.

'And when I posted the reward for that young man it was my earnest wish that he be shot down without mercy. Miranda . . .' He tenderly patted one of her hands on his arm. '. . . she was never so vindictively inclined as I in this matter, but for the first time in her life I refused to indulge her in what she wanted.'

'Mr Randell?'

'Yes, Mr Steele?'

'This is none of my business.'

'But I feel — '

'Eddy Sun told me and some other people about how he let down your daughter. After four of the men looking to collect five thousand dollars were — '

'Yes, yes!' For the first time the rich man from Kansas allowed his obviously difficult to sustain forced humility to slip as a more natural impatience flared up. 'The corporal and one of the ladies told Harvey Baker what happened at the dirt farm worked by young Mr Sun's parents. I simply wish to convince you that, under considerable pressure from Miranda, I have withdrawn the reward I placed on the head of the young man. My daughter is most anxious to see him again and to talk with him. But you have my word that, even if he will agree to nothing she intends to put to him, then he still has nothing to fear from me or anyone connected with me — '

The door in the rear wall swung open and Annie Austin came through, carrying a tray on which there was a plate of strong smelling chili, another heaped with bread, and a large mug of coffee.

'Milton says you folks don't wanna eat here?' she said in a tone of voice that was as bustling as her gait as she set down the tray of food in front of Steele.

'No, that's all right, we already — '

'Thank you to close the door, whichever side of it you wanna be on,' Annie interrupted Randell as she eyed both him and Miranda belligerently before she swung around to return to the kitchen. 'So as my customer can eat his supper with teeth that ain't chatterin'.'

'Look, Mr Steele,' Miranda rushed to say as the door closed behind Annie and her father back-heeled the front door shut. 'I told Daddy at the start that what he was doing would get us disliked and lead to tragedy as likely as not. But it's too late to undo what's been done. And it's all seen to be much more horribly futile in the light of all that is happening with the Indians.'

She had started out to talk with her head still bowed. But as she warmed to her subject and her voice strengthened, she raised her gaze to peer intently at the Virginian who was beginning to eat the chili. And then she felt sure enough of her ground to let go of her father's arm as she went on:

'But despite all that is taking place, I am still desperate to talk with Edward Sun. I don't care how many other people detest and revile me, I must be assured that *he* understands I never agreed to what Daddy did?'

She finished with a note of pleading in her voice and emphasised her sincerity with the look that filled her eyes.

'Miranda, I wish you'd allow me — ' her father started.

'I don't doubt you, Miss Randell,' Steele cut in, and felt enough compassion for the woman to work at an expression on his heavily bristled and trail-dirtied face that he hoped would stress his own good faith. 'I told you the truth about when I last saw Edward Sun as we were coming into Oro City. But he was seen again not so long ago.'

'He was? Where?' Miranda was excited.

Jerome Randell's mood worsened in seemingly direct proportion to his daughter's increasing confidence. He snorted now.

'At the gaol out back of the law office where the local preacher had charge of a Ute prisoner for awhile. Sun tricked the preacher into letting him take the Indian out of the cell.'

'He did?' She was puzzled now.

'For his own selfish reasons, knowing him,' her father added sourly.

'Black Hawk isn't just another Ute brave,' Steele explained. 'He's a sub-chief we had plans to use as a hostage if — '

'To use for the good of all, I'd venture to guess, sir?'

'Reckon so – if it had done any good,' Steele told the scowling Jerome Randell.

'But that sneaky little Chinaboy has taken the prisoner and is trying to secure for just himself safe passage through the — '

'You can't be sure of that, Daddy!' Miranda protested, but she was head down again and her voice lacked conviction.

'Nonsense, Miranda,' he countered, whirling to wrench open the door. 'He's a liar and a cheat and a thief and a womaniser! That sort of no good sonofa . . . well, it seems to me he's far more likely than not to be a self-centred craven coward to boot! Come, Miranda. Thank you for your time, Mr Steele.'

Gunfire crackled outside of town. To the north. The direction in which the soldiers had ridden toward the scene of the train wreck. Miranda Randell threw a hand up to her mouth as she gasped. Her father froze in the act of stepping across the threshold on to the sidewalk. There was a strangled cry from either Annie or Milton from the other side of the door in the rear wall. Steele cocked his head in a listening attitude but pushed a piece of chili-sodden bread into his mouth.

There was an interlude of perfect silence.

Then, from a lot closer than where the opening volley had sounded, gunshots exploded. Bullets thudded and shattered and cracked and whined in ricochets. And Ute warcries and euphoric whoops rang out against the less strident thudding of galloping hooves on hard-packed ground.

'Daddy, what is it?' Miranda shrieked as she snapped up her head and started to turn toward her father.

This as Steele seemed to duck down beneath the table in a display of fear and the door in the rear wall crashed open.

'Back!' Jerome Randell roared as he brought up an arm to swing it toward the woman behind him. And made to take a backward step while he attempted to hook his other hand on the door and slam it closed.

But the shotgun in the hands of a whooping brave discharged its load as the Indian raced his pony across the front of the Paydirt Cafe – the hail of pellets thudding into the timber of the doorway and the flesh of the man who stood on the threshold over a range of just a few feet. And from such close range the force of the multiple impacts sent the tall and thin man staggering backwards: none of his intended moves completed before he was dead on his feet and responding only to the final dictates of a slower-to-expire nervous system.

He backed into the cafe as far as the table nearest the door, which halted him and then prevented him from crashing to the floor. For he sprawled out across it, belly up, with just the balls of his feet on the floor – his arms and head draped over the sides. In such an attitude the overhead lamp dropped cruel light on Jerome Randell to starkly show the ghastly way in which the shotgun pellets had torn the skin off his face to uncover raw tissue and white bone beneath, reduced his eyes to pulp and exposed the worm-like pipes in his throat. There was not much left of his shirt and vest and suit jacket from neck to waist at the front.

'*Ddddaaaaaddddeeeee!*' Miranda screamed and the piercing shrillness of her voice as she drew out the two syllables to excessive length seemed to diminish the clamour from the street. And, as if she could not endure the sound of her own voice, the woman brought up her hands and clapped them to her ears as she stared in abject horror at the bloodily gruesome corpse of her father. Then she managed to take two backward steps from him before her vocal chords were constricted, her mouth became slack and her eyes rolled into the tops of their sockets as the upper lids snapped down. She was totally limp as she collapsed in the faint, glancing off the corner of a table as she fell and bringing the cover and cutlery down on and around her.

Steele was on his feet by then, hat jammed on his head and cocked rifle in a double bare-handed grip. And Milton and Annie Austin were this side of the door – the man holding a Henry rifle like he was afraid of it and she gripping an old Colt revolver as if she didn't have any idea what it was.

'Oh, God!' Milton gasped and swallowed hard.

'The woman, too?' Annie asked despairingly.

'He's gone to hell and she's going to go through it!' Steele rasped as he lunged out from behind the table and headed between others toward the door. 'Take care of her!'

'Good heavens — ' Annie started as she forced a path around her rooted-to-the-spot husband to get the unconscious Miranda Randell.

'Where we all want to go, I reckon,' the Virginian murmured as he reached the shotgun-blasted doorway and came to an abrupt halt. And only he heard the sardonic comment he rasped between clenched teeth and unmoving lips. 'But none of us wants to die.'

CHAPTER FIFTEEN

THE RAUCOUS and violent sounds of the startlingly sudden attack on Oro City had in actuality now faded and so lessened in intensity. The Indians were still galloping their ponies, giving vocal vent to their high emotions, and exploding shots. But they were beyond the first curve of the street out of the downtown area and were racing further up the hill slope with every passing moment. And the Virginian was just one of many men who emerged cautiously on to sidewalks and stoops and the street along the now tensely quiet stretch that had been the first to be ravaged by the fast-riding raiders.

Steele saw Edge at the part-opened double doors of the livery, Winchester in one hand and a bottle in the other. Some troopers, minus their tunics and caps, each holding a revolver or a carbine, were on the stoop of the boarding house. Calvin Brownlow was not armed as he attempted to prevent Mrs Crawford and Mrs Yancy from coming out of the stage-line depot before he was sure it was safe to do so. The fat man with the ragged grey moustache and the sad eyes had a napkin tucked into his shirt collar to indicate he had been eating supper, too, when the Utes hit. The Virginian recognised the ageing and going-to-seed Mayor DeWitt among those who stepped out of the hotel and the redhaired, ruddy-faced loudmouth named Monk was standing next to Arnie Jonas out front of the saloon's batwinged entrance. Only the square-faced trooper with the still-discoloured bruise on his temple had a revolver in his hand.

The bodies of Harve Baker and Dolly Livesey had been removed from the street before the attack was launched. But Trooper Earl Saxon was sprawled on the hard-packed dirt now, a frown of disappointment on his broken-nosed face. A smoking cigar was held between the fingers of one hand. His other hand was fisted around the butt of his revolver that he had been in process of dragging from the holster when the bullet entered his head above his left eye. In contrast with the blood that had oozed from the hole, the scar tissue of the much older wound above his right eye looked particularly livid. He had been caught in the open out front of the boarding house. The Reverend Rice had taken a shotgun blast in the back as he was heading up the hill – perhaps running for the supposed sanctuary of his church. Two other inert forms were sprawled on the street – down near the railroad station where only moonlight fell on them. It was sufficient to show that they were men and had been armed with rifles.

There was a final fusillade of distant gunfire from up near the top of the hill, and then a last burst of whooping that rang with triumph before the thudding of unshod hooves became the only and fast-fading sound of the Utes riding out of the other end of Oro City's main street. The shouting and wailing and howling that erupted afterwards was from the men and women and children of the town as they vented many kinds of emotional reaction to the attack.

'A lot of friggin' use it was puttin' Ed and Ollie on guard!' Monk snarled. 'Look at the stupid sonsofbitches, laying there dead as —'

'Shut your rotten mouth, Ernie!' the town mayor bellowed, and broke free of the men with him to stride out into the centre of the street. And this action served to check a rising babble of talk in a tone that allied the majority of the anxious citizens with the barrel-chested and paunch-bellied Monk. And then the again-silent people began to once more scan nearby patches of shadow and the more distant dark of the night for a sign of further danger. And, likewise, the crowd of angry and afraid citizens who were advancing down the sloping curve of the street quietened and slowed and became aware of as-yet-unseen new danger. 'And listen to me, all you people!'

DeWitt paused and turned his round face in every direction as he clenched and unclenched his pudgy hands. For a moment seemed surprised that he had been able to command such a degree of anxious attention. Then was on the verge of panic as he searched his racing mind for a form of words to fill the void and maintain his control, sounding close to the brink of shrill-voiced loss of control when he demanded:

'Where are you goin'?'

It was Arnie Jonas who had triggered the near shriek, as the scowling trooper stepped away from the saloon batwings and down on to the street. The uniformed man was halfway across the street between The Golden Place and the stage-line depot before he halted, pushed the Army Colt back into his holster and pointedly eyed his fellow troopers on the boarding-house stoop as he said coldly:

'Phil McNally and Jack Irvin' headed out to check on the train wreck. First shootin' we heard came from over in the north. Figure to go see what happened to our boys.'

The baby-faced Roy Egan, the ginger-moustached Goldsmith and the squint-eyed Conran all looked at each other, came to a spontaneous nodding agreement and moved on to the street to follow Jonas round back of the stage-line depot.

'I guess that about tells us plain enough the kind of help we can expect from the United States cavalry!' DeWitt snarled, and once more captured the attention of an audience about to be sidetracked by malcontent muttering.

But then he immediately lost his listeners again, when Edith Crawford pushed by the now submissive Brownlow and the heaviness of her tread on the stage-depot stoop drew all eyes toward her. The grim expression fixed to her fleshy face and the booming tone of her voice kept attention focused upon her as she argued:

'Now see here, you people, what's done is done! Even if the man most to blame for starting this trouble were here, it would be foolish to make an issue of it with him just now! There is an enemy common to all of us close at hand and until we have dealt with the savages, it is essential we set aside whatever differences there are between us!'

She paused and gazed earnestly around, obviously eager for an amenable response. There was stillness and silence on the street for a few moments, during which it was possible to hear the muted sounds of the cavalrymen saddling their mounts out back of the stage depot. Then there was a murmuring and a shuffling of feet among the largest concentration of townspeople: those men, women and some children who had come down the hill and were in a close-knit crowd out front of the law office and the livery stable. It was difficult to tell whether the tenor of the low-voiced talk was approving of the woman's contention or simply nervously impatient. Before Ernie Monk spat at the street in a gesture of unmistakable restlessness and claimed centre stage as he took a step away from the batwinged entrance to the saloon and spoke from the lip of the sidewalk.

'That woman talks a lotta sense, you people! And unless we listen to that kinda talk and do what has to be done to fight off the Utes, we're all gonna end up like Ed and Ollie and the preacherman and Sheriff Rafferty and the Grainger family and Livesey and all the rest . . . all them that tried to run out on the train, too! I have to admit I was one of them thought the Injuns would never hit town! Just take it out on the folks that was easy to jump on the farms in the country! Figured them folks that run scared on the train were . . . well, when we heard that train blow and seen McNally and the rest of the soldier boys come runnin' back in chased by Utes . . . well, we didn't even take it so serious then, did we? Just went our own ways to protect our own, seems to me! And nobody – includin' me – figured Ed Louder and Ollie Knight would get in any trouble just watchin' to see if there was Injuns about!'

He continued to put his point in a forceful tone, but his voice was less loud as he neared the end of what he had to say.

'You have somethin' in mind to — ' DeWitt started to ask disconsolately, as many pairs of eyes shifted to where somebody was moving while everywhere else people were still. But the sight of Adam Steele giving Milton some money for the meal and then starting to pull on his gloves as he ambled away from the Paydirt Cafe did not hold the mass of interest for more than a few moments.

'Wasn't no time to make a proper tally of that bunch that came through shootin' up the town,' Monk went on. 'But I'm pretty damn sure there wasn't so many of them.'

'Fourteen I counted, Mr Monk sir!' a youthful voice called from the largest group of townspeople.

'There you go!' the big, muscular, sandy-haired man exclaimed emphatically. 'Just over a dozen of them whoopin' and hollerin' sonsofbitches come ridin' up our main street and pick us off like apples in a Goddamn barrel! Next time, and you can bet your butt there's gonna be a next time, there'll be more than fourteen of them. And unless we're good and ready to defend ourselves – everybody fightin' for everybody else – I reckon we might just as well throw in our hand now and let the Injuns take whatever they want outta the pot.'

Another brittle silence came to the town as Monk appeared to reach the end of what he wanted to say and Steele went into the livery stable. Then Monk added:

'No tellin' when the whole damn Ute nation might sneak up on us, so I'd thank you folks to reach a decision real fast. On account of if I'm gonna have to throw in my hand I'd like to be roarin', stinkin' drunk when I do it – the mood them Utes are in.'

Inside the livery stable, the half-breed had lit just the lamp on the table in the office section. The pint bottle of good bourbon that he had opened earlier was now less than a quarter full. But he had not been drinking on an empty stomach – there was an empty unlabelled can and some crumbs of food on the table near the much depleted whiskey bottle. He had eased his gelding out of his stall and was starting to cinch the saddle to the horse when the Virginian came into the livery.

'The woman at the cafe cooks a fine chili, Yank,' Steele said against a background of many voices and much shuffling of feet on the street. And the clop of hooves and some equine snorts. The impression of the sounds that carried into the well-kept, aromatic stable was of eagerness to take positive action against future Ute attacks as Arnie Jonas and the other troopers left town.

'The bourbon warmed me where I needed it most, Reb.'

'Fine. You didn't have enough to make you reckless, I reckon?'

'Right. Half the town tried to run and got blown sky high without a chance, sounded like. Them that stayed are just as likely to get themselves slaughtered by the Utes while they're still talking about what they've been doing wrong up until now, seems to me. And this town ain't got anything worth them fighting, is my opinion.'

With the saddle in place on the back of the chestnut gelding, the half-breed checked the ties that held the bedroll on behind. Then he unhooked the two canteens and took them to a trough against the back wall of the stable. He emptied out the stale water and refilled the containers from a pump at one end of the trough.

'I think these people who live in the houses and operate the business in Oro City wouldn't agree with that, sir,' Amy Yancy said from the part-open doorway.

Both the Virginian and Edge were mildly surprised to see the attractive redheaded widow standing there. But she posed no threat and the hubbub of voices and activity out on the street would have more than adequately masked the sounds of her approach.

'The big feller with all the muscles and a lot of mouth told them what to do if that's how they feel, lady,' Edge told her as he returned to his mount.

'And they are going to organise their defences, Mr Edge. But they are not soldiers or . . . or any other kind of fighting men. They are now convinced that they must fight, though. But they lack leadership . . . somebody who will use his experience to — '

'Been a lot of years since I was a soldier, lady,' the half-breed cut in as he hung the canteens back on his saddle. 'And given the choice I only fight for something worth fighting for.'

'But you helped us when the Indians attacked the stage and were about to — '

'He reckoned he didn't have a choice, Mrs Yancy,' Steele said pensively. And when Edge eyed him quizzically, added: 'The Yank and me both.'

'Because you saw that human life was at the mercy of a force of savages?'

'About it, I reckon.'

'But the same is true here! On a much larger scale.'

Edge began to lead his horse toward the doorway where the widow woman stood, trying to keep the despair off her good-looking face. But then he angled to the side, to get the near-empty whiskey bottle.

'People here ain't helpless, lady. There's a whole bunch of them with guns and they got the freedom to choose where to make their stand. Same ain't true here.'

'But they need somebody to advise them how to use what they have!' Amy Yancy insisted as Edge stowed the whiskey in a saddle bag.

'No sweat on that, lady. They got legs, they got horses, some of them got wagons, maybe. My advice is to walk or ride out of this dying town before the Utes come to finish it off. Go west, because the Indians are massing to the east. And Fort Hamilton's to the west. Unlike Oro City, the army post will have been built with defence from Indian attack in mind.' He continued on to the doorway, and the redheaded women backed out on to the street – automatically pulled open one of the doors wider so that the half-breed could lead his gelding through the gap. 'Oh, one other thing,' he went on as he swung up astride the horse after glancing along the street in each direction. 'I could be wrong.'

Steele moved across the livery threshold to stand beside the widow. Made an impassive eyed survey of both stretches of the street himself as he said evenly: 'So you're starting to find out that can happen sometimes, too, uh Yank?'

'Only fools live without learning, Reb,' the mounted man said to the one on the ground, then shifted his steady gaze to the anxious woman. 'Maybe there are Utes all around this town. In which case the people here don't have any choice about where to make their stand. If the Indians want it that way.'

There was very little sound or movement on the street. None at all on the deserted stretch in the area of the livery. And this seemed somehow to emphasise more starkly the dark stains of blood on the moonlight whitened surface of the street. Once again, the area out front of the railroad station and between the saloon and the stage-line depot was where the much diminished population of Oro City was concentrated. To watch in near total silence as Arnie Jonas, Roy Egan, Conran and Goldsmith rode their horses on to the street: returning to town with funereal deliberation from their search of the country out along the railroad track. Egan and Goldsmith were leading two horses by the reins. And even over the distance between the livery stable and the end of the sloping curve of the street, Edge and Steele and Amy Yancy could see that the limp forms draped over the saddles of the led animals were in uniform – and that the tunic sleeve on one free swinging arm bore chevrons.

'Luck to you, Edge,' the Virginian said, moving the rifle against his shoulder in a barely discernible gesture of farewell.

'Obliged, Steele. Maybe next time we'll both be headed in the same direction?'

The half-breed heeled his horse into movement.

'If there ever is a next time for anybody to be going anywhere,' Mrs Yancy murmured disconsolately as she dragged her gaze away from the troopers returning with their dead, spared just a glance for the departing Edge and then looked hopelessly at the Virginian.

Steele ignored her for a few moments to call after the rider: 'Next time I hope to be staying right where I'll be.'

'Luck to you, too,' Edge responded, raising a hand carelessy above his shoulder, then moving it down to delve into the pocket of his shirt where he kept the makings.

'Just your idea to come here, ma'am?' the Virginian asked, and the abrupt change of subject startled the widow.

'Sorry? Oh, yes. Well, Mrs Crawford was to put it to the townspeople while I made the approach to you. You and Mr Edge, I mean. I suppose it seemed as if I was talking only to him. But that was because I was anxious for him not to leave. Oh, dear.' She sighed and was momentarily embarrassed.

'It's all right, Mrs Yancy,' Steele told her evenly. 'He's always looked much more the kind of man for what you and

Mrs Crawford have in mind. And if things work out the way I plan I won't ever have to be in that kind of competition again. Meantime, I have to get out of this trouble in one piece. Alone or with anyone who is of the same mind.'

'We all, I am sure, want to survive, Mr Steele,' the widow replied woefully as she gazed down the street at where Edge had become the centre of attention. This as the half-breed rode around the rear of the crowd who had been listening to Arnie Jonas telling them about how he and the other three troopers found the latest victims of Ute vengeance. 'I don't know if Mrs Crawford had the time to broach the subject before the troopers returned with . . . but since your friend appears to have no confidence in our ability to defend this town in — '

'Just because I happen to agree with him sometimes doesn't make us friends, ma'am.'

'I'm sorry?'

The half-breed had ridden on by the throng of people out front of the railroad station and the saloon, apparently without any words being exchanged. And now, as he moved on by the town-limits marker after striking a match on his revolver butt and lighting his fresh-made cigarette, the widow returned her curious attention to the Virginian.

'We meet up with each other from time to time, ma'am,' he explained evenly. 'And on the whole I reckon it's a pretty agreeable partnership. Which usually gets broken off on account of . . . well, I reckon you could call it ill health.'

'I'm sorry?' she said again, her curiosity expanding to confusion, until she saw his grin that in the low level of light in this part of town was unmistakably boyish.

But she had looked away before the expression was replaced by a pensive frown as Steele murmured: 'Mostly we don't go our different ways until we're sick of each other.'

CHAPTER SIXTEEN

Mrs Yancy's attitude became momentarily despairing, to the point where she looked close to dropping into the same kind of temporary oblivion that had claimed Miranda Randell a few minutes earlier. But then, with an effort of will that brought her near to panting with the strain, she got a grip on self control. And her voice as she stared with mounting disdain at Adam Steele was harsh-toned.

'It seems like a very long time since I felt disposed to laugh at anything, sir. As the fact of my husband's death sank deeper and deeper into my mind. I wanted nothing more than to die and perhaps be with him in an afterlife in which I never previously believed. But the more I have seen of senseless killing and wasteful death since I left Denver to come bring home the body of Cole, the stronger has become my determination to survive. So you will have to excuse me for not finding your jokes in such circumstances as these funny in the slightest extent.'

The Virginian recognised the distinctly enunciated speech and carefully maintained expression as a shield behind which the attractive widow strove to strengthen her hold on composure. And he thought she was succeeding – had been on the point of explaining to her his attitude toward violent death. But she suddenly lunged at him, her arms encircling his neck, to press her slender body closely to him. She started to tremble and to moan inarticulate sounds into the crook of his neck.

For part of a second Steele was frozen by surprise at what she had done. And for another sliver of time was unable to see if anything outside of Amy Yancy's abruptly unbalanced mind had triggered her actions and the new assault of terror. For her auburn hair was flung across his face by the force of her move and he was briefly unsighted by it.

But then a gunshot once again shattered the brief peace that had come to Oro City. And Steele rasped an obscenity between teeth gritted in a scowl of anger as he wrenched himself violently free of the woman's grip. Brought the Colt Hartford away from his shoulder and thumbed back the hammer in a series of instinctive moves. At the same time as he stepped around Mrs Yancy – not so much to protect her as to see who fired the shot and if he might be the next target.

Down near the end of the street, the throng of townspeople and the troopers swung to gaze with shocked eyes in the same direction and curtailed just as it got started a babble of strident talk. From several yards beyond the crowd, Edge watched, too. Turned in the saddle of the gelding he had halted when he heard the gunshot.

It was a rifle that had been fired – the bullet that exploded from its muzzle blasting straight up into the night sky. And when all eyes located the rifle it remained thrust aloft. Its repeater action not pumped in the wake of the shot fired as an attention-getter. The weapon serving now as just a flagstaff, for a piece of whitish fabric was attached to the barrel. Hanging limply for a stretched second, until the man who had a two-handed grip on the Winchester was satisfied he had captured all attention and rocked the gun gently above his head, causing the improvised flag of truce to flutter listlessly from side to side.

The man who held the rifle was Black Hawk. And, Steele realised, it could well have been Edward Sun's Winchester – and the truce flag could be the young man's shirt or undershirt. For the half-Chinese who had tricked the local preacher and let the Ute sub-chief out of the gaolhouse was standing alongside the former prisoner. A prisoner himself now, naked to the waist and with his hands tied behind his back. To either side of Black Hawk and Sun, eight more Ute braves were evenly divided: each with a repeater rifle angled across his chest, aimed skywards but ready cocked and tightly held.

This line of ten men whom Amy Yancy had glimpsed just

part of a second before the shot was fired, were on foot. They were ranged across the centre of the main street where the side street intersected with it between the church and the law office.

'I and my brothers are willing to die here and now if the white eyes do not honour flag of truce!' Black Hawk announced, monotoned, into the hard silence that followed the abrupt cessation of murmuring talk.

'Say your piece, you murderin' sonofabitch!' the instantly recognisable voice of Ernie Monk roared.

This triggered another buzz of talk among the crowd, with a timbre that suggested the big-built redheaded man was being rebuked. This as the redheaded woman who stood behind Adam Steele murmured:

'Oh, God. Oh, God. Please let it end.'

'Easy, ma'am,' the Virginian said softly, and as he made to glance at her found his attention captured by what Edge was engaged in out on the trail. The half-breed was just finishing drinking from what was surely the whiskey bottle – for the moonlight glinted in reflection on the glass as he lowered it from his face. Then he hurled it away, drew the back of a hand across his lips, hung the cigarette from the side of his mouth again and heeled his gelding forward – heading away from Oro City once more as if he were unaware of this latest event.

'Easy,' he told Amy Yancy again, and took a step away from her and out of the moon shadow of the livery stable. Was thus certain Black Hawk and the other Utes were aware of him being the closest white man to them as he canted his rifle to his shoulder again. Raised his voice to offer the assurance: 'Like to think I'm speaking for all of us here when I promise to hear you out, Black Hawk. Long as you and your braves honour that flag, too.'

All the Utes remained wooden-faced, which made the abject terror on Edward Sun's Oriental features all the more plain to see. Then, as the flanking braves continued to rake their dark-eyed stares this way and that – not failing to see the half-breed riding unhurriedly out along the west trail – Black Hawk gave a curt nod and fixed his gaze on the Virginian. A moment later dropped his right hand to his side but kept the Winchester held high over head with the left one.

'It is as I say to you once before, Adam Steele!' Black Hawk answered, speaking as loudly as the Virginian. Which was not shouting. Their voices pitched just high enough so that what was said would carry to the large group of tensely attentive listeners at the end of the street. 'The Utes seek vengeance only against those who make the first move. I now draw my knife to free this man who is neither white eyes nor Indian and who is fool and coward.'

He slid a knife from the sheath on his weapons belt and leaned to the side, his right fist and the blade protruding out of it going from sight behind Edward Sun who was near to collapsing from terror.

'Edward!' Miranda Randell shrieked from the threshold of the Paydirt Cafe.

The youngster's hands, one with a length of rope hanging from the wrist, fell limply into view at his sides. And Black Hawk pushed the knife back in the sheath as he rasped some scornful words at Sun. But Sun seemed physically incapable of moving from the spot on the street where he stood in the line of scowling Indians.

Steele shot the briefest of glances over his shoulder. Focused only on the doorway of the cafe where he saw both Annie and Milton were restraining the homely woman as she fought them in an effort to lunge outside. Then he returned his gaze to Black Hawk and Sun. And growled:

'Jerome Randell's dead, feller. So's the only bounty hunter who came here to collect on you. The daughter's in town to give you another chance. Up to you.'

Sun had been staring frantically between the cafe entrance and the crowd of citizens who were starting to be agitated with impatience by this delaying side issue. Now he gazed intently at the Virginian, mistrustful of everything about his surroundings, and swallowed hard twice before he was able to force out:

'But everybody will want me dead, sir. I tricked the parson and took Black Hawk from the gaol and tried to escape —'

'Edward!' Miranda wailed again.

'This thing's bigger than the both of you, feller,' Steele said, his tone just short of a snarl.

The youngster gulped again, nodded curtly and brought his right hand up to his mouth. Began to chew on the nails as he stepped away from the line of Utes. He walked in a shuffling gait for a few feet, then lengthened his stride and looked even more stiffly unnatural. Finally, after shooting a glance over his shoulder at the Indians, he broke into a staggering run that quickly took him past where Steele and Amy Yancy stood. Some scorn was directed at him but mostly he was ignored: and once he was inside the cafe with the beanpole-thin woman he was forgotten.

'I speak for my grandfather, the great Chief Red Eagle!' Black Hawk said when the door of the Paydirt Cafe had been slammed shut and he was certain he commanded the attention of everyone on the street. 'Red Eagle who is chief of the whole Ute nation. Whole Ute nation has met in council. To consider what must be done to avenge the Massacre of Arroyo Bend.'

As before, the sub-chief with the flag of truce held aloft on the rifle spoke to Adam Steele: but ensured his voice was loud enough so that his words and ominous tone carried through the tension heavy, chill night air to the more distant listeners.

'Seems to us you done enough slaughterin' of innocent white folks on account of what the army done to you — '

'Shut up, Monk!' the Virginian bellowed without turning around, halting the powerfully built man in mid-sentence and also cutting across the mumbling of agreement that had started. 'Let the man have his say!'

Now there was a tone of antagonism in the wave of rasping whispering that followed Steele's censure. But this was in turn curtailed by Black Hawk when he advised:

'You white eyes better listen to what I come here to tell you! And I tell you this, as I am instructed by the chiefs of the Utes who have met in council and come to agreement to take the path of war!' He addressed Steele, and the trembling woman beside the Virginian, as just one section of his audience now. Glanced at them with excitement-fired eyes only every now and then. Just as he looked at the frightened and silent crowd and to either side of the street and up at the star-pricked, moon-glowed sky. Showing his strong-featured face with its frenzied expression to every living being and inanimate object – and even to whatever Gods the living creatures possessed of souls chose to worship.

'There is no escape for any white eyes who has occupied the lands of the Ute nation. Already many have paid the price for the sins of their brothers and their forefathers against our brothers and forefathers. And soon, all here will — '

'Black Hawk!' Steele rasped.

The Ute sub-chief was briefly confused to be stopped in the full flood of his rhetoric. Then anger ignited a different kind of fire in his eyes and the braves flanking him were gripped by the same glowering mood as they all stared fixedly at the Virginian.

'You tell your brothers I am to be allowed to say what Chief Red Eagle sends me here to say, Adam Steele! Now it is you who — '

'Get it said, feller! We know all about the killing the Utes have done since the army started the trouble at Arroyo Bend. And we don't want to hear about settlers stealing Indian lands. Just get to the point, why don't you!'

'That's damn right, mister!' Mayor DeWitt yelled up the street. 'This could all be a part of some sneaky Injun trickery to keep us occupied while — '

Black Hawk threw back his head and vented a burst of laughter at the night sky. Harshly derisive and quick to finish as he once again commanded silent attention that was for the most part fearful. Then, his expression abruptly menacing and his tone earnest, he shouted: 'You were already occupied, concerned with more dead who fell to Ute vengeance! There is no treachery here, white eyes! I come to tell you that more than three hundred Ute warriors are encamped on the far side of this hill where we stand now.'

He continued to thrust the rifle become a flagstaff into the air at the limit of his arm's reach – apparently feeling no undue strain under its weight. This as, with his free hand, he gestured up the hillslope. 'I come to tell you that when the new day's sun rises above the crest of the hill, these Ute warriors will begin the final act that will — '

'You're doing it again, Black Hawk!' Steele cut in, less vehemently than before.

And this time the Ute sub-chief was only momentarily irritated by the interruption. And perhaps his nod was of agreement with the Virginian and even appreciative acknowledgement. He addressed himself exclusively to Steele again, but loud enough for all to hear.

'You will know I speak truth because of what fool and coward tells you?'

'Had to be some reason you let him live and turned him loose, feller.'

'That is right, Adam Steele. But because he is fool and coward, he could not be trusted to return and tell all he has seen. Now you know all, I and my brothers who are not cowards because we have come here will go back to far side of hill.'

'Neither cowards nor fools, I reckon?'

'Because you are warned that we Utes will come to kill you white eyes at sun up? That is not foolish, Adam Steele.' Now he raised his voice and peered down the street again, to emphasise that he was addressing himself to all in a position to see and hear him. 'There are many ways to die! You will have heard of and perhaps seen some of the many ways in which the avenging Utes can inflict terrible death upon their enemies!' He used his free hand to gesture toward the quartet of now wooden-faced braves aligned to each side of him. 'I and my brothers have come with the warning of what fate awaits you as the new day starts! So that in the hours of the night that are still to pass before the sun rises above the crest of the hill, you may die a thousand times in your — '

'Grateful to you for the message, Black Hawk,' Steele said as he heard Mrs Yancy catch her breath and felt the brush of her fingertips against his jacket sleeve as she reached out for a comforting contact with him but then decided it might be unwise or to no avail to touch him. 'Don't reckon there's any reply.'

'I got a whole lot I want to say to him and his bunch of — ' Ernie Monk started.

'The truce!' Black Hawk roared, and moderated his voice when Monk's voice and the many raised in agreement were silenced. 'The truce will remain until I and my brothers have withdrawn?'

'Kill him,' Amy Yancy rasped, and perhaps intended that only Steele should hear what she said. Or maybe the mixture of terror and vindictiveness that had a grip on her was having a constricting effect on her vocal chords. 'Kill all of them . . . there'll be that many less to come for us when the sun — '

'Long as your flag stays high and the rest of the braves don't do anything stupid, Black Hawk!' Steele promised – making the offer quickly as he detected a shrillness in the widow's voice that might signal a much louder outburst which in turn could trigger a panicked reaction from the jittery crowd.

'Men of honour are rare breed among white eyes, Adam Steele,' Black Hawk replied, and for the first time his voice was pitched so that just Steele and the frightened widow could hear him as he and the other Utes backed away across the intersection. 'Why do not you and this woman follow example of your friend and make escape to the west? To the fort?'

The gap between them, that got wider by the moment, kept the Ute's voice from being a conspiratorial whisper. But it was obvious the sub-chief was trying not to move his lips over much while his dark eyes expressed cunning intrigue that came close, perhaps, to the Ute equivalent of a white man's wink. Then the backward-stepping braves moved into the moon shadow of a building, where they were seen to whirl hurriedly before they broke into a swift run that carried them out of sight around the bend in the street.

'You should have — ' Amy Yancy began, still softly but with a note of shrillness in her voice.

'Shut up and listen!' Steele snapped, his own voice lower but more insistent than that of the woman. And, before lengthening distance augmented by a furor of fervid talk from the crowd made further concentrated listening futile, both the Virginian and she heard the tell-tale sounds of many more than nine pairs of moccasined feet scampering away through the town on the slope.

'There were reinforcements hidden in back of them!' the woman gasped. 'So if you had done as I pleaded . . . ?'

'Good few of us wouldn't have lived to fight another day, I reckon,' he replied pensively as he continued to rake his dark-eyed gaze over the street that curved into the mid-town area up the hill. Unable to hear any sounds from up there against the body of vocal noise from down near the foot of the slope, but putting to the test that sixth sense for lurking danger that was no longer as reliable as it used to be. Tonight he experienced no warnings that he was being watched with hostile intent from out of the dangerous darkness.

But, as Amy Yancy did tentatively touch his coat sleeve, was not rebuffed and so fastened a loose grip on the crook of his arm, he was aware of a mass of less than friendly attention being directed toward him from the quietening crowd on the brightly lit stretch of street.

'It was because you and Mr Edge kept him from being murdered by the troopers, I expect,' the woman murmured as they started down the street.

'Uh?' he grunted, still deep in thought.

'The reason Mr Edge was allowed to leave unmolested and that Indian offered you safe passage away from this town.'

'That's how you understood it, ma'am?' he asked, and allowed her to continue to hold his arm as he used the gloved knuckles of his hand gripping the Colt Hartford to rasp over the bristles on his jawline. There continued to be a quality of distance from the here and now in his voice and expression.

'Why else should he choose to be so merciful toward you and Mr Edge? Me because I was with you and heard the offer, of course. I do not feel able to come with you, but if you feel you would rather the others know nothing of what was said, I am prepared to remain silent until after you have left. Because I am another of those saved from . . . well, had it not been for you and Mr Edge, I would not be here now — '

The crowd of people had packed more closely together between the saloon and the stage-line depot and the agitated talk had lessened as the good-looking redhead and her escort drew nearer. And eventually just the bulkily built, bloated-faced Edith Crawford could be heard – delivering a fast-spoken speech to the townspeople closest to her.

' — I was just starting to tell these folk of the proposition you have put to Mr Steele, my dear!' the older woman broke in on what the widow was whispering to the Virginian. 'Since his companion has left Oro City, I can presume he was not interested in — '

'What proposition, lady?' Ernie Monk demanded from a section of the crowd that had previously been beyond earshot of Mrs Crawford's voice.

'Yes, ma'am, as strangers to this town, I hardly think it's right that you oughta make arrangements for the rest of us — ' Mayor DeWitt hurried to proclaim as he stepped up on to the sidewalk at the front of the saloon, which compensated for his lack of height by placing him in a position where he could be seen by everyone.

'Well, I think it's a fine idea!'

'Though what good it'll serve if there are more than three hundred savages ready and waitin' to hit us, I'm darned if I know!'

'He don't look like much to me!'

'If he can use that rifle good as they say?'

'Reckon there's enough rifles in town for every man, woman and child to have one, Ezra! And I reckon all we can do is barricade ourselves in our homes and — '

Many of the townspeople had rifles and revolvers they had brought out on to the street and down from the hill in the wake of the raid by the Utes. Now some of these thrust the weapons in the air and yelled agreement or disagreement with this. Until, his round face crinkled with an angry frown, DeWitt snatched a revolver from a nearby hand: grasped it around the barrel and used the base of the butt to hammer on a sidewalk roof support. It took a number of violent blows to restore order. The exertion compounded by earlier fear and anger left the grey-haired little man in the shabby city-suit breathless. But his glowering stare raked back and forth over the assembly and served to maintain the disquiet peace until he was recovered sufficiently to ask:

'Now, Mrs Crawford, ma'am . . . in our present situation we must be prepared to give a hearin' any proposition that may mean our salvation. But unless all interested parties – that is, everybody in Oro City – is made aware of — '

'Charlie DeWitt!' a woman yelled angrily, 'you're soundin' off worse than that there savage that just told us we got until sun up to get ourselves defended! That kinda talk ain't gonna help nothin', seems to me! Unless it's the savages, by wastin' time!'

On this occasion the sudden chorus of voices was exclusively in accord with what the woman had said. Against the barrage of competing in agreement sounds, Steele eased out of Amy Yancy's undemanding hold on his arm and drawled:

'That lady talked a lot of sense, ma'am. Be grateful if you don't mention Black Hawk's offer yet awhile.'

'Where are you going?' she asked anxiously, dividing her nervous attention between the Virginian and Edith Crawford who had broken from the crowd to come toward her.

'I reckon I'll be leaving soon. But not how the Utes want me to.' His dark eyes asked for her pledge.

'All right,' she called after him, surreptitiously agreeing to his request for secrecy on the Ute chief's escape plan as she was joined by Edith Crawford who had no reason to ask about her non-committal parting comment to the Virginian.

This as Adam Steele stepped up on to the sidewalk out front of the Paydirt Cafe and DeWitt allowed in a disgruntled tone:

'Very well, then let us have Mrs Crawford tell us all what she has in mind to . . .'

Steele failed to hear the rest of what the mayor said as more than a muted mumble, for he had stepped inside the cafe and closed the door behind him. Noted in passing that just a bloodstain on the floor revealed there had been a violent death in the place – and this had been scrubbed at to fade its vividness at the same time as the two disarranged tables had been reset. Annie or Milton or both had also taken the time to remove the dirty dishes and reset the table by the stove where he had eaten his meal. Miranda Randell and Edward Sun sat at opposite sides of this table now, the young half-Chinese wearing the plain woman's coat slung cape-fashion around his bare shoulders. The two of them, each holding both the hands of the other, had obviously been deeply involved in intense conversation before the opening of the door and intrusion of the Virginian put a stop to it.

'God willing that we survive this terrible time, Mr Steele,' the woman said with high excitement bubbling just beneath the surface of earnest solemnity as she looked constantly from the uneasy Edward Sun to the impassive Virginian and back, 'we are to be married at the first opportunity.'

'Miranda does not seem to appreciate how serious our situation is, Mr Steele,' the youngster explained apprehensively, and tried without success to ease free of her clasping hands.

'Three hundred Utes about right, feller?'

'Yes, sir. At least that many.'

'So it's going to be quite a fight, I reckon,' the Virginian drawled. 'And with a wedding due, I guess we have to make sure that more than just the best man wins.'

CHAPTER SEVENTEEN

THE SKY domed over the dying community of Oro City was in process of lightening from star-pricked black to a featureless grey shade of blue, but the leading arc of the new day's sun had not yet risen above the brow of the hill on which the town stood, when the two strings of horses were spotted far out along the west trail.

Because the Ute sentries and lookouts had the advantage of elevated positions up on the hilltop, they were first to see the movement of something dark against the lighter shade of the trail: that gradually came closer and took on the material form of thirty or more horses in a column of two.

But even before one of the Indian sentries had moved stealthily away from his secret watching place and then run swiftly down the blind side of the hill to report the new development to Red Eagle and the sub-chiefs at the encampment where battle preparations were nearing completion, many of the townspeople and enforced overnight visitors on the lower slope of the hill's western side had become aware of the approaching column.

Just one of the weary watchers, peering out of a dusty window of the railroad station's spartan waiting-room, glimpsed the distant dark specks when they first moved into view at this level. This was the baby-faced Trooper Roy Egan, who fisted the grit of sleeplessness from his eyes and instinctively snatched up his carbine as he did a double-take. Then, as soon as he was certain of what he saw, the young cavalryman shook the muscular shoulder of the dozing Ernie Monk who had shared this sentry post during the long night hours.

'He did it, sir!' the trooper told the irritable-on-waking

redhaired man excitedly. 'That guy you figured for a weak-kneed dude with no backbone done what he said he would!'

Monk, recalling where he was and the circumstances that had brought him here, ceased his ill-humoured cursing and rose from the floor to peer from the window along the daybreak-lighted trail that stretched westward. Then allowed grudgingly: 'So I was wrong about Steele, soldier. But what's a handful of troopers gonna do against all them Utes over the other side of the hill?'

'Obliged if you'd tell the others, sir,' Egan muttered to the scowling civilian as he tried to make an accurate estimate of how many riders were in the distant column: and was conscious of his initial enthusiasm draining out of him because of Monk's pessimism. 'But best not to make too much noise about it, in case the Injuns ain't spotted our boys yet.'

Monk's ruddy complexioned face showed disdain for the trooper's naiveté, but complied with the request: and started a chain of muted shouts, eerie-sounding in the brittle surrounding stillness of early morning, that conveyed the news up the curve of the street and back and forth between the facades of the flanking buildings.

The strained softness of Monk's tone that was imitated by the others who passed on what he said served to affect everyone else who heard about or was in a position to see the far-off column of riders approaching Oro City. And the various reactions to this turn of events were tautly muted. Responses that ran an uneven gamut between the kind of spirit elevating joy that Egan had initially experienced to the heart-sickening gloom with which Monk had greeted the sight he patently had never expected to see. A large majority of the rest of those who had spent the night in the besieged town had also not counted on seeing it, either.

The passing on of the news and the suppressed excitement or despondency that it triggered extended no further into town than the church and the law office opposite where the main street curved across the intersection with the lowest side street. For from this point up to where the Ute lookouts were positioned in stands of timber and thickets of brush between the brow of the hill and the start of the street's twisting and turning route down the slope, Oro City was a no-man's-land. The utterly deserted thoroughfare flanked by lifeless houses and stores and other commercial premises; the streets that cut off to either side were just as empty between closed-up and abandoned buildings.

Just where the surviving former occupants of these vacated buildings aligned along the forsaken streets should spend the fraught-with-fear hours of darkness had been left for them to decide after all the talking was done and the strategy agreed upon. But, because by and large the human animal has a herd instinct that is particularly compelling at times of danger, only one elderly couple had wanted to see out the night and what the morning would bring in their own small house along a side street.

However, soon after they realised they were the only exceptions among their hundred or so fellow citizens, the old lady convinced her near-senile husband they should remain with the rest. In the railroad depot, The Golden Place saloon, the Ingot Hotel, the Paydirt Cafe and the church along the northern side of the western end of the main street. And in the depot of the Central Western Stageline Company, the Miner's Rest boarding house, Livesey's Livery Stables and the law office on the south side of the final curve before the town-limits marker and the open trail beyond.

Just Egan and Monk were in the exposed railroad depot. Diagonally across from here stood the stage-line depot where Calvin Brownlow, his eyes sadder and his moustache more ragged after a sleepless night, had Edith Crawford, Amy Yancy, Miranda Randell and Edward Sun for uneasy company. At the other end of the stretch of street where all the whites were concentrated, Troopers Jonas and Conran and Goldsmith kept watch from the law office and gaolhouse at the rear. While the most devout of the local population waited in the church, seemingly unconcerned by the macabre knowledge that the vestry was a temporary storehouse for the unburied dead of the past two days.

Women with children had been given first choice of rooms with beds in the hotel, saloon and boarding house. The old couple, who had been the last to agree that it would be best for everyone to stay close in the most solidly constructed and easiest to defend buildings in town, had chosen to share the livery stable with all of Oro City's livestock: which included chickens, roosters, dogs, four burros and three milk cows in addition to two dozen horses.

Every able-bodied man over the age of sixteen was in possession of a rifle or revolver. Females from a much younger age were charged with the reloading task. A half dozen of the oldest and frailest women had volunteered to take care of the youngest children while their parents were engaged in fighting off the attacking Utes.

This was how it had all been arranged or came about without organised planning after Adam Steele rode away from Oro City in the cold wake of Edge last night. And now, as many of the animals within the foul-smelling confines of the livery stable began to whinny and bark, crow and low in apprehensive greeting of the new day, everyone moved with varying degrees of reluctance to undertake his or her appointed or voluntary role in whatever drama was to be enacted as the leading arc of the bright yellow sun showed above the smooth ridge of the hill to the south east.

A few seconds later, the crest of the rise over a distance of perhaps fifty yards on and to each side of the trail was a mass of unhurried movement as thirty or so Utes astride their ponies rode into sight.

The braves and their mounts were starkly skylined against the constantly lightening blueness of the backdrop of fully broken dawn as they came to a brief halt. At the centre of the row, attired in a double-tailed war bonnet of eagle feathers, buckskin war shirt, breechclouts and leggings, was the old and frail Chief Red Eagle – the crimson colouring with which his headdress feathers had been dyed leaving none in any doubt that this was the chief of the whole Ute nation. Less resplendently dressed, his son, Straight Arrow, was to Red Eagle's right and his grandson, Black Hawk, sat astride a pony to the old man's left. But what the lesser-ranked Utes lacked in the quantity and colourfulness of their garb they made up for with the vividness of war-paint that was daubed on their broad faces and muscular bodies. Yellows and greens and whites and reds in streaks and patches and zigzags and arrowhead designs.

The braves below the rank of suc-chief who were spread out to either side of the centrally placed trio were less brightly adorned and few wore more than one feather in the back of their headbands. Here and there a Ute wore the hat of a white man. Some were garbed in other items of clothing undoubtedly stolen from the body of a white corpse or taken by force before the owner was put to death. But most were dressed only in leggings or breechclouts so that their upper bodies and faces were left bare and unshaded to display crudely or skilfully applied war-paint designs.

A fear that seemed to chill the air that should have been warmed by the rising sun had suddenly entered the inhabited section of Oro City as the line of Indians heeled their ponies forward and then reined them to a halt at the top of the hill. And the animals in the livery were caught up in the same eerie spell that acted to constrict throats and trap the breath in the lungs of the terrified humans – and not a hoof nor paw nor claw was scraped or scratched as heads were cocked, ears were pricked, nostrils flared and eyes blinked.

'Ten times that many is what the Injun and the Chink told us, Arnie,' the near-bald, ginger-moustached Goldsmith rasped from where he stood at the cracked open door of the law office, peering up at the hill crest with one eye to the gap.

The short and broad Jonas, his square face impassive instead of fixed with the usual scowl, stood at a nearby window which, because of the way the street curved, gave him a viewpoint to the ridge almost as good as Goldsmith had from the doorway and Conran commanded from a barred side window of the gaolhouse behind the office. This oldest of the troopers – who had assumed command of the uniformed men and improved in temperament after Corporal McNally was killed – nodded briefly and answered:

'Just the top brass, I guess, Kris. Big chief with all the head feathers. Black Hawk up there with him, I see. So I guess that's Black Hawk's old man – the big chief's son – on the other side. Rest will be somethin' special, I figure. Here come some more.'

Elsewhere in this part of Oro City, pent-up breath was released noisily from straining lungs. And some muted squeals of fear were vented through gritted teeth.

The animals jostled each other and complained about their uneasiness in subdued versions of their various cries. That perhaps suggested some of them were close to panic.

A baby howled and another whimpered.

Fists tightened around revolver butts and rifle barrels. Forefingers toyed with the triggers and thumbs caressed hammers.

Children old enough to understand the menacing situation began to question the people who had charge of them. And were shushed into lip-chewing, tear-threatening, dry-swallowing silence.

Those in a position to see to the top of the hill rasped a terse commentary on what was taking place up there to the men and women unable to see for themselves.

Some of the heavily bristled faces of the men and the drawn features of the women were dry and shiny with the sensation of icy coldness of which they could not shake free. Others were slickly sheened with sweat which had erupted in the wake of the initial jolt of fear that had seemed to interrupt their circulation and freeze the blood in their veins for long seconds.

The Utes were on the move.

Within a minute, Chief Red Eagle's entire army of vengeance-bent braves had ridden into sight on the brow of the hill where the trail ran past the town-limits marker to become the meandering main street of Oro City. Rank after rank of war-painted Indians rode up and over the crest of the rise as the first line to emerge into view advanced down the slope at a measured pace. Whatever sounds were made by the scowling Indians and their docile ponies were not loud enough to carry down the slope to the lower end of the street. If any hand signals were given they were not sufficiently emphatic to be seen by the anxiously watching whites.

But what the whites could not fail to be aware of was the perfect order that prevailed among the mass of serenely unimpassioned Utes as they all now came to a smooth halt. To wait patiently for the command that would transform them into a charging horde of raging savages: giving vent to bloodcurdling whoops and war-cries as they raced down the hillside to commence the slaughter of the white eyes they hated.

Were there three hundred or more of them, as had been claimed? Nobody had the inclination to make a head count of the calmly waiting braves who sat their quiet ponies as the sun inched higher into the azure sky. And, probably, nobody thought there would be enough time left to do more than make a start on such a futile exercise before the attack was launched. But certainly those watching and waiting whites who were not driven into total mindlessness by their fear at the mere sight of so many war-painted Indians were able to estimate that that number looked to be about right. Which meant that Red Eagle was not holding many, if any, warriors in reserve. Why should he . . . ?

'What the frig they waitin' for, Arnie?' the stockily built and squint-eyed Conran called into the law office from his post at the cell window in the gaolhouse. 'I figured for sure they'd come chargin' over the hill and down at us with the sun behind them soon as — '

'The boys from the fort and that pint-size dude have got them interested, I guess,' Jonas answered inattentively from where he continued to stand at the window, a frown of deep thought on his square face. At present he had one of the best vantage points in town to keep watch on both the motionless mass of Indians at the top of the hill and the slow-moving column out on the west trail. And he constantly turned his head one way and then the other as the frown cut deeper lines into his element-burnished, unshaven face. Then he did a double-take to the west and vented a soft grunt of comprehension as he snapped his fingers.

'You figured something out, Arnie?' Kris Goldsmith asked eagerly and hopefully from the part-opened door.

Then despair fastened a grip on his features as he was given a reply.

'Dead! They're all friggin' dead!'

Not all. Not the Virginian and the half-breed who rode at the head of the double-file column, each wearing a sheepskin coat against the chill of the night that was no more and a kerchief over his mouth and nostrils to combat the sickening stench of death that grew more powerful in the warming air.

Adam Steele said evenly: 'I know we're hauling a lot of dead weight, Yank . . .'

'Sure, Reb,' Edge answered in the same tone. 'But it's time we started to look alive.'

CHAPTER EIGHTEEN

BOTH MEN asked their mounts for a trot and the chestnut gelding and black stallion complied at once to the touch of heels to their flanks.

Just for a few seconds the increased pace was a little ragged as the strings of animals on lead lines behind each of the front runners took the time to understand what was meant by the tautening of the linking ropes and to adjust to the different speed. But then all the horses trotted with the same will as those of Edge and Steele: eyes bright, ears pricked and nostrils flared as they relished the much-needed exercise after too long cooped up in the Fort Hamilton stable block and then the slow trudge through the early hours from the post to this close to town. And maybe, too, their equine minds considered the increased speed might carry them clear of the insidiously sweet smell of mass death with which they had become so uneasily familiar in recent days and nights.

But, since there was the decomposing corpse of a man lashed to the saddle of each of the cavalry horses in the column, there was to be no escape yet from the putrid stench of the long-time dead for these hapless creatures.

The gelding and stallion in the lead were more fortunate, and their riders also welcomed the turn of speed – for the slipstream it created which acted to sweep the stink of death behind them after it had hovered around them for so long at the fort and during the journey back to town. And first Steele, then Edge, jerked down the largely ineffective kerchief masks that had been covering their mouths and nostrils. After which each man spared a brief but intent glance into the dirt-streaked, unshaven, gaunt-with-weariness face of the other.

'You've never looked good to me, Yank!' the Virginian said as he returned his dark-eyed gaze to the still-motionless mass of Utes on the hilltop. 'But right now you could look a whole lot worse.'

'Likewise, Reb,' Edge countered, and returned his glittering-eyed gaze to the lower section of Oro City. 'Figure soon we're going to see a whole bunch of people looking a lot sicker than you look and I feel.'

'You know something?'

'You're going to tell me.'

'I really never expected to find you at the fort fixing this up.'

Steele jerked a thumb over his shoulder at the strings of horses with the thirty soldiers, all dead from disease, draped over their saddles. The corpses were bent over backwards and unshrouded, so that their smallpox-ravaged and putrifying faces were exposed to left and right of the double lines: and, too, the extent of emaciation to their frames could be seen from the way the uniforms hung on the wasted bodies. Each of these uniforms adorned with the insignia of the wearer's rank: from lowly trooper to full major.

'Never did think to have you lend a hand with the chore, Reb,' Edge replied as he and the Virginian rode past the town-limits marker and on to the first stretch of street across the front of the railroad depot. 'About time now, you figure?'

'I reckon.'

Both men reached forward with a right hand to slide his rifle from the boot. And thrust it high into the air – to ensure that the Utes massed at the top of the hill could see the makeshift flags of truce that fluttered from the barrel ends in the slipstream of the trot.

Even had there been need of further talk between the two sheepskin-coated, Stetson-hatted men leading the corpse-burdened horses into Oro City, it would have been futile to attempt an exchange against the barrage of vocal sounds that exploded from the buildings to either side of them. But everything that needed to be said between them had been exhausted at Fort Hamilton.

Where Edge had gone with the conviction that he would

find more dead than living cavalrymen. And had it in mind for his own reasons to bring all the unburied corpses he could find back to Oro City in just such a way as he was doing – except that he had not counted on the Virginian's assistance.

Just as Adam Steele, who had reached the same conclusion as the half-breed about the situation at the fort – and how it might be used to combat the Ute threat – had been more than a little surprised to find Edge already started on putting into effect the plan he had in mind when he rode out of Oro City in the tracks of the half-breed. He considered he had good reason for what he was doing, too. But such issues were unimportant in the context of what both men had to do.

And all the talking that needed to be done now was to Red Eagle and his sub-chiefs. If that had the desired effect, then maybe what was important to each of these men as individuals might get to be spoken of – but the circumstances would have to be right.

Right now, the ice-blue eyes of Edge flicked back and forth between their slitted lids, making a careful study of the building facades with the gun-toting men poised at their doorways and windows with equally fearful women in back of them. His face remained impassive as he rasped:

'Maybe it wasn't such a good idea not to tell them what you had in mind, Reb?'

'Didn't hear you yelling it from the rooftops, Yank,' Steele answered, and knew that most of what he said had been lost under the tumult of noise from behind them.

Although he had chosen to concentrate his attention on the massed Utes, the Virginian had been peripherally aware of the high emotion that had been generated among the whites as he and Edge brought the gruesome moving tableau into Oro City. But, like the half-breed, he had not had the time to offer even a tacit sign of reassurance to the citizenry, strangers and troopers who were stunned into silence and suddenly shocked into turmoil. And perhaps neither stone-faced man could have succeeded in such an aim even if there had been ample time to try – since they had no confidence to spare in what they were attempting to do.

Then the two living riders led the horses of the thirty dead ones beyond the church and the law office and around the curve of the rising street. And were briefly lost to the view of the screaming and shrieking, yelling and cursing whites whose response to the sight of the flags of truce was as nothing as they saw at close quarters the brutal and macabre manner in which the smallpox victims of Fort Hamilton were displayed in the light of the new day, brightening by the moment.

But soon the clamour was drowned out by lengthening distance and the even-paced thudding of many hooves at the trot. And the sense of being stared at with a multitude of powerful emotions was no longer affecting either Steele or Edge when they knew they had ridden far enough up the snaking street to be in sight of the whites again. And the itch that had made itself unnervingly felt between the shoulder blades of each man was suddenly gone.

For the silently glowering horde of Ute Indians who continued to wait, stock-still, at the top of the hill, was directing toward them a near palpable emanation that demanded every iota of their awareness. And, too, each man would have been prepared to admit there and then that an ice-cold fear in the pit of his belly was also a contributing factor.

'Sonofabitch, Reb, if these Utes don't go for this, it's going to be a crazy way for us to die!' Edge rasped through clenched teeth as he began to rein in his mount.

'It was your idea before it was mine,' the Virginiar growled, moving his lips even less than the half-breed as he began to slow his stallion to the same extent.

'You could have told me there are exceptions to every rule. And it ain't always great minds that think alike.'

All the horses were moving at an easy walk again as the two riders at the head of the strings came within a hundred yards of where Red Eagle, Black Hawk and Straight Arrow sat their ponies in the centre of the street level with the town-limits marker.

'Let's hope we're not all that exceptional, Yank.'

'If I had some more of Livesey's sipping whiskey, I'd drink to that, Reb.'

'Hadn't been for whiskey, feller, none of this would have happened,' Steele reminded.

Edge directed a globule of saliva into the dust and muttered: 'That's a sobering thought.'

Red Eagle spoke some fast words of command and to either side of him Black Hawk and Straight Arrow thrust their rifles forward and upwards, in single-handed grips and sideways on to the advancing white men. Gestures that were patently meant to tell Steele and Edge that they should halt. And this they did, some thirty feet away from the centre of the front rank of Utes. The army-trained horses, familiar with drilling in columns, came to a calm halt in back of the leading animals.

The half-breed and the Virginian, their right arms still thrust into the sky to hold the Winchester and Colt Hartford at the limits of their reach, found it virtually impossible to read anything significant in the faces of the massed Utes. For the countenance of the aged chief might have been carved from inanimate brown rock while his entire band of warriors, because of the intended effect of the war-paint, expressed solely savage aggressiveness.

'So, Edge and Adam Steele, you are not the cowards you appeared when — '

Black Hawk was forced to curtail what he was saying when Red Eagle issued another command in his native tongue. An order that triggered his son and grandson into lowering their rifles. And caused all the other Utes to bring their rifles into sight – but angled across their paint-daubed chests, as yet not pointed at a target. Red Eagle spoke again when the noise of movement diminished and, as before, only his lips and the slack skin at his throat moved to vent the words. Everything else about his face and body and limbs remained eerily unmoving.

Black Hawk spoke a short sentence in his own language, then continued in American: 'The white eyes honoured Ute flag of truce in the night. The chief of whole Ute nation will hear what you wish to say.'

Straight Arrow, who was closer to the age of his son than to his father, spoke in an undertone to the chief, obviously able to understand what Black Hawk was saying and giving Red Eagle a translation.

'It isn't much,' Steele said flatly, it having been agreed back at the fort that if they got this far, he would be the spokesman. 'Reckon Red Eagle and all the Utes here can see what we've brought from Fort Hamilton?'

Because of the slope of the ground, the lines of Indians with vividly daubed pictographs on their hard-set faces were ranged in a tier-like formation – all of them looking down and clearly seeing the two living white civilians and thirty dead soldiers.

'I was able to tell Chief Red Eagle of the sickness that struck down many horsesoldiers at the fort, white eyes,' Black Hawk replied flatly. 'Do you think you can light the fires of fear of such sickness in us by bringing — '

Once again the stone-faced chief uttered a curt order that cut off his grandson in mid-sentence. And this time, despite the war-paint that was like a mask, it was possible to detect irritation in the attitude of the sub-chief as he translated:

'You are to get said quickly what it is you have to say.'

Both Edge and Steele were sweating, and this not just because of the rising heat of the sun and the physical strain of keeping the heavy rifles high in the still air that did not flutter the strips of white fabric tied to the barrels. Rather, fear of the outcome of what they were doing was no longer a cold and controlled feeling. Had been in danger of breaking free of a lifetime of constraint until the inscrutable Chief Red Eagle made it plain that he meant what he said about being ready to hear them out.

Steele swallowed hard and Edge held back from a spit as he realised it could be misconstrued.

'It's our belief that Chief Red Eagle can't now finish this fight how he intended,' the Virginian said, and his voice had a tremor for the first few words but then steadied. 'Because all but for a handful of the men from Fort Hamilton who he blames for the Arroyo Bend Massacre and what happened afterwards are dead. You and your braves accounted for many of them and the smallpox killed the others. Including Major Crawford.'

Adam Steele paused, inviting the aged chief to say

something after this had been translated for him. But Red Eagle continued to stare fixedly ahead, and might have appeared to be rigidly dead himself had it not been for the way in which he infrequently blinked and the manner in which his nostrils flared almost indiscernibly with his measured breathing.

'Red Eagle wanted more than just the slaughter of whites here, there and everywhere,' the Virginian went on. 'That's why you were sent into this town last night, Black Hawk. To tell us there would be no more killing until sun up. And to plant the idea that we should all leave Oro City and head for Fort Hamilton. But we would never have gotten through the gate, would we? Not the way Edge and I figured it out.

'The idea was to let us get within reach of the post and then move in for the slaughter where the men at Hamilton could see it happening? And with this many braves on the warpath, up against a cavalry force he knew was reduced by smallpox . . . well, taking Hamilton after the massacre of the civilians wouldn't have been a problem.'

Now, attempting to convey a degree of confidence to the Utes which, at close range, Edge could see was a lie, the Virginian glanced at the half-breed and asked: 'That about it, Yank?'

'I guess, Reb. Except to say again, maybe, that it'll be pretty pointless to carry on the killing now there's nobody left alive to — '

'You will be silent, white eyes!' Black Hawk snarled, and held up his rifle in the manner of a bar again as Red Eagle began to speak.

The unpainted and time-lined face of the aged chief was a little more animated now, by the light of anger and perhaps hatred that gleamed in his dark eyes which constantly switched the direction of their gaze from the sweat-beaded face of one white man to the other. His voice was a monotone as he made his episodic speech, obviously irritated by the need to wait while his words were translated.

'Chief Red Eagle tells me to say, white eyes, that you are not so clever as you think you are. You cannot read into his mind to discover his plans . . . But you are right to think it was his wish to put to death the people of this town before the horsesoldiers of Fort Hamilton . . .

'But it was not the plan to then attack the fort, white eyes. Plan was to allow the horsesoldiers to live. So that they perhaps have long lives in which to know that what was done at Massacre of Arroyo Bend and afterwards caused entire Ute nation to do much worse. And to do so where they can see . . . So that their every waking hour will be filled with memories and their sleep be troubled by nightmares and — '

Abruptly the old Ute chief seemed to be drained of the energy needed to sustain high emotion. The heat went out of his eyes and his voice dropped to little more than a murmur as he changed the subject from what might have been to what was.

'Chief Red Eagle asks me to tell you,' Black Hawk passed on in a suddenly disgruntled tone, 'that he has admiration for you and for you, Adam Steele and Edge. In hours of darkness after you have gone from Oro City, no Ute is able to tell if you have deserted your own or if you have plan to bring horsesoldiers here from Fort Hamilton . . . It was hoped that you would bring the horsesoldiers after you tell them of the great danger of Utes on warpath at Oro City. That hope is reason we keep pledge given under flag of truce and make no attack until the sun rises over top of hill . . .

'It was never expected, Chief Red Eagle says to say, that you bring the horsesoldiers here in such a manner . . . He admires you for running risk of being infected by the disease that has killed them all. And he agrees that further killing now that the horsesoldiers who commit Massacre of Arroyo Bend are dead is no longer so important to him . . . And finally, he says to tell you, that admiration for white eyes from any Ute is not large. He will not feel sadness if all in this town are infected by the disease you bring here and die.'

Red Eagle's dark eyes, momentarily alight with hatred rather than respect, flicked between the faces of Edge and Steele as the two white men looked suddenly drained to near exhaustion. And then the aged Ute chief showed a brief smile of relish as he perhaps mistook the signs of bone-deep physical and emotional weariness as symptoms of mortal illness.

'You're a real silver-tongued devil, Reb,' the half-breed murmured as he bent his aching right arm to bring the Winchester down so that it canted to his shoulder.

'We Southern gentleman are supposed to be charming, aren't we?' the Virginian answered in the same husky tone as he lowered his rifle in the same way.

This as Straight Arrow barked an order as he and Red Eagle and Black Hawk wheeled their horses. And the other ranks of Indians parted at the centre to allow the head men passage between them toward the top of the hill. Then, after he had slid the Colt Hartford back in the boot with the flag still fixed to the barrel, Steele put his left hand to his throat and massaged it with gloved fingers, as if it pained him.

'The chief starting to get what he wanted?' Edge asked, and reached into the long hair at the nape of his neck.

'If talking over much always makes a man feel this lousy, I'm glad I don't usually have so much to say,' Steele answered, and as Edge drew the razor from the neck pouch, reached into the slit in the outside seam of his pants to bring out the knife from the boot sheath.

The two of them reached behind them to cut through the lengths of rope that linked their own mounts to the horses immediately in back of them. And the half-breed said with a weary sigh and a quiet smile:

'Sometimes a man's just gotta do what a man don't wanna do.'

The Virginian displayed a grim smile as he replaced the knife in the sheath and shook his head wearily, murmured: 'That doesn't sound right, but I reckon it surely is, Yank.'

Then, from the east beyond the hill where the horde of Utes were in process of turning their ponies as Red Eagle and his two flanking riders neared the crest, came the strident blast of a bugle call.

And Edge snarled: 'But that sure sounds a wrong note, Reb!'

CHAPTER NINETEEN

FOR A stretched second it was as if time stood still and all movement was frozen. And during that same eerie moment the only sound in the entire world might have been the distant bugle call. Distant, but fast coming closer.

Closer to where the mass of Indians at the top of the hill had brought their slow and orderly withdrawal to a halt, every brave and sub-chief looking to Red Eagle for leadership. And to where the people had spilled out of the flanking buildings on to the stretch of street at the foot of the hill: Mayor Charlie DeWitt, Ernie Monk, Annie and Milton Austin, Calvin Brownlow, Mrs Harper and the rest of Oro City's citizenry; and Troopers Arnie Jonas, Conran, Kris Goldsmith and Roy Egan; and Edward Sun, Miranda Randell, Edith Crawford and Amy Yancy. Everyone of them fleetingly trapped in an emotional vacuum between enervating relief and many degrees of fresh fear.

And to where Adam Steele and the man called Edge sat their mounts: shifted their cold-eyed gazes from the Utes, to each other, to the column of corpse-burdened horses and to the people at the other end of the winding slope of the street. Then it was as if the wrenching around and back of the heads of the half-breed and the Virginian acted to trigger all other motion. And the rasping words that they vented through clenched teeth between drawn-back lips were the signals to unleash the barrage of pent-up sound.

Edge snarled: 'The frigging cavalry, Reb!'

Steele growled: 'It sure as hell isn't Gabriel blowing his horn, Yank!'

The whites whirled to lunge back into the cover of the buildings where they had spent the dread-and-tension-filled night – bellowing and shrieking their dismay and despair at this latest assault on their nerves for which they had been totally unprepared. This as the Utes, responding without pause to the signal of Chief Red Eagle's upthrust arm and the single word of command he roared, wheeled their ponies. And gaped their mouths to shriek a cacophony of strident warcries that seemed to generate an invisible but somehow discernible wave of depthless hatred. A current of sound that could have no substance and yet which Edge and Steele were able to feel reaching toward them and billowing about them like a dry and dusty desert wind as they made their move.

A move that was one of retreat with the help of a diversion.

The Virginian had wheeled his stallion first, and the half-breed was perhaps a second later in wrenching on the reins to turn his gelding as the clenched fist of Red Eagle was punched in a gesture of fury at the sky above the fully risen sun. And the taller of the two sheepskin-coated riders was this much behind the other as they raced down each side of the column of cavalry mounts: cracking open-handed blows against the rumps of the animals at or close to the head of the two single-file strings.

Then, as the opening fusillade of gunfire sent bullets flying past and over them, both the retreating white men were able to abandon their attention to the corpse-burdened animals and crouch low in their own saddles as they thudded in their heels to demand the best that the stallion and gelding were able to give. For the diversion was fully launched – the linked-together horses galloping away up the hill. Toward the charging Utes: not all of whom were so enraged by apparent treachery that they failed to remember what had caused the mass dying at Fort Hamilton.

And there was suddenly a break in the centre of the now-ragged ranks of advancing at the gallop braves: fury giving way to panic among the Indians desperate to veer away from the diseased bodies of the unburied dead. Because of the tightness of their formation, this swerving to the sides that was started at the centre of the lines was forced by pony against pony to be carried out to either end.

And the barrage of rifle fire faltered and for several seconds was silenced while the still-shrieking, paint-daubed braves gave their full attention to staying astride their mounts and keeping the ponies from stumbling amid the panicked disorder.

This allowed the bugle-call sounding attack from the far side of the hill to blast out clearly again against the yelling and the thudding of galloping hooves. And could, perhaps, have urged the cavalry horses with their sickeningly sweet-smelling burdens to greater speed as they recognised the familiar sound. This as the double string of animals raced on up the trail through the gap that had opened between the mass of Utes to split the attackers briefly in two.

But, just a moment after the last pair of cadaver-carrying horses had gone by, the front runners of the Utes closed the gap again. Along a shorter line of hell-for-leather advance now, as the braves, no longer hampered by terror, reformed into a snaking column to take account of the constantly narrowing street. Their warcries were once again filled with near-palpable anger and hatred, defiance and contempt, frenzy and perhaps insanity. But nothing more solid than the sounds of this fury and the thunder of their mounts' hooves on the hard-packed ground was sent down the hill ahead of them now. For the two white men whom they held most accountable for the treacherous use of the flag of truce and who were the prime objects of their hatred were for the moment out of reach of their vengeance. And no bullets were wasted on trying to blast them out of their saddles as they raced further ahead of the Utes with every stride of the gelding and stallion beneath them.

Then the Virginian and the half-breed were lost to the sight of their pursuers, as they swung around the final curve before the straighter stretch of street at the foot of the hill. They should just have been hidden for two or three seconds as they raced around a rock knoll: before they emerged on the intersection with the church on one corner and the law office facing it from the far side of the street.

But it took all of five seconds for the two riders to bring their mounts to skidding, rearing, near-halts. And power out of their saddles, sliding the Winchester and Colt

Hartford from the boots as part of the same frantic series of movements. So that when the two horses were once more seen by the Utes, they were riderless as they trotted a zig-zagging path along the street's final easy curve, snorting and tossing their heads in a show of petulance at how they had been mistreated.

Adam Steele burst in through the law office doorway first, to send the ashen-faced Goldsmith staggering away from the threshold. Edge was close on the heels of the Virginian and now the ginger-moustached trooper with the prematurely bald head moved further back of his own volition after the impetus of the crashing-open door was lost. Both intruders ripped the white fabric from their rifle barrels, as Jonas and Conran stared at them with as much hostility as Goldsmith: and a citizen who had chosen the church for cover began to set the bell tolling.

'You want us to start yelling *unclean* too?' Steele snarled at the troopers as he swung around to assume the position his entrance had forced Goldsmith to vacate.

'It's a sick society we're living in!' Edge growled as he went to the window and the grimacing Arnie Jonas backed off. Then he used the stock of the Winchester to smash the glass and, against the sound of falling shards, added: 'But it's going to change for some of us pretty soon!'

'Be dying to get out of it!' Steele snapped.

And this was punctuated by the Colt Hartford and the Winchester exploding shots that were close enough together to sound as one. And, as the hammer of one rifle was thumbed back and the lever action of the other was pumped, a fusillade of gunfire sent a hail of bullets up the final slope of the street. Spurts of black powder smoke seemed to show at every window and doorway of the railroad station, the saloon, the hotel and the cafe on the north curve of the street. And from the hayloft hatch of the livery across the vacant lot from the law office on the south side. To pitch several of the Ute frontrunners off the bare backs of their ponies. Some of those behind, too.

Suddenly, as this new burst of gunfire delivered blood spurting fresh death to the dying but not yet dead town, the warcries and whoops of the enraged Utes rose to a crescendo that transcended all that had gone before – from the moment when Red Eagle had ordered the attack in the wake of the cavalry bugle call, to when the enraged warriors saw the riderless gelding and stallion. And, in such an all-consuming frenzy for vengeance, the garishly painted Utes knew no fear so that it seemed the insanity which had affected a scattered few earlier now took a grip on every brave.

A second barrage of gunfire exploded toward the horde of shrieking Indians surging down the street, with guns from the church now added to the firepower. And the carbines of Goldsmith, Jonas and Conran triggered from the threshold and shattered window of the law office. And more deadly bullets cracked out of the boarding house and the stage-line depot as the frontrunning survivors of the first volley of shots either remained astride their galloping ponies or flung themselves to the ground. The riders to race down to the end of the street while those on foot darted to the flanking buildings. On pony or on running feet, the Indians now began to return the fire of the whites.

Whites began to respond vocally to the cries and shrieks of the Indians. And, too, some matched the screams of pain and the terror of dying as bullets from Ute guns thudded into their flesh.

Kris Goldsmith took a bullet in his right shoulder that knocked him into a half turn. From beside him, Steele triggered a shot that drilled a bullet into the heart of the brave who wounded the trooper and the Indian dropped in his tracks. Two more war-painted figures leapt from their ponies to flank the falling brave. Steele yelled at the wounded trooper and ducked behind the doorframe, but Goldsmith was slowed by pain and fear. Both Utes fired at him and he was hit in the side of his hairless head and in the belly. Steele was sprayed by droplets of the dead man's blood as he swung back into the open doorway and snapped off two quick shots. The first blasted a hole in the decorated forehead of one brave and the second went over the head of the other whooping Ute who dived full length for the doorway as the bullet that missed him hit a galloping pony and brought the animal and rider and several others down into a flailing, snorting, shrieking, bellowing heap.

The diving brave had misjudged his dive and came too close to the doorway to get off a shot from his rifle. Close enough for the Virginian to launch a vicious kick that smashed the toe of his boot full into the face of the Ute. With sufficient force to snap up his head and break his neck.

Edge and the two troopers who flanked him at the glass-less window fired into the confusion of struggling-to-rise ponies and riders who had been sent pitching to the centre of the street by the stray bullet from the Colt Hartford.

Then Conran was drilled through the heart and took two further bullets in the head before his stocky form and squint-eyed face dropped from sight below the ledge of the window. The half-breed's Winchester and Arnie Jonas's Army Colt dropped the Indians who had blasted the trooper.

Across the street, littered with dead and wounded Indians and ponies and veiled by drifting gunsmoke, a man stood in the porched entrance of the church, deliberately aiming and firing with a revolver at the frenetically riding braves. Until a Ute with a shotgun – perhaps the same one who had killed Jerome Randell the previous night – took less careful aim and squeezed both triggers. And all that remained of the man in the church doorway was his discarded handgun and a massive splash of blood on the flagstone threshold.

Steele's six-shot rifle was empty and he snatched up Goldsmith's revolver. Arnie Jonas worked calmly to reload his revolver within the cover of the wall beside the window. Edge tossed down the Winchester when its firing pin clicked into an empty breech, and ripped his coat unfastened to draw his Frontier Colt.

Into the acrid tainted, smoke-filled atmosphere of the law office came for the first time in what seemed a long while the clarion call of the bugle.

'Sounding better all the time now, uh Yank?' Steele yelled against the rattle of distant and cracking of close gunfire. And, despite the undiminished clamour of reports, it was clearly heard that the bugler was much nearer to the centre of the battle now.

'Music to my ears, Reb!' Edge roared in reply.

This just before a deafening barrage of rifle fire drowned

out every other sound of the tumultuous clash. And then a vociferous roar of approval rang out as a whole bunch of Utes were lifted off the backs of their ponies and sent crashing to the street amid spraying blood and billowing dust.

The church bell began to clang again.

The thunder of countless shod hooves competed with the uproar from other sources. Another barrage unseated another group of braves as they spurted their ponies around the curve of the street.

'That's it, boys, give the bastards hell!' Jonas roared as he swung to the shattered window again, and saw the latest casualties tumble to the ground under the hail of bullets triggered by the pursuing cavalry.

Then he and Edge and Steele opened fire with their revolvers at the braves who galloped past, briefly out of range of the guns of the cavalry behind them.

A man who had taken the place of the one blasted by the shotgun made frantic signals from the doorway of the church to the front of the law office – gesturing with the blood-dripping revolver that was apparently empty.

Four braves flung their rifles away and twisted off the backs of their galloping ponies before the revolvers in the hands of Jonas, Edge and Steele were certainly spent of live shells.

And, in the moment that followed the first second of no gunshot cracking out of the law office doorway or window, four more Utes powered into the building. Two lunging across the threshold and two more leaping over the window sill. All giving vent to shrill-pitched cries to augment the ferocious appearance of their paint-daubed faces and torsos and the menace of the knives which each of them brandished in tight fists.

All three white men had been aware of the man in the church doorway, but had assumed the waving of his arms to be a part of his celebration as he saw the welcome sight of the rescuing cavalry galloping down the hill with bugle blasting and pennant flying, buttons and badges gleaming and guns blazing. For in the split second between seeing this man and seeing the Utes inside the law office, Steele,

Edge and Jonas caught a glimpse of the uniformed men at the head of the relief column as they galloped around the corpse-littered curve of street.

But then there was no opportunity to be concerned with what was taking place beyond the dangerous confines of the law office. Where two braves rounded on Steele, making slashing motions with their knives as the Virginian hurled away his confiscated handgun. At the same time as he stood suddenly on one leg – to bring up his right knee so that he was able without stooping to draw the knife from the boot sheath. While, a few yards away, the Utes who had dived in through the window picked themselves up off the floor with smooth agility and turned to face the trooper and the half-breed. Edge drew the razor fluidly from the neck pouch and threw his revolver at the brave who was threatening Jonas and snarled:

'Lousy colour scheme!'

His Frontier Colt bounced off the chest of the brave closing with Jonas. And the trooper now flung his Army Colt at the same vividly decorated brave as he countered:

'Needs more red, I figure!'

'You got it, feller,' Edge replied, and held both Utes beyond lunging range by brandishing the razor in the same manner in which they were slashing their weapons back and forth. Then, as Arnie Jonas powered himself into a backward roll over the window sill and out on to the street, the half-breed added in a rasping tone: 'Didn't plan on sending out for — '

Across the office, Steele swung his knife hand down and back, then forward and up – the second part of the move far more forceful than the first. He let go of the knife when his hand was just above hip level, to send the finely balanced weapon spinning straight and true on an upward trajectory, so that it flew some six feet through the smoke-tainted air to bury its blade deep in the throat of the brave on the right. Who gagged and dropped his own knife as he brought both his hands up to clutch at the haft of the one in his flesh. He tried to wrench it out, but died in the attempt.

The Ute at his side was momentarily stunned by the sudden and lethal action of the white man.

The dead Ute collapsed into a heap, blood gouting from his mouth.

Arnie Jonas rose to his feet outside the window, the Winchester of another dead Ute levelled from his hip. He squeezed the trigger and another brave was dead – sent staggering into an ungainly backward run with blood blossoming from a hole in his chest.

Edge lunged at the brave who faced him, his right wrist turning one way and then another as he slashed with the razor from side to side, on a level with the daubed face of the shorter Indian. Who backed off, then came suddenly forward, mouth gaped to vent a hate-filled shriek that could be comprehended as his attempt at the taunt:

'You trick!'

'No, feller,' the half-breed rasped, and proved once again that cool composure is better than the heat of rage in face-to-face mortal confrontation – especially when there is also a physical advantage such as longer reach. 'But you won't like the treatment you're gonna get.'

He had waited for the Ute's knife hand to move across in a final slashing motion, then reached out to fist his free hand around the wrist behind the knife. Took a long stride forward to compensate for the brave's instinctive backward step. Then smashed the side of his right fist into the Ute's painted belly, so that the blade of the razor sank its full length into the flesh.

The Ute gasped and ceased to struggle against the restraint of the grip on his wrist. Then he started a scream as the razor was ploughed upwards, the blade forced to make a shallower cut as it scraped over the bones of his chest. He was dead from the shock before the razor came clear at his throat of a gaping wound that gouted blood from navel to Adam's apple. His knife was still clutched in a dead-handed grip as he dropped limply to the floor before the half-breed who stepped back from him.

'Dear God in heaven!' Arnie Jonas gasped. It sounded a strangely mild response to come from the lips of a frontier-toughened soldier who had seen his fair share of violent death. Among the enemy and his fellow troopers. But he had patently never seen such a ghastly wound inflicted with such assured composure to torrent so much blood.

'Maybe, feller, but all sure ain't right with the world,' Edge muttered as he stooped to wipe the blade of the razor clean in the lank hair of its latest victim. 'But okay with you, Reb?'

The query was a sardonic one, for it was obvious Adam Steele was well able to take care of the immediate problem. Had already pulled the scarf with weighted corners from around his neck, hurled it toward the perplexed Ute and jerked the suddenly terrified brave forward as soon as one end of the Oriental weapon of strangulation whirled around the wrist of his knife hand and gripped there. Now the Virginian powered up his knee to thud it into the crotch of his victim. Agony doubled him forward and the knife clattered to the floor as his hand spasmed open.

The white man wrenched the scarf clear of the wrist of the Indian, swung behind him as he straightened. Made a second forward motion with the scarf and brought up his other hand to catch the flying end. Then crossed over his hands at the back of Ute's neck to tighten the silken fabric across his windpipe. His scream of pain at the impact of Steele's knee in his crotch was suddenly choked off as he was forced to straighten up by having the same knee thudded into the small of his back.

He clawed vainly at the constricting fabric until the lack of air in his lungs drained him of the strength to struggle and his hands dropped to his sides. His mouth fell open, his tongue lolled out and his eyes bulged. He ceased to make pathetically weak sounds of pain and terror just a few moments before the glaze of death made his eyes opaque.

Steele sensed his death and stepped back, allowing the falling weight of the corpse to free the scarf with weighted corners.

'Shiiiiitttt!' Arnie Jonas gasped as he began to recover from the shock of what he had seen. And spoke into a near silence that had come to Oro City after the bell had ceased tolling a few seconds before the Virginian finished off the last Ute in the law office. 'You two guys are sure full of surprises.'

'Two take longer, Yank,' Steele replied to Edge's rhetorical question as he draped the scarf back around his neck, then crouched to draw his knife out of the throat of the Ute.

'Wasn't a complaint, feller.'

'Speaking of complaints, how d'you feel?'

'Shit, I guess I oughta go report to somebody in the . . .' Arnie Jonas murmured, letting go of the Winchester like it might be contaminated as he backed slowly away from the window. Then allowed his voice to trail away before he swung into a turn and started down the corpse-and-carcase-littered street at the double.

'Dead on my feet, but I figure a lot of people are feeling like that right now, uh?'

'Reckon so.'

They stowed the knife and the razor in their accustomed places, then Steele moved to the doorway and Edge to the window to survey the morning-sunlit street with its scattered dead and increasing signs of life. And, just as Arnie Jonas had been able to do at a much earlier hour, they could see far out to the west of Oro City. Where a much diminished group of Utes were galloping their ponies into the distance. While a much larger force of blue and yellow clad cavalrymen were being recalled from pursuit to commence an orderly return to town.

'You know what I think Reb?'

'You're going to tell me, Yank.'

'I think at least one of the fellers at Hamilton lived through the epidemic and got to Floyd or Bridger.'

'Could be.'

'Or maybe with so much Ute trouble all over, word just reached one of those posts and the troopers followed the trail of Indian-style killings to here?'

'Whatever, Yank. Those fellers can't be blamed for what happened here. They had no way of knowing we'd headed off what the Utes had planned.'

'That's right.' He had been rolling a cigarette and now he struck a match on the frame of the shattered window to light it. 'Guess we're just hexed to have no way out of trouble except more trouble.'

Steele shook his head wearily. 'I don't believe that any more, feller.'

'That ain't a belief. That's just a hope.'

'No, feller,' Steele insisted grimly. 'Hope is what I have that there's a doctor with that bunch of US cavalry out there.' Now he showed a weary grin as he added: 'Just have to be careful that hope doesn't reach fever pitch, I reckon?'

On a stream of expelled tobacco smoke, Edge answered through teeth displayed in a tight smile of his own: 'No sweat.'

CHAPTER TWENTY

ADAM STEELE and Edge slept an uninterrupted sleep for a day and a night in separate bedrooms of one of the large abandoned houses near the top of the hill on which Oro City was spread. Watched over in their isolation by two of the six troopers who had survived the disease that had taken such a high toll of the men at Fort Hamilton.

By surviving, these troopers had shown themselves to be immune to the sickness that had stricken the rest. But their nerve had finally cracked under the strain of watching so many men die and the digging of grave after grave. And so had they left the post, with many corpses unburied and eight men on the brink of dying. To ride for Camp Floyd. Reached the Department of Utah Headquarters in time to join the large force of men being despatched to check on and deal with a rumoured uprising of Utes.

The half-breed and the Virginian learned of these events that resulted in Fort Hamilton being abandoned and the cavalry reaching Oro City at the tragically wrong time when they woke at dawn after almost twenty-four hours of sleep and met up in the kitchen of the once fine house: where the two medical orderlies detailed to watch for signs of sickness had already set a pot of coffee to brewing on the stove.

'Either of you guys thrown up?' was the first anxious question to be posed.

Steele answered: 'Not me, feller,' and Edge shook his head as he lit the cigarette he had rolled on his way down from the bedroom.

Both civilians were heavy-eyed with sleep and their heavily bristled faces doubtless were made to appear even more unhealthy by the bright-eyed and freshly shaven countenances of the smartly uniformed troopers.

'No shivers?'

'You crappin' as usual?'

'You got no signs that I can see.'

'You got any redness on your backs or your bellies or chests?'

Both troopers continued to peer intently into the impassive faces of the civilians, who shook their heads or nodded to the queries.

'You itch any place?'

'Soles of my feet is all,' Edge replied, and this caused the gradually lightening mood of the soldiers to suddenly go into reverse.

'The Yank means he's got itchy feet for leaving this place, fellers,' Steele explained as he moved to the stove to see if the coffee was ready.

'Oh, yeah.'

'That's fine. If you feel as good as you look, I figure you're gonna be okay. Maybe guys that are already dead from the smallpox ain't so easy to catch it from as them that are still alive and kickin'?'

'Could be. But you guys oughta watch for any of the signs for a few days yet. And stay away from other people. That's real important.'

Steele poured coffee into the four tin mugs that were on the table where the two troopers sat.

'That's real important to him and me, too,' Edge said as he and the Virginian joined the soldiers in sitting down.

'Course, we ain't medical orderlies as a usual thing,' one of the troopers said, and got started on the explanation of what had happened to lay the groundwork of the events that led to the Ute attack on Oro City.

'Some folks – military and civilian alike – figure it was a damn shame we showed up when we did. After it looked like you two guys had fixed for it to be ended without no one else gettin' killed,' the trooper who had said least so far now added to the account. 'But a whole lot more are glad about it. Now it's over.'

'With him and me around,' Edge growled, gesturing with his mug toward the Virginian, 'I figure we were on a loser from the start: looking for an easy way out.'

'Easy?' a trooper gasped. 'Exposin' yourselves to smallpox and riding right up to that bunch of Utes with just a couple of white flags for — '

'That's what rankles most with me,' Steele said across the table to Edge. 'The way it looked as if we used those truce flags as part of — '

'*We* know we didn't, Reb.'

'Reckon so.' Now Steele shared a glance between the two troopers. 'I'm not saying smallpox isn't a bad way to die, but the Utes know of some worse ones?'

First one soldier, then the other one nodded in acknowledgement of this. Then both made to speak at the same time, until the less garrulous man became gratefully silent and attentive.

'There's sixty-four of them won't have the chance to torture whites no more, mister. That's how many of the bastards got themselves killed yesterday mornin'. And, like we told you already, whole lot of people were real happy to have a part in that. Liked the taste of revenge for all the killin' the Injuns been doin'. Army and civilians the same.'

'Yesterday morning's fight wasn't one-sided?' Steele said in the manner of a question.

'No,' the talkative trooper allowed, briefly downcast. 'We lost ten men dead and had another fourteen shot up pretty bad. And sixteen of the local people got killed, ten wounded, when the Injuns came on that crazy run through town. That ain't countin' the sixty-two that got blown all to pieces in the train wreck. That was a real mess out there along the track.'

While he paused to grimace at a recollection of carnage he had witnessed to the north of town, the other trooper supplied:

'Arnie Jonas and Roy Egan came through it okay, Arnie said to tell you. They've left now, with the rest of our boys. Local folks didn't want any army help on clearing up after we took care of our own and the Injun dead. And rounded up them horses with the dead from the fort tied to them. Folks around here don't think so well of the army right now.' He grimaced, too. 'And I guess they can't be blamed for that. Oh, and Mrs Crawford and Mrs Yancy give us a message for you. Before they left on the eastbound stage. Said to say goodbye and good luck to you.'

'And if you guys say you feel as fine as you look, I guess that's what me and him will be sayin' to you?' the other trooper asked with arched eyebrows as he pushed back his chair and rose.

'Obliged for looking out for me,' Edge replied.

'Grateful to you, too,' Steele added.

The second trooper got up from the table. Started to follow the first toward the door, but paused to explain:

'Your horses were caught and they're in the livery. The couple who run the Paydirt Cafe have been sendin' grub up to us. They leave it on the front step. Breakfast for two oughta be here any time now. We won't be needin' it.'

'Obliged.'

'Grateful to you.'

'Just one other thing . . . Town'll look a little empty if you to out there this mornin'. But that's because most folks have taken off to lend a hand with buryin' the dead out where the train was blown up. Can't understand it myself, but everyone wants to keep on livin' in this town where there ain't nothin' that makes life worth livin', seems to me.'

The trooper went through the doorway, shaking his head in mild perplexity as the half-breed muttered:

'Seems to me as well.'

'Only because the girl was killed?' Steele murmured.

'I'll never know, Reb.' He dropped the butt of his cigarette in the dregs of his coffee and the dousing of the hot ash made a low hissing sound.

'I know I'll find what I'm looking for, Yank,' Steele said. 'And the sooner I leave here, the sooner that'll be.'

Edge aped the Virginian's move of rising from the table and answered: 'I'm with you, Reb. But only in a manner of speaking. East is east, uh?'

'Right. And west is west.'

The two troopers had ridden out of sight along the trail where it humped over the crest of the hill above which the sun had already risen. There were no breakfasts on the front step of the big, deserted house. And no sign of life – even a wisp of woodsmoke from a chimney – as the two civilians moved down the meandering main street of Oro City, each with a rifle canted to one shoulder and a sheepskin coat draped over the other.

Bullet-scarred stonework and timber, smashed windows and stains on the surface of the street were the most evident signs of the fierce battle that had taken place in the town.

In Livesey's Livery Stable, where they checked that their gear was all in order and then saddled their horses, Steele reminded:

'That gelding needs new shoes.'

Edge answered: 'There's a few miles in these yet. Keep an eye on — '

'Horses are going to be my business,' Steele cut in.

Then they became silent as they completed readying their mounts for riding, and led them outside into the sunlit morning. Where they saw that there was one other man remaining in town – the young half-Chinese in his dishevelled city suit who emerged from the doorway of the Paydirt Cafe and stepped down off the stoop, a plate of food in each hand.

'The Austins have gone with the others out to the train wreck, gentlemen,' he announced as he started across the street. 'I'm no cook, so it's just cold food. But a token of my personal appreciation to you for — '

'Miranda Randell's left town?' Steele asked as he and Edge checked their move to swing up astride their saddles.

'She was killed,' Edward Sun answered dully, and perhaps sorrowfully. 'By the Utes. A bullet in the heart. It was very quick. Just one other fact to be grateful for – she was not going to have a baby. That was a lie she told to her father because she was so angry that I — '

The young man stopped abruptly in his tracks. And a dark hole showed at his left temple just above and to the left of his eye. There was no exit wound for the bullet had been fired over too long range for any velocity to be left after it penetrated Edward Sun's skull. And very little blood trickled out of the hole as he dropped the plates, vented an almost inaudible groan and collapsed: dead before his knees hit the street and he sprawled out forward. Probably did not hear the report of the shot that caused Edge and Steele to snap their heads around – raking their gazes away from the dead youngster to peer up the hill toward his killer.

Both needed to tilt their heads to bring down the brims of their hats and shade their eyes against the dazzling brightness of the newly risen sun. And were in time to see a black-clad figure astride a black horse as the marksman slid the deadly rifle back in his boot.

'That's a frockcoat he's wearing,' Edge growled.

'Something like it,' Steele answered.

They swung up astride their own horses as the man on the hilltop wheeled his – and doffed his hat in an arrogant gesture before he plunged out of sight at the gallop.

'Blond hair, Reb.'

'Pants inside his shiny boots, Yank.'

'Gunbelt slung around the outside of that long coat with the fancy cape. Sure looked like that Barnaby Gold kid.'

'Well, if it was that character, when he finds out Jerome Randell's dead and can't pay him, it will maybe take some of the shine off his brashness, you reckon?'

'Could be. But I heard he'd been killed by a bunch of troopers out in the Mohave Desert.'

'I never believed that.'

Edge shrugged his shoulders. 'You know something, I never believed Barnaby Gold.'

'Not too many people did.'

Steele turned his stallion toward the east and Edge tugged on the reins to head his gelding in the opposite direction. Then each heeled his mount into a slow walk, moving away from where the body of Edward Sun was sprawled in the dust on the centre of the street.

'Two like us are enough, feller,' the Virginian said over his shoulder.

'Most of the time I'd say one,' the half-breed answered.

'But not in this case.'

'I'll buy it.'

'Need two . . .

. . . BOOKENDS.'*

*As this one does at this point. But both men will reappear in the next stories of the two series.

